# One Night with an Irish Billionaire

## By

## Dee Markwith

# Contents


Chapter One *Vivian*..................................................1

Chapter Two *Beau*...................................21

Chapter Three *Vivian*...............................42

Chapter Four *Beau* ..............................102

Chapter Five *Vivian*..............................131

Chapter Six *Beau*.................................182

Chapter Seven *Vivian* ...........................209

Chapter Eight *Beau*...............................284

Chapter Nine *Vivian* .............................337

Chapter Ten *Epilogue*...........................384

# Chapter One

## *Vivian*

"I don't want to do this anymore," Vivian said, stopping Marcus mid-sentence.

"Excuse me?" he asked, setting his fork down.

"This," she said, gesturing between them. "Us."

He looked at her with a mixture of confusion and concern. "What are you saying?"

"It's just not working anymore. We're two different people with two different goals."

Marcus looked around the restaurant anxiously and leaned in to whisper, "Are you seriously doing this right now?"

"I'm sorry," she shrugged. "You're a great guy, and I'll always love you... just as a friend."

"So you're saying you're not *in* love with me?" he asked, pushing his plate aside and crossing his arms. He looked at her with resentment, awaiting her answer.

"I'm not," she sighed. "Again, you're a great guy, but I think it's time we called it quits. We both want different things out of life."

"You're breaking up with me in a goddamn restaurant?" he hissed through gritted teeth.

"I'm sorry, I really am," she told him gently. "I didn't plan this. I've just been thinking a lot lately, and it's clear we're not exactly on the same page."

Arms still crossed, he looked around the room again and shook his head in frustration. "It's because I've been pushing the marriage and kids thing, isn't it?"

She cleared her throat and took a sip of her wine. "I'd be lying if I said that wasn't a part of it, sure."

"For fuck's sake, Vivian, you're twenty-eight. You're not getting any younger. We've been together for three years. It's only natural that I'd bring up marriage and children."

"It's not like you mention it now and then, Marcus. It's constant. I'm just not ready for either right now, especially with somebody I'm not in love with."

She could see the hurt in his eyes and swallowed hard. She hadn't planned on breaking things off with him tonight, but the words had just come pouring out. She also pushed her plate aside, having barely touched her meal, and watched as he processed her words.

"You're really not in love with me?" he spoke after a long moment.

"I love you deeply as a friend," she replied in an attempt to soften the blow, "but I'm not *in* love with you."

"Ouch," he said, wincing. "That stings a bit."

Having noticed they weren't enjoying their meals, their waiter returned to their table to ask if everything was okay. Vivian assured him there wasn't no problem with the food and asked for the check and boxes for the leftovers. Sensing the tension between the two, the waiter politely nodded and rushed off.

"So... what are we going to do about the living situation?" Marcus asked.

"I'm one of Denver's most successful real estate agents," she reminded him, hoping it didn't sound as arrogant as she thought. "I think I can find a place easily enough."

Doubtful about buying a home with somebody she wasn't sure she had a long-term future with, they'd moved into a small yet pricey apartment together two years earlier. Without kids or even any pets, it had been working out well for them. Marcus would regularly suggest upgrading to a larger place more suitable for children, but she'd always shoot the idea down, citing her desire to focus on her career. It wasn't an excuse.

The small real estate business she'd launched from home had taken off like wildfire and quickly grown into one of Colorado's largest and most lucrative firms. One employee had turned into a team of twenty skilled agents operating out of a spacious office on the top floor of a modern commercial building.

The lease was steep, but with the money her firm was generating, paying the bills was a breeze. She'd built a sterling reputation with her combination of looks, intellect, and charisma, and clients loved her staff of knowledgeable, friendly agents that she'd handpicked personally. They were the best and had helped her firm achieve the success she'd only dreamed of.

"So you want me to keep the apartment, then?" he clarified, looking relieved. She didn't blame him. It was a nice place in a decent area, and the apartment was filled with more of his belongings than hers, anyway.

"If you can afford it," she replied.

"I might have to pick up a few more hours or get a roommate, but I'll figure it out."

Marcus did okay for himself as the sales manager of a local office supply chain. It was a painfully dull job, and Vivian often found it hard to focus on his work-related stories. She certainly wouldn't miss those.

"Okay, good. I can be out by the end of the month."

"Jesus," he gasped, "that's only two weeks. You're not fucking around, huh?"

"No use in dragging it out," she shrugged. "I'll help you out with next month's rent until you can pick up those hours or find a roommate who won't murder you in your sleep."

"Funny," he chuckled, finally cracking a smile.

"You know I really care about you, right?" she asked, offering her hand. He took it and looked at her apologetically.

"I know you do," he sighed. "I'm sorry I couldn't make you happy. Maybe you're right. We just want different things. I want to settle down. You want to expand your business, which I totally respect. I love you a lot, so this isn't going to be easy for me, but it's probably for the best."

She felt as though a weight had been lifted from her chest. Marcus was a gentle guy with no temper she'd ever experienced, but she wasn't sure how he'd take the break up. She'd never seen him lose his cool or get emotional and was relieved he was handling the situation as stoically as usual. The waiter cautiously returned with the check and two boxes for the remainder of their meals. He thanked them for their patronage and hurried off again, not wanting to interrupt.

The ride home was awkward, to say the least, and things didn't get any more comfortable once they arrived home. They slept on their usual sides of the bed, only farther apart than expected and without the obligatory goodnight kiss. When the morning came, Marcus quietly left for work while Vivian was in the shower. She'd called into her office to let her team know she wouldn't be coming in—something she had the luxury of doing as the boss—opting to stay home and house hunt. She'd recently listed a few beautiful homes for sale, all within her budget, and wanted to look at them again. After toweling off and slipping into sweatpants and a baggy t-shirt, she grabbed her laptop and plopped down on the sofa to review the listings a little more closely. She was glad she didn't have too many things since packing was always such a pain. If all went well, this would be her final move. Whatever home she decided on would be it for her. She'd settle in, build her life there, and wouldn't invite a man to move in unless she was sure they had a lifelong future together. At only twenty-eight years old, she wasn't in any rush, especially after a three-year relationship. She needed to focus on her career, not finding Mr. Right. If she decided she needed companionship, she mused to herself, she'd just get a dog.

She'd just booted up her laptop when her phone sounded from beside her. Figuring it would be work-related, she was surprised to see it was her old friend phoning her from overseas. She'd met Samantha during her freshman year of high school, and the two had become fast friends, forming an inseparable bond that had remained strong over the years. When Samantha had visited Ireland and met the love of her life there, she'd decided to stay and regularly kept in touch with Vivian with phone calls, text messages, or video chats. With Vivian keeping so busy, video chats were rare. Today, however, her friend was in luck.

"Top o' the mornin' to ya," Vivian greeted in her terrible Irish accent.

"Not exactly morning here," Samantha pointed out, rolling her eyes. "Time difference, remember?"

"Yeah, yeah," Vivian laughed. "It's morning here, so bite me."

"You know I love me some chocolate," her friend smirked, referring to Vivian's dark complexion. The two couldn't look any more different, yet their similar personalities had drawn them together.

"You look great," Vivian smiled, noting her friend's freckled pale skin and red, curly hair. Samantha often referred to Vivian as the pretty one, but the girl didn't give herself enough credit. She was quite attractive in her own right and had no problem turning heads.

"Thanks, love. You look stunning, as always. It's nice to see you finally. How long has it been since we video chatted?"

"Jesus, I can't even remember," Vivian groaned. "Too long, that's for sure."

"I'm surprised you even answered. I figured you'd be busy with work, as always."

"I took the day off."

Samantha let out an exaggerated gasp. "Shut up. Where is my best friend, and what have you done with her?"

"Your best friend is officially single," Vivian replied. "I took the day off to house hunt."

"Wait, what? Are you being serious right now?"

"Very. I broke things off with Marcus."

"Holy shit. That's huge news," Samantha said. Vivian watched as her friend got comfortable on her own sofa over four thousand miles away. "I need details. When did this happen?"

"Just last night. We were at dinner, and he was telling another one of his boring work stories. I just kind of snapped."

"Wow. How is he taking it?"

"Honestly? Better than I thought he would. I mean, I can tell he's hurt, but he's doing his best to hide it."

"So you're moving out, not him?"

"That's right. There are a few houses on the market that caught my attention. I'm toying with the idea of buying one."

"This is all so sudden," Samantha said, shaking her head in disbelief. "Why did you break up?"

"He's all about getting married and having kids. I'm just too wrapped up in my career right now. I might consider it if I were in love with him, but I'm just not."

"I kind of suspected as much," her friend sighed. "I could tell you cared about him, but I never thought you loved him."

"Was it that obvious?"

"Yeah... no offense. I didn't want to say anything, but he never seemed right for you." She paused and added, "Don't get me wrong, he's a great guy, but..."

"You can say it," Vivian grinned. "He's boring."

Samantha blew out a long breath and chuckled. "Yeah, just a bit. I'll never forget that party where he talked to me for ten minutes about some scene from Star Trek. Or was it Star Wars? I was completely zoned out within the first minute, so I can't even remember."

"God, that was so humiliating," Vivian laughed, shaking her head at the memory.

"I'm sorry, but what did you even see in him? I mean, he's good-looking and nice, but he has the personality of drywall."

Vivian covered her smile, her chest heaving as she giggled. "You're awful!"

"Was the sex good, or was he boring in bed, too?" her friend asked.

"I'll be nice and say that it was average. Very, very average."

"I can't believe you hung in there for… how long? Three years?"

"He treated me well," Vivian shrugged. "And he was nice to look at. I was hoping I could work on the personality thing."

"Yeah, I see that worked out," Samantha laughed.

"Enough about me. How are things in your world?" Vivian asked, smoothly changing the subject.

"Great. Brian and I have been talking about starting a family."

"No shit?"

"No shit. Who'd have thought, right? Me, married and thinking about having a baby?"

"Seems like just yesterday we were only fourteen and swearing we'd never have kids."

"Right? Funny how time changes things."

"I'll say. Remember how I wanted to be a lawyer? Now I sell houses."

"And you're thinking of buying one," Samantha reminded her. "Listen, before you rush into moving, why don't you come visit me over here?"

"I told Marcus I'd be out soon…"

"For the last two years, you've told me you'd come to see me, yet it's been one excuse after another. Now's the perfect time. Fly here for a week or two, clear your head, and then move out. Come on. You'd love it here. I'll show you a good time, I promise."

"I don't know. I said I'd be out by the end of the month. I need to buy a house to make that happen."

"So pick out a house, get the paperwork rolling on it, and come visit me while everything processes. Move when you get back. You're finally single again, Viv. You know how much fun you could have over here?"

"What's that supposed to mean?" Vivian laughed.

"I'm just sayin', there are a lot of hot guys over here who would love a shot at you," Samantha smirked.

"Oh, great, that's just what I need. Some pasty-faced Irish guy was slobbering all over me." Remembering Samantha's husband was Irish, she winced and added apologetically, "I mean… no offense."

"None taken," her friend chuckled. "I happen to love my pasty-faced Irish guy. Now book a flight and get your sexy ass over here. Your passport is still valid, right?"

"That it is," Vivian nodded. Before Samantha's move to Ireland two years earlier, she'd helped Vivian get a passport in hopes it would rope her into visiting. "But I'm not sure now's the best time to take a vacation."

"Stop. You know if you don't come now, I'll be bugging you for another two years. You'll buy a house, get caught up with the move and work, and it'll be excuse after excuse again."

Vivian sighed, knowing her friend was right. The responsibilities of being a homeowner would likely make her work even harder as if she didn't work hard enough already. If she did postpone her move by a couple of weeks, it would give Marcus more time to find a roommate or pick up the extra hours he'd need to cover rent. He certainly wouldn't mind her waiting a bit longer to move out.

Watching her friend mull over the idea, Samantha sweetened the pot in a singsong voice. "I'll buy your ticket."

"No, no," Vivian replied, shaking her head. "It's an expensive flight, and you'll need to start saving if you're going to have a baby. I'm doing very well for myself. I can get the ticket."

Samantha's face lit up. "So that means you'll actually come?"

"Looking up flights right now," Vivian smiled, pulling her laptop closer.

"Shit, I didn't think you really would."

"Hey, when you're right, you're right. If I don't do it now, it could be a while before I get the chance again. I miss you and could use a week of fun. Breakups are never easy. It will be the perfect way to take my mind off it."

"You'll have a blast," her friend beamed, grinning wide. "Oh my God, this is so awesome. Brian will be excited to meet you. I talk about you all the time."

Vivian had waved hello to Samantha's husband once during a video chat but had never met him in person as her friend's wedding had been so spontaneous that nobody had been invited. They'd met, fallen in love, and married so quickly that Vivian could barely wrap her mind around it. One month, her best friend was single, and the next, she was walking down the aisle to wed a man she'd met while vacationing. Samantha was always impulsive, so she shouldn't have been so surprised. Still, having her best friend move so far away had been hard. She missed the girl deeply, and a visit was long overdue.

"I'm excited to meet him, too. I finally get to meet the man who stole my best friend," Vivian joked. "I take it things are still good between you two if you're talking about starting a family."

"Very good. We still act like newlyweds."

"I'm looking at... next week. Does that work for you?" Vivian asked, eyeing a morning flight that would work best for her.

"Wow, that's soon. But, yeah, that's great."

"I'd be flying into Dublin, right?"

"Right. We can either pick you up at the airport, or you can rent a car."

"How far of a drive is it to… what the hell is the name of your town? I can never remember."

"Killarney!" Samantha laughed. "It's about five hours."

"Yeah, I'd never ask you to drive ten hours. I'll rent a car."

"Are you sure? We don't mind."

"I'm sure. I think it would be fun to drive on the wrong side of the road for once," Vivian laughed. "And the drive will help me decompress after the long flight."

"You really want to do more sitting after being on a plane for so long?"

"Well, I'll want to stop and do some sightseeing. Stretch my legs. Buy some souvenirs. Take some photos. You know, all that touristy crap."

"I don't blame you. There's a lot to see. It's a very scenic drive here. You'll love it."

After a few keystrokes and a couple of clicks, Vivian took a deep breath and secured the ticket. "Done. I'll be there next Friday."

"Oh my God!" Samantha squealed in excitement. "I can't believe you're coming!"

"I got the earliest flight I could. Red eye that leaves a bit after midnight. I land in Dublin a little after 5:00 p.m., so that I won't be at your place until 11:00 p.m. I hope that's okay."

"We're old but not that old," Samantha chuckled. "We'll still be up, no worries. I'll be so excited to see you. I won't be able to sleep anyway!"

"Good answer," Vivian quipped. "At least I'll get to see some of the country before it gets dark."

"Brian will have to work over the weekend, but I have it off. I'll show you around."

They hammered out a few more details before ending the video call by blowing each other a kiss, as always. Riding the high from the unexpected decision she'd made to visit her friend overseas, Vivian hummed to herself while browsing the homes her firm had listed and settled on one that stood out from the others. It was a beautiful two-story house with modern architecture that had been recently constructed in a wonderful neighborhood reasonably close to her office. The price was steep, but she'd squirreled away enough money for the down payment, and with how successful her firm was, the mortgage payments wouldn't be a problem. It was a prominent place with more than enough room to grow should she ever decide to follow in Samantha's footsteps by starting her own family. She didn't see it happening anytime soon, but when the time did come, she would be ready.

She got the paperwork together for the purchase, knowing if everything went well, she'd be ready to move in after her trip. It didn't take long to prepare since she'd done it so many times over the years, and with a bit of help from her team, the offer she'd submitted had been approved by the end of the day. She shared the news with Marcus and asked if he'd be okay with her staying a bit longer. It would only be a few days if that. As anticipated, he was fine with it and assured her she could take all the necessary time. He even offered to help her move, which she politely declined. She didn't have enough stuff to warrant his help and wasn't comfortable with the idea of having him in her new home anyway. She wanted to start fresh, with no memories of him ever stepping into her house. Of course, she'd never say that out loud since it admittedly sounded cruel, but she was looking forward to a new chapter of her life. A vacation in a foreign land she'd never seen would be the perfect segue to her new beginning.

# Chapter Two
## *Beau*

"Don't you dare throw that," he warned, pointing at her sternly.

Across the room, Jessica stood poised to throw the thick porcelain vase in her hand. In the heat of the moment, she'd snatched it from the closest shelf and had her arm cocked to launch it.

"Seriously, don't you throw—?"

Beau ducked out of the way as the vase whizzed by his head and shattered on the wall behind him.

*"Are you fucking crazy?"* he growled, looking down at the remnants of the antique vase they'd bought together at an art exhibit six months earlier. Masterfully hand-painted with silhouettes of cherry blossoms, the vase from Japan's bygone feudal era had set him back close to five thousand dollars. Now, laying in hundreds of pieces all over the kitchen floor of his Manhattan townhouse, it was completely worthless. It had survived three centuries of war and a trip halfway around the globe to suffer at the hands of a scorned lover. Before he could say another word, she reached

for its smaller counterpart—this one valued at nearly two thousand dollars—and rocketed that at him. He ducked again, and the vase exploded into fragments just below where its big brother had made an impact.

*"Seriously?"* he yelled, shielding his face from the flying debris.

*"You are not breaking up with me!"* Jessica screamed, her face twisted in anger.

He knew she wasn't going to take the break-up well but hadn't expected this sort of reaction. Breathing heavily with her chest heaving and face red, she looked like she was ready to kill. She was known to fly off the handle, but he'd never seen her this unhinged.

"Just calm down," he said gently. "Let's discuss this like rational adults."

*"I suck your dick, and you fucking break up with me?"* she roared, taking a step toward him. Pieces of shattered porcelain crunched under his feet as he backed away from her, disturbed by her skewed perception of reality. Yes, his cock had been in her mouth minutes earlier, but certainly not of his own volition. She'd taken it upon herself to slide his boxer

briefs down and wake him with a blowjob, a gesture he might have appreciated had things been going well between them. They'd spent the night before bickering, something that had become increasingly frequent in recent weeks thanks to her growing neurosis. A wake-up blowjob had always been her go-to way of smoothing things, but this morning he hadn't been in the mood and hurriedly pulled away, tugging his boxer briefs back up as she looked at him with contempt. To put it mildly, his reaction to her played-out tactic hadn't gone over well. Within seconds, she was screaming obscenities at him with her nostrils flared and eyes full of rage.

*"Oh, now I'm not fucking good enough for you?"* she'd spat. *"Most men would kill to have a girl like me, you fucking prick! You think you're such hot shit, don't you? Just wait until you're begging me to suck your dick. Just wait until you're begging me to suck it, and I fucking laugh, you piece of shit!"*

Always one to avoid confrontation, he'd calmly gotten dressed while she continued to yell, then headed downstairs in hopes she wouldn't follow. She did, and unable to hold his tongue, he'd suggested they sever ties. That didn't go smoothly and brought them to where they stood now.

"You need to lower your voice," he said, concerned by the look of murder on her face. A part of him was glad he didn't have neighbors within earshot, while another wished he did in case she turned violent.

Fuming, she hissed through gritted teeth, "We are *not* breaking up."

"Look, I'm sorry, but this just isn't working out. I know it, and deep down, I think you know it, too."

In an instant, her face turned from bitterness to sorrow. She closed the distance between them and took his hand in hers. Her voice was almost pleading as she told him, "We can make it work. We need to talk. We can get through this."

He slipped out of her grip and brushed by her into the living room. "No, Jessica. I think it's best if we just go our separate ways. You're a great girl, but—"

"I did *not* just waste a year of my life with you," she snapped, reverting to anger as she followed behind him. He was used to her moods changing at the drop of a hat, so he wasn't overly surprised by the sudden change. She was an undeniably gorgeous girl whom he'd met at a fashion show he'd helped sponsor. A tall, leggy blonde with a slender build, she'd made a name for herself as a runway and print model, but she was more than just looks. She was also quite intelligent, having earned a degree in nursing before a modeling opportunity presented itself and derailed her interest in the medical field. It had been her combination of beauty and brains that had caught his attention. She conducted herself the best she could initially, trying to conceal her bipolar, manic behavior. However, she couldn't keep the facade up forever, and cracks began to appear in her act within the first few months. Her unpredictable mood swings, as was her constant paranoia, were hard to deal with. She'd regularly accuse him of cheating and would look at him with skeptical eyes when he assured her he hadn't strayed. At her persistence, he regrettably allowed her to move into his upscale townhouse, hoping it would quell her doubts about an affair. If they lived together, he surmised, she wouldn't feel the need to question what he was doing when they weren't together. It didn't work; she'd still interrogate him if he arrived home even one minute late. His attempt to comfort her, to ease her concerns, had backfired, and he'd been dealing with the consequences ever since. After months of putting up with it, he'd finally had enough.

"I'm sorry, but it's over," he said as apologetically as he could. He was trying to remain collected, but his patience was wearing thin. "Listen, you're a great girl, you really are, but we're just not good together."

"Where is this coming from?" she asked. "Did somebody put this idea in your head? Because last time I checked, we're *very* good together."

He couldn't help but chuckle at that. "In what universe are we good together? For fuck's sake, I got home from a crucial business trip last night, and the first thing you do is accuse me of cheating… again. No, 'Hi, honey, I'm so glad you're home!' I walk through the door, and you instantly grill me about who I was with." Frustrated, He shook his head and added, "I just can't take it anymore. I really can't. How you treat me isn't right, and it's unfair."

"I'm sorry," she said meekly, in almost a mumble. Her mood had changed yet again, this time to self-pity in a desperate ploy to tug at his heart. Looking down at the floor, she continued softly, "I love you so much, I'm always afraid of losing you. It's stupid, I know, but I can't help it."

He sighed in exasperation and ran his fingers through his dark hair. "You held onto me so tightly you crushed what could have been a good thing."

"Is this because you can't have kids?" she asked, referring to the fertility test he'd failed a few months earlier. He'd taken it at her insistence after she accused him of being infertile and regretted the results. She'd learned to use it as a weapon against him, bringing it up every time they fought. "Is it because you don't feel like a man?"

"What?" he scoffed. "Of course not. It's because of how you act. You're all over the place. One minute, you're smiling. The next, you're freaking out. I can't deal with it anymore."

"We can fix it," she replied, touching his chest. "I'll be better, I promise."

He wasn't buying it. Knowing the next words out of his mouth would trigger her temper again, he took a deep breath and braced himself for the storm. "Jessica.

It's over. I'm leaving, and when I get back, I want you and your things gone."

*"Fuck you!"* she shrieked, punching him in the chest. *"I can't believe you!"*

Thankfully, his time spent in the gym paid off, and her punch didn't make much of an impact. His muscular chest absorbed her blow quickly enough. When she took another swing, he blocked it and grabbed her wrist.

"Behavior like that is exactly why it's over," he hissed. "Pack your stuff and get out. I want you gone by the end of the day."

He released his grip on her wrist, and she stepped back, her blue eyes welling with tears. "Baby... baby, please don't do this. I'll do anything. I'll... I'll..."

"The only thing I want you to do is leave," he replied, unphased by her sobs. He steeled himself for another punch and was relieved when one didn't come.

She sniffled and wiped away the tears that had escaped her eyes. "I can't have everything out today, and you know it. I... I have too much stuff."

He groaned, knowing she was right. Her collection of shoes alone could fill the bed of an average pickup truck. He briefly debated helping her move but decided it would be too awkward and settled on a solution that worked for them both. "Okay, look. I'm going to take off for a few days, and when I get back, I'd appreciate it if all of your things were gone. You can leave the key on the counter."

"Okay," she agreed, her lower lip trembling as she fought back more tears. "Beau... I'm so sorry. About everything."

"Me too. Just..." he trailed off, stopping himself before asking her not to trash the place in his absence. He didn't want to give her any ideas. Instead, he changed direction and finished with, "Just try to have everything out, okay? I'm sorry things didn't work."

"Okay." She wiped her eyes again and composed herself. "Maybe we can try again someday?"

"Yeah, maybe," he replied dismissively. Moving by her and into the kitchen, he grabbed his keys, watch, and wallet from their home on the counter and patted his pocket to make sure he had his phone. "I'm taking off."

"Where are you going?" she asked, sounding concerned.

He knew what she was thinking but no longer needed to explain himself. "Out."

She opened her mouth to speak but thought better of it. It was obvious that she was fighting hard to hold back her accusations. He heard her say "I love you" as he headed out the door, but he didn't respond. She said those three words to him regularly, even though he'd never returned them. He simply didn't share the sentiment and wasn't going to make such a powerful statement if he didn't truly mean it. Yes, he'd been taken by her beauty and her intelligence, but he'd never been close to loving her. It was a fling that snowballed into a relationship, and he'd grown to care about her deeply, even with her erratic, unpredictable behavior. He knew he was taking a risk by allowing her to move in, but foolishly thought it would improve their strained relationship. For a savvy venture capitalist who took calculated risks for a living, he couldn't believe he'd made such a mistake. Matters of the heart, it seemed, were far more complex than matters of finance.

Making his way around the corner to his Mercedes, he sank into the driver's seat and gripped the steering wheel tightly, the pronounced muscles in his forearms flexing as he released the tension he'd been holding. He prided himself on always remaining calm and controlled, but Jessica had come close to breaking that composure. He was glad he'd made it out of the house before he'd snapped, though he couldn't help but worry about what she was doing inside. He wished he could feel relief at having ended things between them but was too concerned she was destroying his property. She'd already cost him seven thousand dollars between the two vases she'd so carelessly wrecked. If she decided to go on a rampage, the damage could cost him tens of thousands... if not hundreds. As an avid art collector, he'd amassed a wealth of paintings, sculptures, and relics that dated back centuries. Thankfully, he'd had the foresight to insure his more valuable pieces.

He shook his head and dug his cell phone from his pocket to reset his focus. After collecting himself, he called his secretary, who answered on the second ring.

"Hello, Mr. Sullivan, what can I do for you?"

Eyes closed and gently pinching the bridge of his nose, he did his best to sound chipper. "Hi, Gabby. I need you to do me a favor."

"Sure. What's up?"

"I need you to book me a flight."

"On it. Where to this time?"

He paused, mulling over his options. He wasn't quite sure where he wanted to go. He just knew he wanted to get far away from Jessica. His most lucrative investment flashed through his mind, and he blurted, "Ireland. Get me on a flight to Dublin as soon as possible."

"Leaving again so soon?" Gabby asked. He could hear the click of keystrokes as she questioned this unexpected trip. "Didn't you just get back from Seattle last night?"

"I did," he answered, trying to keep the coolness in his voice. His secretary didn't need the details of his personal life. "But something came up. You know how it goes."

"I'm sure you're looking forward to flying again," she replied sarcastically, still clicking away on her keyboard.

"Oh, you know it."

"You going to visit your family?"

He could tell she was just conversing casually as she searched for flights and wasn't trying to pry. "Yes."

"How long are you planning on staying?"

"Let me think," he answered, considering her question. The meeting in Seattle had gone well, and he'd decided to invest in the old music hall he'd flown there to look at. With some renovations, he knew the place had serious potential. With that decision made, he didn't have any meetings scheduled for another two weeks. It was an opportune time to take the much-needed vacation he'd been thinking about. "Let's make it a week."

"Okay, just a second." She paused for a moment and continued, "I found a flight leaving in two hours out of LaGuardia. Is that too soon?"

"That's perfect," he replied, glancing at his Rolex.

"Okay, locking it in now. Don't forget your passport."

He was glad she'd reminded him. Perhaps he hadn't regained as much focus as he'd thought, he mused as he started the car and rolled off toward his office in Lower Manhattan, thankful he'd had the foresight to keep a copy of his passport there. The last thing he wanted to do was brave his townhouse again and deal with Jessica, who was indeed having a meltdown of some sort. Sure, she'd seemed calm as he was leaving, but with how quickly her mood could change, he knew she could be in there setting his clothes on fire. As long as she didn't burn the townhouse down, he supposed he could live with whatever damage she caused. At least, that's what he tried to convince himself of as he navigated the busy city streets.

When he pulled up to his office building that proudly displayed the name *Sullivan Investments* in big, bold lettering, he darted inside. He nodded to Gabrielle as he rushed by her to his private office just beyond her desk. He pulled his passport from the wall safe he kept concealed behind a Renaissance-era oil painting and returned to say a few quick words to his secretary.

"Thank you for reminding me, Gabby," he said, flashing her a smile as he held up his passport.

"You seem like you're in a hurry. Did you even have time to pack?" she asked, looking at him worriedly.

"I'm traveling light," he replied. For once, he would be traveling with just the clothes on his back and looking forward to the experience. With no bags to check or stow, it was one less thing he had to worry about. He'd buy whatever he needed when he landed. "Send the flight information to my phone. I need to get going if I want to make it."

"Mr. Sullivan?" she called after him, stopping him in his tracks as he headed for the door. When he turned to acknowledge her, she asked, "Are you okay?"

Gabrielle, affectionately known around the office simply as "Gabby," was a nerdy, pixie-cut blonde in her early twenties who was socially awkward but a whiz at her job. He'd hired her personally a year earlier at the recommendation of a friend, and she'd proven herself a valuable asset. As she looked at him with worry through the lenses of her horn-rimmed glasses, he couldn't help but tell her the truth.

He returned to her desk and said, "I just ended things with Jessica."

"I'm sorry to hear that," she replied. The look in her eyes said otherwise. Jessica had stopped by the office on more than a few occasions over the course of their relationship, mainly to make sure he was really there, and he'd gotten the vibe that Gabby wasn't a fan. "Are you alright?"

"I am," he nodded. "I figure now's a good time for me to take some time off."

"You certainly deserve it. You work so hard…"

"Thank you." He shot her another smile and moved to leave, but she stopped him again.

"If you need anything, I'm here for you."

Her tone seemed almost suggestive, as did the look in her eyes. He hoped he was reading too much into it and replied, "I appreciate that."

Hurrying out the door, he glanced at his watch again and knew he had to get rolling if he wanted to make the flight. Thankfully, traffic was light, and he made it in plenty of time. He wasn't thrilled about leaving his $150,000.00 car parked at the airport but figured it was safer there than with Jessica. Arriving home to find "DICKHEAD" keyed into the hood was something he could envision a bit too easily for his comfort.

After passing through security and finding his terminal, he pulled his phone from his pocket to check his messages while waiting for his flight to board. He'd heard his text message alert sound off several times on the drive to the airport, but he'd ignored it, knowing who they'd be from. Only one person was known to blow up his phone like that. Jessica had messaged him eight times, with each message more desperate than the last.

*Where did you go?*

*Hello? At least tell me when you're coming back.*

*Are you with another woman?*

*Have fun with whatever slut you're with.*

*Baby? Just come home. We can work this out.*

*Fine, fuck you. You'll beg for me back someday, and I'll spit in your face.*

*I didn't mean that. I'm just upset. I'm sorry.*

*Okay, wherever you are, be safe. I love you.*

Groaning, he put his phone on silent and shoved it back in his pocket. The break-up was proving that she was more unstable than he thought. If he returned to his possessions intact, it would be a miracle. He tried to push those concerns from his mind so he could focus on enjoying himself, not wanting her to ruin the vacation he so desperately needed. It was no coincidence that his workload had increased after Jessica moved in. He'd intentionally overbooked his schedule, keeping himself as busy as possible to avoid her. That led to more suspicions of an affair, but it beat the alternative. Things had gotten so bad between them that they couldn't spend more than an hour together without fighting if you could call it that. It mainly was her yelling at him over something absurd while he sat there taking the abuse, not wanting to escalate things further by losing his cool.

"You're acting crazy," he'd once snapped after she'd thrown their dinner out the window in a fit of irrational jealousy. That remark hadn't gone well, making things twice as bad.

"Oh, now I'm crazy for loving you?" she'd screamed, twisting his words completely. "If you want to see crazy, I'll show you crazy!"

He'd watched in shock as she began throwing dishes out the window as well, plates and glasses shattering on the sidewalk below until he had no choice but to apologize.

"Okay, okay, I'm sorry! You're not crazy. Please, just... calm down."

They were fine together in small doses, but anything beyond that ended in disaster. He'd allowed the relationship to go on far too long and chastised himself for not having cut the cord sooner. He supposed deep down he was hoping the sweet, kind girl he'd first met would return but had grown to realize she was never those things in the first place. She'd played the part well, but it had just been a ruse. The honest Jessica was an angry, bitter woman who liked to get her own way and didn't care who she stepped on to make it happen. There was a reason he hadn't introduced her to his parents in Ireland, despite their persistence. They'd been asking him to bring her to Killarney with him on his next visit, understandably wanting to meet her. Thirty-four years old, he'd had his fair share of flings, but she was the first woman he'd allowed to move in with him. Because of that, his parents assumed things were much more serious than they were and would jokingly ask when the wedding was. As the old saying goes, a lot of truth is revealed in jest. They clearly wanted him to settle down, but the thought of marrying Jessica had never crossed his mind. If he ever did marry, he envisioned his wife to be genuinely compassionate and understanding, two traits Jessica lacked. As he boarded his flight, he knew they'd be thrilled by his surprise visit yet disappointed to hear he'd broken things off with her. He was confident that, had they met her, they would have understood his decision. They were very perceptive people who wouldn't have been blinded by her beauty and would have seen through her act. She was good, so that it might have taken them a couple of days, but they would have seen through it and agreed that she wasn't the right fit for him.

Pushing Jessica from his mind, he buckled into his seat, excited to see his parents. It had been far too long. He'd promised them that he'd visit but had kept himself so busy with work that he hadn't made time.

That time was now, and as the plane ascended into the sky, he vowed to make the most of the trip. For the first time in a year, he was going to let loose and have fun.

# Chapter Three

## *Vivian*

The flight from Denver to her layover in Heathrow, London, felt every bit as long as she feared it would. Vivian slept for half of the ten-hour flight and spent the other half stressing out about work. In the seven years since launching her business, she'd never taken a week off from work. She'd take the occasional sick day, but never more than that. Having taken an entire week off was causing her anxiety to skyrocket. She helped calm her nerves by ordering a drink and focusing on the in-flight movie that was terrible but enough distraction to occupy her mind.

From Heathrow, it was a short flight to Dublin. She breathed a sigh of relief when she stepped off the plane, glad to be out of the sky finally. She'd seen an aerial view of the land from her window seat and was looking forward to seeing more along the drive. From what she'd seen from the air, it looked just as incredible as Samantha had described. Marcus had asked her to call him when she landed to let him know she'd arrived safely, but she'd gently reminded him that they needed to start living independently of one another. His face had fallen, but he'd agreed that she was right. Instead, she texted her friend to let her know that she'd arrived in Ireland safely and would be heading in her direction soon.

After picking up her rental car, it took her a few minutes to adjust to driving on the left side of the road. She practiced in the airport parking lot before punching Samantha's address into her GPS and starting toward Killarney. The drive was truly breathtaking, and though the sun was already beginning to set, she managed to snap a few photos of the green hillsides before losing all daylight completely. She drove the last three hours of her trip in darkness, trying not to let the narrow, winding roads scare her. Her GPS announced that she'd reached her destination when she pulled up to a modest two-story home a hair after 11:00 p.m. She'd never seen Samantha's house from the outside. However, any worries that she might have the wrong address were quickly assuaged when her friend bolted out the front door with her arms outstretched.

"I can't believe you're actually here!" Samantha shrieked, wrapping Vivian in a warm embrace.

"Neither can I," Vivian laughed. Looking over her friend's shoulder, she saw a tall, slender redhead approach with his hand outstretched. Though she'd never met him, she immediately recognized him as Samantha's husband.

"It's nice to finally meet you," he greeted with a kind smile. Vivian got a kick out of his thick Irish accent. He wasn't her type, but she could see what her friend saw in him. He was boyishly handsome, and his pale, freckled complexion matched Samantha's.

She broke from her friend's hug and shook his hand. "Likewise. Thank you two for having me."

"It's our pleasure," Brian replied, making his way to the trunk of her car. "Let me help you with your luggage."

"You're a sweetheart," she gushed, popping the trunk. "It's been a long day. The last thing I want to deal with is this damn suitcase."

"That's what these manly muscles are for," he joked, flexing his skinny right arm. With Samantha by her side, they watched as he fought to get the suitcase out of the trunk.

"I never claimed he was the most masculine man," Samantha leaned over to whisper in Vivian's ear. She turned her attention back to her husband and asked, "Need some help with that, babe?"

"Very funny," he groaned, struggling to lift the luggage. He finally wrestled it from the car, and it landed on the ground with a heavy thud.

"Please tell me you don't have anything valuable in there," Samantha winced.

"Thankfully, I left my fine china at home."

After guiding her inside, they sat in the living room and talked briefly before Brian politely excused himself for the night as it was well past midnight, and he had to work early the next day. He shook Vivian's hand and assured her they'd spend more time together the following week when he wasn't so busy. A handshake seeming too informal, she stood to hug him and thanked him yet again for the hospitality. He was a kind, outgoing, outrageously funny man who had kept her laughing from the moment she'd stepped inside. She was glad her friend had found such a gentle soul to spend the rest of her life with.

"He's great," she smiled, returning to her seat on the sofa by Samantha's side.

"Right? I scored a winner for sure." She cleared her throat and looked at Vivian apologetically. "I'm sorry about you and Marcus. I know you weren't in love, but it still sucks."

"I'm already over it," Vivian shrugged.

"Is he?"

"He tries to act like it, but I know he's not."

The two stayed up for another hour, catching up on each other's lives between reminiscing. They laughed as they relived their glory days, recalling what cut-ups they'd been back in high school and how their lives had turned out nothing like they'd planned. Vivian was well known around Denver thanks to her pictures being plastered on real estate billboards throughout the city, but that was a far cry from the famous criminal defense lawyer she'd aspired to be. She'd given up on that dream years earlier when she discovered the joy of buying and selling homes. Her father had made his living in real estate and had handed her the tools she needed to excel in the trade. Samantha longed to be a superstar, briefly singing in karaoke bars before realizing that achieving international fame was easier said than done. She ended up working many dead-end jobs before meeting Brian while vacationing with her family. They hit it off so well that he'd flown her back three weeks later, and they'd been married in a quiet ceremony in Killarney National Park. Now, she worked part-time as a cashier in a small craft store in town and was looking for something else with better pay.

"Girl, I'm beaten," Vivian yawned. "I forgot how tiring traveling can be."

"Let's get you to bed," Samantha said, gently slapping her friend on the knee. "We have a busy day tomorrow."

"We do?" Vivian asked, confused.

"You think I'm going to have you come all this way and have nothing planned? Trust me, you're going to love it."

"This could be dangerous," Vivian playfully groaned, following her friend upstairs to a small room that looked like it hadn't seen much activity.

"It'll be nice to finally use the spare bedroom before it becomes the baby's room in a year or so."

Even though Brian had gone to bed and was out of earshot, Vivian leaned in and whispered, "Are you pregnant already?"

"Not yet," Samantha laughed, "but soon, if all goes well."

Vivian noted her suitcase sitting by the bed. "Tell Brian I said thank you for lugging that thing up here for me."

"He'll probably be sore from it tomorrow," Samantha laughed. "He's a wimp, but he's a loveable one."

"Mind if I take a quick shower before I crawl into bed?"

"Make yourself right at home, girl. What's ours is yours. Help yourself to anything. If you get hungry, the fridge and pantry are all stocked up."

"Thank you for everything. You and Brian… you've both been so amazing already," Vivian said, bringing her friend in for a long hug. "I needed this more than I thought."

"I needed it, too. Three years is a long time to go without seeing your best friend."

"Any specific time I should be up?" Vivian asked, breaking the hug and opening her suitcase.

Samantha waved her hand dismissively. "You're on vacation. Sleep in as long as you want. The fun will begin whenever you haul your ass out of bed."

"You're the best."

"I know."

Alone in the room, Vivian moved the contents of her luggage into the small dresser positioned across from the bed. Since she would stay an entire week, she preferred not to spend every day rooting through her suitcase for an outfit. With her clothes neatly folded and put away, she crossed the hall to the bathroom to take a quick shower. After drying off with the fresh towels Samantha had left out for her, she quietly returned to the guest bedroom and crawled into bed wearing only a baggy t-shirt, her usual nightwear. Despite being in a strange, new land, she fell asleep quickly, exhausted from the long day of traveling, and comforted by knowing her best friend was nearby.

She awoke around 10:00 a.m., shocked that she'd slept so long. She was typically lucky to sleep five hours a night, so getting nearly seven full hours was a welcomed surprise. The smell of eggs and bacon lured her downstairs, where she found Samantha in the kitchen preparing what appeared to be a late breakfast.

"Morning, sunshine," her friend greeted with a smile. "Manage to get some sleep?"

"One of the best nights of sleep I've had in ages, actually. Thank you," Vivian replied as she sat at the small kitchen table.

"Good. I was hoping you'd wake up in time to join me for breakfast."

"Sorry, I slept so long. It was just nice not to have any worries for once, you know? No work, no boy troubles, and knowing my best friend was in the next room knocked me right out."

"I'm glad to hear it," Samantha grinned. "You're going to need your energy today."

"Oh, God," Vivian groaned. "We're not going on one of your crazy ten-mile hikes or something, are we?"

"No, no," her friend laughed. "I wouldn't do that to you."

"Good. I'd hate for this friendship to end in murder."

Samantha laughed again and divided the scrambled eggs she'd made into two plates. "No need to sharpen your knife. You're going to love what I have in store for you, trust me."

"Which is?" Vivian asked with a slight look of concern.

"Well," Samantha began, serving Vivian breakfast before sitting across from her with her plate. She poured them both a glass of orange juice from the pitcher centered on the table. "First, I want to take you to Killarney National Park, where Brian and I married. It's beautiful. There's an old castle there you have to see."

"Oh?"

"Yeah, you probably saw it in the background of our wedding photos. It's called 'Ross Castle' and was built in the 15th century. Very historic place."

"I'm down! Let's do it."

"Then I want to show you around town. There are a few shops I know you'll love."

"I can get behind that idea."

"After that... well, you'll have to wait and see," Samantha said, grinning mischievously.

Vivian paused a forkful of eggs halfway to her mouth. "Okay, now I'm scared."

Samantha laughed and took a sip of her orange juice. "Don't be. You'll love it, I promise."

"Do I get any hints?"

"Nope! Now finish up because I want to head out soon."

With breakfast out of the way, the two returned upstairs to get ready for the day. They bounced jokes off each other while they changed into presentable yet casual outfits and did their makeup, feeling like they were back in high school again as they giggled until their eyes watered and their sides hurt. An hour later, they were finally ready and driving toward the National Park in Samantha's mid-size SUV, taking the scenic route so Vivian could soak in the land. She was moved by the unique architecture of the houses and the sprawling green hills scattered with sheep and gasped at the sight of St. Mary's Cathedral. Its brick construction and tall lancet windows held a Victorian-era feel, its tall spire shooting upward into the blue afternoon sky.

"Beautiful, right?" Samantha asked, noticing her friend's awestruck look.

"I love it here," Vivian replied, glowing as she absorbed her surroundings. She was also taken by the National Park and quietly relieved that Samantha didn't want to spend the entire day walking it. She didn't mind exercise, but the energetic redhead was a bit of a fanatic who could hike countless miles without breaking a sweat. She admired the girl's enthusiasm but couldn't match her endurance. After a short walk to the stone bridge where Samantha and Brian had exchanged wedding vows, they ventured over to the 500-year-old Ross Castle, which had become a major tourist attraction over the years. Vivian took her fair share of photos of the old tower house before they drove into town to check out the local shops lining the historic Main Street. She noted how, in Killarney, everything seemed to hold some historical significance. She was reasonably sure that if they passed a McDonald's, that would be of historical value, too.

They took their time perusing one shop after another, with Vivian fighting hard not to overdo it with the souvenirs. She didn't have space in her luggage for much and limited her choices to a magnet, a shot glass she hoped wouldn't break on the trip home, and a few postcards. When Samantha insisted they hit a high-end clothing store named *Weardrobe Boutique*, Vivian quickly found out why.

"We're getting dolled up tonight," Samantha informed her, leading her to a selection of beautiful but pricey dresses.

"You're up to no good, aren't you?" Vivian grumbled, rolling her eyes. Samantha was known to get wild but thought her friend had outgrown those days. She couldn't keep up with her friend's workouts, and she certainly couldn't keep up with her drinking. She'd learned years earlier not to even try.

"Shush, you. We're having a girls' night, but we have to look our best."

"I packed a few nice outfits. I can just wear something I brought."

"No, you don't understand. Where we're going, we have to…" Samantha trailed off as she began browsing the dresses.

"We have to what?" Vivian prodded, studying her friend's face. The girl wasn't giving anything away.

"Just trust me and pick out a damn dress." She grabbed a yellow number from the rack and held it up to herself. "Would I look good in this or not? Be honest."

"You'd rock that," Vivian nodded. "Can you please give me a hint?"

"What about the color?" Samantha asked, ignoring her question. "Is it okay?"

Realizing she wasn't going to get any information out of her friend, she sighed and answered, "Yes, it's fine. You look good in any color."

After poring through the dresses for nearly an hour, Samantha decided on the long, empire-cut yellow dress that had initially caught her eye. Vivian settled on a sheath cut with a slit that showed off a hint of leg and a deep enough v-neck to display just the right amount of cleavage. She was iffy on the color, but Samantha assured her that the lavender contrasted nicely against her dark skin. The dress was a perfect fit, looking like it had been tailored just for her. Samantha, on the other hand, wasn't so lucky. Being rail thin, her dress was a bit too loose for her liking, but with a tailor right around the corner, adjusting it wasn't much trouble. While they waited for the tailor to make the alterations, they hit up *O'Connor Pub* just down the street to grab lunch and a drink. Vivian was surprised when Samantha showed restraint, ordering only one drink with her burger. She also limited herself to one drink, knowing her friend's plans for the evening would likely involve a lot more alcohol.

Vivian wouldn't take no for an answer and paid for lunch. She was delighted by the pub's warm, friendly atmosphere and could see why it was such a local hot spot. With welcoming smiles that were genuine and not forced, the staff made total strangers feel like family, and the food didn't disappoint. Their bellies were full, so they walked back to the tailor to pick up Samantha's dress. It was a bit tight around the middle, given how much she'd eaten, but Samantha knew it would fit perfectly once her food settled some. From there, they hit up a few more shops to find shoes matching their new dresses. Already tall enough and not wanting to tower over anybody, Samantha chose white leather flats, while Vivian found a pair of lavender heels that matched her dress perfectly. They picked up a few accessories to complete their outfits—clutches, bracelets, and hair clips—before returning to Samantha's home with Vivian, still clueless about what her friend had planned. At Samantha's insistence, they left their shopping bags in the car.

"Grab your makeup," Samantha said over her shoulder as they trudged upstairs. "We'll get changed when we get there."

"Get where?" Vivian asked, following behind her friend.

"It's a bit of a drive, but you'll see. Just grab your makeup and whatever else you'll need to get dolled up."

"Are we going to the opera or something?"

"Yes, Viv, we're totally going to the opera," Samantha replied sarcastically as she darted into her bedroom to grab her makeup. She returned seconds later and handed her friend a plastic bag. "Here. Put your stuff in this."

Vivian did as told and filled the bag with her makeup, razor, lotion, and hairbrush. "I think that's all I need."

"Anything else we can get along the way," Samantha assured her. She glanced at the time and added, "Shit, we must get going. Come on."

Before heading out the door, Samantha stopped to leave a note for Brian, who was still at work. She could have sent him a text message but chose to write him a couple of sentences that she left in plain sight on the kitchen counter. Vivian smiled at the gesture and stole a quick glance at the note that read:

*4:00 p.m. Just left with Vivian for the night. We'll be back tomorrow. I'll call you later, baby. I love you!*

"So we're going out for the entire night?" Vivian asked, unable to hold back the question. Her curiosity was truly piqued now. "Should I bring a change of clothes?"

"You shouldn't need one," Samantha replied, ushering her out the door. They climbed back into the SUV and were off again, a destination unknown to Vivian.

They spent the next hour laughing as Vivian spit out her ridiculous, over-the-top ideas of where they could go. Samantha played along, adding to whatever silly scenario her friend concocted.

"We're going to the theater, aren't we? To watch a play?"

"Close. We're actually going to be *in* the play."

"Shit, I better start rehearsing my lines."

"Don't worry, we're just extras. The whole play is just a cover, anyway. We're secret agents, and our mission is to dig up dirt on the leading man. We just need to linger backstage and eavesdrop on his conversations."

"Will we get guns?"

"Guns *and* grenades," Samantha grinned. "You know, in case shit goes down."

"Good thing I'm an expert marksman with a mean pitching arm."

"Aren't you also a karate master like me?"

"Kung-fu, actually."

The two laughed and kept the routine going. Vivian took in the passing scenery, but when another half an hour passed, she found it harder to appreciate the foreign land.

"Okay, seriously, where are we going?" she asked, shifting in her seat. "We've been driving for over an hour already."

"And we're only halfway there," Samantha smirked. "Get comfortable. I'll let you know when we're close."

"This better be good," Vivian grumbled.

The sun was sinking behind the treeline when they arrived, the destination making Vivian's jaw drop. Mouth agape, she was speechless as they pulled up to a sprawling, well-kept castle that dwarfed the more miniature, run-down castle they'd toured earlier in the day that, in her mind, had seemed more like an old brick fort than anything. She gasped at the sight of this majestic, almost intimidating castle that stretched across the landscape and high into the twilight.

"Tell me this wasn't worth the drive," Samantha smiled, pleased with her friend's reaction.

"It's... It's incredible," Vivian muttered, leaning forward in her seat and admiring the view as they made their way past a grand stone gate and continued down the long, paved driveway toward the sweeping castle. It was well-illuminated from the outside, with light pouring out its many windows from the inside. A large, circular fountain had been carefully positioned in front of the castle and shot streams of water into the air. The property was meticulously cared for, the grass freshly cut and trees neatly pruned. When they approached the main entrance, they were promptly greeted by two gentlemen wearing matching red suits.

"Welcome!" the shorter, portlier man smiled with outstretched arms.

"Let me help you with your bags," the other man said, rushing to Vivian's side.

"I got it," Vivian laughed, holding up the bag to show him how light it was and that she only had one.

"I insist," he replied with a polite grin, taking her bag anyway.

"They refuse to let you carry your things here," Samantha explained quietly, handing the man her bag as well. She tossed her keys to the shorter man, and he quickly drove off with the car. "Valet parking, too."

"Fancy," Vivian nodded, watching the car disappear behind the castle.

Standing with their two bags, the remaining man cleared his throat before speaking. "Ladies, my name is Paul McKinley, and it's my pleasure to introduce you to Ashford Castle." He paused and motioned to the main entryway. "Right this way, please."

Vivian's heart raced as they followed him inside. The lobby was immaculate; its paneled mahogany walls adorned with what appeared to be original oil paintings, not reproductions. The spacious room was decorated in shades of burgundy and magenta, adding to its royal feel, with glass chandeliers suspended above. Antique vases and artifacts sat atop the marbled surface of tables with elegantly carved legs. Red armchairs, trimmed in gold, were positioned throughout the room. In one corner, two of these chairs sat facing each other with a raised chess set in between. A suit of armor standing against a wall looked to be authentic and fit the atmosphere well. The Victorian-era influence wasn't lost on Vivian, and she gasped again as she processed her surroundings with wide, unbelieving eyes. She was no stranger to high-end real estate, but this was posh, unlike anything she'd ever seen before, even in magazines.

"Oh my God," she breathed, looking around the room in wonderment.

"And this is just the start," Samantha grinned, lightly elbowing her in the side.

"Oh my God," Vivian repeated, unable to gather her thoughts. When she finally came to her senses, she asked, "What is this place?"

Her friend looked at her with a smirk. "Only one of the most luxurious hotels in the world."

Paul guided them to a small reception desk and waited while a woman wearing a red blazer checked them into their room. She showed genuine enthusiasm as she welcomed them to the castle and detailed its many amenities before handing their room key to Paul.

Bags in hand, he led them up a flight of stairs and down a long hall, stopping at their room and unlocking it for them. Ushering them inside, he carefully set their bags on the bed and handed them the room key before turning on his heel to ask if there was anything else they'd need. Vivian was impressed with the service, having never stayed anywhere that walked you through the check-in process. Samantha assured him they were fine and gave him a few bills. He thanked her for the gratuity and slipped out, closing the door behind them and leaving the two alone.

Their room didn't disappoint. Both queen-size beds were dressed in matching light blue bedding that was trimmed in gold, their headboards upholstered in the same style. Curtains that matched the bedding decorated a large bay window overlooking Lake Corrib, and cream wallpaper printed with branches and leaves contrasted nicely with the eggshell white ceiling. Two light blue armchairs were seated in the corner of the room with a gold-trimmed end table positioned between them. A flat-screen television was mounted on the wall across from the beds with a desk below it, a bowl of fresh fruit resting on top. Vases stuffed with real flowers were carefully arranged around the room and added a relaxing touch. A few gold lamps were placed, and original artwork featuring birds hung from the walls. Whoever was in charge of decorating had done an excellent job making the room feel luxurious yet homey. Vivian spotted a crystal decanter filled with brandy and two Lismore-pattern Waterford Crystal tumbler glasses sitting atop another small table. She wondered how much her friend would be charged if they dipped into the alcohol. Peeking into the bathroom, she noted a shower stall adjacent to a beautiful clawfoot bathtub. Across from it, his and her sinks sat below an elegant mirror with leaves carved into its gold frame. The walls were lined with golden velvet wallpaper, the floors tiled in what appeared to be marble.

"Well?" Samantha asked, studying her friend's face. "What do you think?"

"It's incredible," Vivian replied as she stepped toward the bay window to admire the view. It was almost dark, yet she could still see the lake below. "This isn't what I was expecting at all!"

"Surprise!" her friend laughed. "We have the room until Monday morning, so we can do it up tonight and spend tomorrow recovering."

Vivian looked over her shoulder and asked, "Recovering?"

"We're getting nice and drunk tonight, baby," Samantha grinned devilishly. "Just like old times."

"This is nothing like old times," Vivian said, gesturing to the lavish room they were standing in.

"Okay, just like old times but only classier," Samantha chuckled. "Come on, let's get changed."

"Sammy, I haven't drunk in… God, it's been so long I can't even remember."

"Good. You'll be a cheaper date," Samantha joked.

"You're not kidding. Two drinks, and I'll probably be passed out."

"You pass out, I'm drawing dicks all over your face."

Vivian laughed, knowing that her friend likely wasn't kidding. As she waited for her to take a quick shower, she got comfortable on one of the beds and did a bit of research on the castle. She learned that it was over eight hundred years old and, at one point, had been owned by the Guinness family. It was a name she was familiar with, though she'd never tried their line of stouts. The castle was expanded over the centuries and eventually sold to a businessman who converted it into a hotel. The place had swapped hands a few times since then and, thanks to help from a number of investors, had grown into what many considered to be the finest luxury hotel in the world. She could see why it received such high praise.

When Samantha finished in the shower, Vivian hopped in to rinse off. By the time she was out, Samantha had already squeezed into her dress. She slipped into hers, and the two did their makeup together using the large bathroom mirror. Side by side, in front of the his-and-her sinks, they applied their makeup with painstaking perfection, both choosing shades of eyeshadow that matched their dresses. When satisfied with the results, they moved on to their hair, ensuring every strand was in place. It took nearly an hour, but when they were finally done, Vivian couldn't deny how good they looked. Samantha was equally pleased.

"Goddamn. We look so good," she beamed, fluffing her curly red hair as she admired herself.

"I'd fuck us," Vivian smirked. She did a little twirl and looked over her shoulder at her reflection while she spun.

"I'd fuck us twice, even," Samantha laughed. She grabbed her purse and added, "Come on, let's go have fun."

Vivian straightened her dress again, reached for her new purse, and followed her friend out the door. Samantha gave her a tour of the castle, doing an impressive job recounting its history as they made their way from one side to the other.

"Were you a tour guide here or something?" Vivian joked.

"No, but I could be with how much I know about this place. It's where Brian and I spent our honeymoon. I fell in love with it and had to know everything I could."

"It's truly incredible. Thank you for bringing me here."

"I've been itching to come back. Your visit gave me the perfect excuse. Let me show you the rest. There's—"

"Think we can do that tomorrow?" Vivian interrupted to ask, casting her friend a pained look. "Heels were a bad choice. My feet are killing me right now. I don't think this place would appreciate it if I took them off and walked around barefoot."

Samantha looked down at Vivian's lavender high heels and winced. "Yeah, about that. I probably should have warned you not to wear heels. My bad."

"It's fine. I just need to sit down for a bit."

"You hungry at all?"

"Starving, actually." They hadn't eaten since the pub, and that had been five hours earlier.

"Let's grab some food, have some fun, then see the rest of the place tomorrow if you're not too hungover to walk. Deal?"

"Deal, but no heels tomorrow," Vivian chuckled.

Samantha guided her to an exquisite dining room lined with the same paneled mahogany walls found throughout the castle. Sparkling crystal chandeliers hung above tables draped in white, each table set for four with fine china, wine glasses, and silverware Vivian suspected was made from actual silver. Four mahogany chairs upholstered royal blue surrounded the tables and matched the curtains decorating the room's large windows. In the corner, a pianist played softly while guests enjoyed their meals. The two settled in for a dinner that was every bit as delicious as it was expensive, and at Samantha's insistence, Vivian made sure she left room for dessert. That dessert, she would soon find out, was of the liquid variety in a breathtaking bar just down the hall known as "The Prince of Wales Room." High-back leather stools sat in front of a marbled bartop, and behind the bar, tall liquor cabinets stood stocked with a variety of the world's finest liquors. Throughout the room, leather armchairs sat around small tables also topped with marble. Oil paintings of British royalty hung on the wall, and as common throughout the castle, bowls of fresh fruit and vases filled with beautiful flowers were placed about.

As wonderful as the room was, Vivian was drawn to the handsome man sitting by himself in one of the leather armchairs. One of the only patrons in the bar, he was dressed to the nines in a black suit, his perfectly coiffed dark hair contrasting nicely with his fair complexion. She noticed him immediately as he sat sipping a glass of what appeared to be whiskey. He also took notice of her, giving her a polite nod while flashing a welcoming smile. Flustered by his piercing blue eyes and angular jawline, she turned to sit at the bar with her friend by her side.

She cleared her throat as she climbed atop her stool, trying to focus on the decor instead of the man whose eyes she could still feel on her. "This bar is gorgeous."

"And so isn't that guy behind us," Samantha replied with a smirk. "Don't think I didn't notice him, too."

"Right?" Vivian whispered, fanning her face with her hand. "Think he's a model?"

Samantha stole a glance at him over her shoulder. "Could be."

Vivian could see his reflection in the mirrored interior of the liquor cabinet. "That is one fine white boy," she muttered.

"I'm off the market, so he's all yours."

"Ha! Thanks, but no thanks. I came here to see you and get away from Marcus. The last thing I'm looking for is a random hookup."

"Who says it has to be random?"

Before she could answer, the barkeep approached and greeted them with a thick Irish brogue. "Well, well! Don't you two just look lovely? Stunning, I must say. Stunning!"

He was an older man with kind eyes and a slight hunch to his shoulders. His face glowed as he looked them over, admiring their beauty. Had he been a few years younger, he might have come off as perverse, but age had given him the innocence of a sweet old man.

"What can I get you two?" he asked with a smile, still looking them over.

"I'll have a—" Vivian began, only to be cut off by her friend.

"No," Samantha told her sternly. "No to whatever girly drink you were going to order."

"I was going to order sangria…"

"Yeah, I figured. None of that fruity crap tonight. We're getting torn up."

"I'm telling you, I can't drink like I used to," Vivian protested.

Samantha quickly countered, "No offense, but you were never very good at it back in the day."

The barkeep shook his head as he laughed at their playful banter, patiently waiting for their order. He didn't have to wait much longer.

"You know what? Bring it on," Vivian challenged, slapping the bartop. Smiling at the older man, she pulled a move that caught Samantha entirely by surprise. "Line up six shots of Jameson… and a pint of Guinness."

"Shut up," Samantha gasped in disbelief. "You can't be serious."

"You want to get wild? Let's do this thing."

"Now you're talking!" Samantha laughed. The barkeep joined in on her laughter, amused by their exchange, and got to work preparing the drinks. He moved slowly but poured them with a steady hand, filling each shot glass equally before expertly pouring the pint of Guinness.

"I'm on vacation in Ireland," Vivian announced. "So, screw it, I'm letting loose."

"This is music to my ears," Samantha beamed, watching as the old man lined up the drinks in front of them.

"I've never tried Guinness before," Vivian confessed. "But when in Rome, right?"

"There you go, ladies," the barkeep grinned, sliding the drinks closer to them. "Feel free to stay and drink until I look young and attractive again."

The two burst into a fit of laughter, and when Vivian regained control of herself, she cautiously took a sip of the Guinness, unsure of what to expect. She allowed a moment for her palate to process the unfamiliar taste before reaching her verdict.

"It's good," she nodded. "Not like I thought it would be at all."

The two divided the shots and quickly downed all six, sharing the Guinness as their chaser. It didn't take long for the three shots of whiskey to hit Vivian. Head spinning but feeling very good, she daringly ordered another round while her friend looked at her in admiration.

"Damn, girl. You weren't kidding about letting loose, huh?"

"How often am I in Ireland with my best friend?" Vivian smiled, her cheeks feeling flushed from the alcohol.

"Bottoms up," Samantha smiled, raising a shot glass. Vivian raised hers as well, and they gently clinked them together before throwing their heads back and swallowing the whiskey. Vivian winced and sipped the Guinness, while Samantha didn't bother with a chaser. This time, they waited before gulping down the remaining two shots. Neither of them wanted to get too drunk and risk making a scene in such an upscale place. Samantha looked like she was doing okay, which was no surprise to Vivian since her friend was of Irish descent.

On the other hand, Vivian was already heavily buzzed and didn't want to cross into total inebriation yet. Even with the alcohol numbing her senses, she could still feel the eyes of the handsome gentleman behind her. Casting a glance at the mirror in the liquor cabinet again, she could see him smiling at them, entertained by their revelry. He seemed to be trying not to look but couldn't help himself. She didn't blame him since they were the only liveliness in the otherwise dead bar. Half an hour had passed since they started drinking, and aside from their attractive admirer, everyone else had called it a night.

"Well, I'm officially drunk," Samantha giggled after downing her ninth shot.

"Do I look sexy yet?" the old barkeep quipped, batting his eyes at them.

The girls erupted in laughter, and Vivian slammed back her sixth shot, drinking considerably slower than her friend. She was feeling good but still in control of herself.

"One more round!" Samantha insisted, her pale, freckled face now red from the booze.

"Are you sure?" Vivian asked, questioning her friend's decision. She knew the girl could drink, but it had been a few years, and neither of them was getting any younger.

"Baby, I'm just getting started!" Samantha proclaimed boisterously, slamming her fist down hard on the bar top. She ordered six more shots, and the barkeep, with a look of concern, hesitantly poured them.

"Maybe you should slow down," Vivian leaned over to whisper, noting the barkeep's souring mood.

"Maybe you should suck my clit!" Samantha returned with a loud cackle.

Embarrassed, Vivian flashed the barkeep an apologetic look. His jovial mood had been replaced by one of irritation, and she sensed he was dangerously close to cutting them off. Distancing himself from them, he moved to the other end of the bar and began wiping it down with the small towel that had been slung over his shoulder.

"I'm kidding. Relax!" Samantha added, picking up on the tension. Quickly downing her tenth shot, she spun around in her seat and winked at the man in the black suit. "You can suck my clit anytime, though."

"Oh, Jesus," Vivian groaned, hanging her head and covering her face in humiliation.

The man took it well, roaring in laughter. He spoke in a deep voice, and she detected a hint of an Irish accent. "Well, it looks like you two ladies are having a mighty fine time tonight."

"You're hot," Samantha blurted, the whiskey having removed her filter.

"Thank you," the man replied, blushing from the compliment.

Vivian tugged on her friend's arm and hissed, "You're married, remember?"

Samantha turned her back to the man again and finished the remaining Guinness. She smacked her lips and replied, "Hey, I may be on a diet, but I can still look at the menu."

"Yeah, how about you *don't* look at the menu. I don't want you to be tempted."

"Oh, come on," Samantha said, rolling her eyes. "You know I'd never actually do anything."

Vivian wasn't so sure but reeled her friend in any way. "Just... ignore that guy, okay?"

"Okay, Mom," Samantha scoffed. She let out a small burp and added not-so-quietly, "But you should totally fuck him."

"Sammy!" Vivian gasped, covering her face in embarrassment again. Her drunken friend's attempt to be discreet had failed miserably, and she knew the man had overheard.

"What?" Samantha laughed. "Don't you want to get lucky in Ireland?"

"Okay," Vivian replied, "I think it's time we go. You've had enough."

"I remember when you used to be fun," Samantha complained. She cocked her head back and poured the eleventh shot of Jameson down her throat. "Come on, Viv, do one more with me!"

Vivian had no interest in the shots sitting in front of her. She was already buzzed enough and needed to sober up so she could spend the remainder of the night babysitting her friend. "No, I'm good. Maybe we should just go back to our room."

"And waste these bad boys?" Samantha said, gesturing to the four shots they still had left. "That's just alcohol abuse, baby."

Without warning, she polished off two shots in a row and let out a loud belch. She laughed and reached for another shot, but Vivian stopped her by covering the glass with her hand. "Just chill for a few, okay? Let those settle. I want to have fun, but you're already wasted, and we've only been here for an hour."

"Okay," Samantha conceded with a hiccup. "I can do that for you. I love you, Vivian. I really do. You're my best friend."

*Great, she's in her drunken "I love you" mode,* Vivian mused to herself, knowing there would be more to come. She wasn't wrong.

"Vivian," Samantha began, swaying in her seat. Her speech began to slur as she continued, "I love you. Do you love me? You need to say it back."

"Yes, Sammy, I love you, too," Vivian replied. She sat poised to catch her friend should she fall from her bar stool.

"Can I have another one now, please?" Samantha asked, looking at the shots with an exaggerated pouty face.

"Nice try," Vivian laughed. "Just sit with me for a bit. You're smashed."

Her friend's eyes were glassy and distant. She sat in silence for a moment before saying, "You know I'd never really cheat on Brian, right?"

"I hope not. He seems like a really good guy."

"He is. I love him tons. I just wanted to let loose and have fun tonight. Feel young again. I might flirt, but I'd never actually do anything. Brian's my world."

"That's good to hear. I was a bit worried there for a second."

"I know. But don't be." She paused and hiccupped again. "The room is spinning."

Vivian chuckled. "I'm not surprised. You've done thirteen shots already."

"You better drink those, then," Samantha smirked, looking at the two leftover shots. "Before I do."

"Let's make a deal," Vivian sighed. "I'll do one right now if you wait half an hour before doing another. Good?"

"A half an hour? That's, like... forever. Can I order a beer or something while I wait?"

"No."

"A glass of wine?"

"No!"

"Fine," Samantha groaned in defeat, crossing her arms in indignation.

Satisfied with the negotiation, Vivian reluctantly did her shot without a chaser. It burned all the way down, but within minutes, she was feeling good again. Against her better judgment, she did the final shot as they once again relived their younger days, laughing as they recounted stories from their past. The barkeep's mood seemed to lighten some as Samantha appeared to sober up. Behind them, the attractive man in the black suit sat sipping a fresh glass of whiskey while reading a book. Vivian couldn't help but sneak more glances at him in the mirror.

"I need to go pee," Samantha announced. It came as no surprise since she'd drank so much without having gone yet. "I'll be right back."

Vivian watched as her friend clumsily stepped down from the stool and hurried out of the room, leaving her alone at the bar. Despite the liquor in her, she was overcome by a sudden wave of awkwardness as she felt the handsome stranger's eyes on her again. There seemed to be some sort of energy between them, but she didn't dare act on it. Unsure of what to do, she ordered another pint of Guinness and two more shots. She took a sip of the stout, letting its unique taste linger, but the silence in the room was too much for her to bear. Turning on her stool, she waved at the man and mustered the nerve to speak.

"Hello. I'm sorry if we've been a nuisance tonight."

He set his book aside and smiled at her warmly. "No need to apologize. You've been quite entertaining."

"My friend can be kind of a handful."

"The amount of whiskey she's drank would turn anyone into a handful," he laughed. "It's okay." He motioned to the open chair across from him and asked, "Would you care to join me?"

"Thank you, but my friend will be back any minute now."

"I wouldn't hold your breath on that one," he chuckled.

She looked at him in confusion. "What do you mean?"

"I heard her say she had to go to the bathroom. I wasn't trying to eavesdrop. She's just a bit… loud."

"What are you getting at?" she asked with a raised brow.

"Well, she went that way," he began, nodding to where Samantha had stumbled off. "But the bathroom is that way," he continued, pointing in the opposite direction.

Vivian craned her neck and followed his finger to two bathroom doors.

"Oh, goddammit," she muttered, realizing he was right. Her friend had drunkenly wandered off the wrong way, and she really didn't want to chase after her. "I suppose I should go find her."

He leaned forward and patted the chair across from him. "Come sit with me for a few. She's probably just using one of the bathrooms down the hall. She'll be back."

She didn't want to be a bad friend but certainly wasn't in the mood to hunt the girl down. The man also had a magnetic charm that made it hard to say no, especially with the drinks clouding her mind. Assuring herself that Samantha could find her way back, she took him up on his offer and carefully climbed off her stool, not wanting to embarrass herself by falling. She grabbed her drinks—two shots in one hand, the pint of Guinness in the other—and approached him.

"Okay," she said as she settled across from him and set her drinks on the table between them. "But if she's not back in five minutes, I must go look for her."

"I respect that," he smiled. Setting his drink down, he offered his hand and introduced himself. "Beau Sullivan. Nice to meet you."

She shook it and could feel his strong yet gentle nature. "Vivian Clark. Nice to meet you, too."

"Forgive me if you caught me staring a few times," he said as he reached for his drink. "You're just stunning."

The unexpected compliment made her blush, but she was quick to return the sentiment. "I could say the same about you. Are you a model or something?"

He threw his head back and laughed. "Me? You're too funny." He took a sip of his drink and volunteered, "I'm a venture capitalist. I've been mistaken for many things over the years, but never a model. I'm flattered."

"Venture capitalist," she repeated, kicking the words around in her head. "So you're an investor?"

"That's right. Let me guess… you're an entertainer of some sort. An actress, perhaps?"

Now, it was her turn to laugh. "No, no. I run my own real estate firm."

"Oh, wow," he replied with his eyebrows raised. "That's very impressive. With your looks, I assumed you were in show business."

She felt her cheeks flush. "You're quite the flatterer."

"Just being honest."

"Well, for the remainder of our time together, you can be a model, and I'll be an actress," she joked, raising a shot glass.

"Deal," he chuckled, lifting his glass to meet hers.

Vivian downed her shot, chasing it with a sip of the Guinness, and looked over her shoulder. Still no sign of Samantha. She'd give it a bit longer, then go looking.

"So… do you live here?" she asked.

"Just visiting. I'm guessing by your complete lack of accent that you're just visiting, too?"

"I am. It's my first time."

"Oh? What do you think about it so far?"

"I love it!" she burst, unable to contain her enthusiasm. "Everything is just so beautiful, and there's so much history. Everyone's been really nice, too."

"It's a wonderful place," he agreed.

"You have a slight accent. Are you originally from here?"

"My parents live here," he explained. "I moved to the States when I was only eighteen. I love it here, but there's a lot more opportunity there, as far as investing goes."

"That makes sense," she replied, completely captivated by him. It took a lot to hold her interest, but he was doing it in spades. Not only was he gorgeous, he was clearly successful and driven. Whatever cologne he was wearing wafted her way and added to her intoxication. She silently scolded herself for being so completely taken by his looks, charm, and intellect.

"So, Vivian Clark," he started, his eyes locked on to hers. "You're just here visiting your friend?"

"I am," she answered, taking another sip of her Guinness. "I just... I really needed to get away."

"Oh?"

"I broke things off with my boyfriend and just needed to get away."

"What happened?" he prodded gently.

"We were together for three years, and I just couldn't take it anymore. He's a good guy, but it wasn't working. He wanted to get married and have kids, but I didn't. Not with him, anyway. He was just so… boring. I wanted to focus on my career." She wasn't sure if it was the alcohol or his kind, inviting eyes that made her open up, but she feared she'd rambled and overshared. Feeling exposed and vulnerable, she poured one of her shots into her stout and took a swig. "Anyway, yeah. I ended things, my friend invited me to visit, and here I am."

"So you're here kind of as an escape?"

"You could say that," she shrugged.

"Well, then. Cheers to being in the same boat," he smiled, lifting his glass to hers. "I just ended things with my girlfriend. We were only together for a year, but it was a total disaster. I'm rather ashamed that I let it go on so long."

"Are you being serious?"

"Unfortunately, yes. I made the brilliant decision of letting her move in a few months ago." He shook his head and let out a long, deep sigh. "Boy, was that a mistake."

"That bad, huh?" Vivian asked, genuinely interested in his story.

"You have no idea," he chuckled. "I told her it was over, asked her to move out, and hopped a flight here. I'm just hoping she's really gone when I get back."

"Think she really will be?"

"I think so, yes." He paused and swirled his whiskey around in his glass. "I just hope she hasn't burned my place to the ground."

"Yikes. I take it the breakup didn't go well?"

"That's putting it lightly," he laughed. "Yours?"

"I have to say, he took it much better than I thought he would. If I'm being sincere, I was a bit disappointed he didn't put up more of a fight."

"It seems you made the right choice, then. If he wasn't willing to fight for a beautiful, intelligent woman like you, he clearly didn't deserve you."

"Thank you," she blushed, shifting in her seat.

"I'm sorry," he said, noting her sudden discomfort. "I wasn't making a pass at you."

"It's okay," she assured him with a smile. "If I hadn't sworn off men, I'd be just fine with you making passes at me."

He laughed and replied, "I get it. The last thing I'm looking for right now is another woman. Besides, I've learned firsthand that there's much more than beauty and brains. Personality goes a long way."

"That it does," Vivian agreed, remembering how monotonous Marcus was. He was handsome and smart but painfully dull. "Was your ex as boring as mine?"

"Truthfully, I probably would have welcomed boring," he smirked. "She was a bit dramatic, to put it gently. And not a very nice person."

"No?"

"Don't even get me started," he groaned. "The stories I could tell you..."

"Oh, come on. Give me at least one."

He finished off his whiskey and set the empty glass by his book. "Okay," he began. "Get this. Seven months into our relationship, I found out she'd been lying about being on birth control. When I confronted her about it, she told me it didn't matter anyway since I was infertile. That came as news to me. I was skeptical, but she had me take a test. Turns out she was right. I failed it miserably." He stopped and asked, "I'm sorry, is this too much information? Perhaps the whiskey is making me share a bit more than I should."

"No, it's fine," she told him, amused by how similar their thought process was. "Please, go on."

"Anyhow, after I failed, I thought that would be the end of it. Instead, she'd use it against me every time we fought... which was a lot. She'd belittle my manhood. Mock me for 'shooting blanks,' as she so eloquently said."

"Oh my God, that's awful," Vivian gasped, covering her mouth in shock. "What a horrible woman."

"Yeah, she'd pull that card every time we'd argue. 'I'm not acting crazy. You're just insecure because of your broken balls,' she'd tell me. Nice, right?"

"Nobody deserves to have that used against them. I'm so sorry."

He cocked his head and chuckled in amusement. "Did I really just tell you all that? What a lousy thing to dump on somebody I just met. Where are my manners? I'm the one who should be apologizing. I just got way too personal there."

"Stop," she said with a comforting smile. "It's fine."

His deep blue eyes were mesmerizing, but she managed to break from them long enough to steal another glance over her shoulder. Again, there was no sign of Samantha.

"I'm enjoying your company, but I know you need to find your friend," he said with an understanding look. "You should probably go look for her."

"I should," Vivian nodded. "Thank you for—"

She was interrupted by Samantha's slurred voice blaring through the bar. "Party time, motherfuckers!"

Their heads spun around to see Samantha stumble into the bar with a glass raised in one hand and a crystal decanter half full of liquor in the other. Vivian immediately recognized the set as the one she'd seen in their room earlier.

"Seriously?" she groaned, piecing together where her friend had really been. The girl was clever. She had to give her that.

"Sorry, but I couldn't wait half an hour," Samantha grinned, drunkenly making her way over to them and taking a seat on the arm of Vivian's chair. She chugged the rest of her drink and noisily slammed the glass down on the small table along with the decanter. "Don't be mad at me, mom."

Before Vivian could even speak, the barkeep had hurried over to scold the inebriated redhead for bringing the decanter of whiskey into the bar. "Ma'am, I'm sorry, but I'm afraid I will have to ask you to leave. Outside food and beverages aren't allowed in here."

"What the fuck?" Samantha spat. "It's from our room. It's not like you're losing money on it. I didn't get it from a goddamn convenience store."

"Ma'am," the older man said, trying to keep his cool, "rules are rules, and I think you've had enough to drink anyway."

"It's okay," Beau interjected, waving a hand at the barkeep. "If you could let it slide just this once, I'd be indebted to you, William."

"I don't know, Mr. Sullivan..." the barkeep, now identified by name, replied as he considered the situation. "Look at her. She's right pissed."

Vivian reminded herself that "pissed" had a different meaning in Ireland. Here, it meant "drunk," and that's precisely what her friend was.

"I'll take full responsibility for her, I promise," Beau told him with a look of sincerity. Glancing around the room, he appended, "There's nobody else here. She won't be disturbing anybody."

"Okay," William conceded, "but if she pukes, you're cleaning it up."

"Deal," Beau smiled, nodding his head in agreement.

"Oh my God, I'm not going to puke," Samantha scoffed as she rolled her eyes. "I'm not an amateur."

The barkeep shuffled back to his position behind the bar, leaving the two girls in the company of the handsome man in the black suit.

"Beau Sullivan," he greeted, extending his hand to Samantha. "Pleased to meet you."

She shook it and released a small hiccup. "Samantha Berney. You're really hot."

"Sammy!" Vivian quietly hissed, poking her friend in the side.

"Thank you," he laughed. "I believe you mentioned that earlier."

"How did you do that?" Samantha asked, jerking her chin in the direction of the barkeep. "Are you famous or something?"

"No, no," he laughed. "But I do have a little clout."

"I see you've met my friend, Vivian," Samantha said, teetering on the arm of the chair. "Isn't she gorgeous?"

Beau looked deep into Vivian's eyes and smiled. "She is... and that's not a word I toss around."

"You two…" Vivian waved dismissively, trying to play off the compliments. She felt her cheeks flush once again and reached for her drink.

"Give me a sip of that, you black hooker," Samantha blurted, intercepting her friend's whiskey-laced Guinness and gulping half of it before Vivian could pry the glass from her hands.

"That's enough!" Vivian snapped. "Seriously, no more for you tonight, got it?"

Samantha ignored the warning. Smacking her lips, she mumbled, "Shit that was good."

Unlike Vivian, who was visibly annoyed with her friend, Beau looked amused by the freckled redhead. "I see you've got some Irish in you, huh?"

"Damn straight. Thank you for putting—" She paused to hiccup again and continued, "Thank you for putting up with us. Vivian's my best friend. I love her so much but don't get to see her much anymore."

"I probably would have left an hour ago had you two not been so entertaining," Beau smiled.

Beginning to lose her balance on the arm of the chair, Samantha wrapped an arm around Vivian to help brace herself. Once again glassy and distant, her eyes reflected just how drunk she was. Beads of sweat peppered her forehead, and her clammy skin looked even paler than usual.

"You doing okay?" Vivian asked, gently patting her friend's leg.

"I'm good. I just need a sec—"

She was mid-sentence when she unexpectedly vomited. It poured down the front of her dress but miraculously didn't get on Vivian, who had recoiled at the sight, pushing herself away from her friend.

"Sammy, what the fuck?" Vivian growled, springing to her feet.

"I'm sorry!" Samantha cried, her yellow dress now stained with puke.

Hearing the commotion, the barkeep looked over, but Vivian quickly stepped in front of her friend to shield her from his view.

"Everything's fine," Beau assured the old man. "Nothing we can't handle."

"This is a first," Samantha burped, looking down at the mess she'd made of herself.

"Okay, we're done here," Vivian huffed. "Come on. We're going to our room. I'm cleaning you up, and you're going to bed, you hear me?"

"I'm so sorry. I didn't mean to ruin the evening," the intoxicated redhead sobbed, tears streaming down her reddened cheeks.

"Thank you for the conversation," Vivian told Beau with an apologetic look. Turning her attention back to Samantha, she guided her friend to her feet but knew the girl couldn't stand alone. "Goddammit, Sammy," she muttered, slinging her friend's arm over her shoulder to help support her.

"I love you," Samantha slurred.

Vivian cringed as the stench of the vomit hit her nose. She wasn't sure how to handle the predicament her friend had placed them in. The old barkeep was still unaware of what had happened, but they needed to pay their tab. There was no way Samantha could walk without her help, which made it impossible to square up without him finding out. Sensing her dilemma, Beau chimed in to offer his help.

"Just get her back to your room," he said, rising to his feet. "I'll cover your tab."

"I can't have you do that," Vivian replied. "We both drank a lot. It would be way too expensive."

"I insist. It is my fault, too. I'm the one who wanted her to stay."

Samantha looked down at her dress and commented satirically, "I hope this doesn't stain."

"Come on," Beau persisted. He smirked and added, "I can't have William mad at me now, can I?"

Realizing she didn't have many options, Vivian sighed and accepted his help. "Okay, but I'm paying you back. Will you still be here tomorrow?"

"I'm leaving in the morning. Seriously, it's fine. I got you."

"Thank you," Vivian smiled, her friend's arm still slung over her shoulder.

"You're hot *and* sweet," Samantha blurted, running a finger down his chest.

Beau laughed and shook his head. "You're a character, Samantha Berney. It was nice meeting you."

Samantha stumbled, but Vivian caught her and helped her out of the bar. The barkeep eyed them suspiciously but didn't notice the vomit painting the front of Samantha's dress. It was a challenge, but with a degree of work, Vivian was able to get her friend back to their room, where she got sick again, a hair short of the toilet, covering the bathroom in puke. After cleaning it up, she placed the stained dress in the tub to soak and put her friend to bed. She was about to climb into bed when a gentle rapped on their door. She feared it was management asking them to leave, which would have been wrong since neither of them was in any condition to drive. Samantha was passed out drunk on her belly and breathing heavily. As for her, she was still quite buzzed and in no shape to pack up and go.

She nervously cracked the door, and relief coursed through her at seeing him.

"Hello, stranger," she smiled. "What a pleasant surprise."

# Chapter Four

## *Beau*

"Those two left in a hurry," William said as Beau approached the bar, noting how quickly the girls had left. "They better be back. They didn't pay their bill."

"I got it," Beau assured him, pulling a billfold from the inside pocket of his suit jacket. He tugged a few bills loose and threw them down on the bar top. "Keep the change."

"Ah, you're too kind, Mr. Sullivan," William smiled.

"You have yourself a good night," Beau replied, returning the old barkeep's smile.

Being a key investor in the luxury hotel allowed Beau certain privileges. He used his influence to get Vivian and Samantha's room number but lingered in the lobby, unsure if he should use the information. Deciding against it, he returned to his suite and loosened his tie before sinking into one of the red armchairs. Propping his feet on the matching ottoman, he dug his cell phone from his pocket to see what he missed. After arriving in Ireland earlier that day, he'd put his phone on silent and had made a point not to check it. He was proud of himself for having avoided it this long.

Ten new text messages awaited him. One of them was from Gabby, confirming a meeting with a potential partner the following week. The other nine, as he expected, were from Jessica.

*Were you serious about me moving out?*

*Now that we've both had time to cool down, I think we can work this out.*

*Where are you?*

*Does your whore know about your broken balls?*

*I'm sorry. Please just come home.*

*You got some mail. I left it on the counter. Miss you.*

*Seriously, where did you go?*

*Are you okay?*

*Fine, whatever. Have fun with your slut.*

"Oh, for fuck's sake," he groaned. He didn't want to but knew he had to reply if he really wanted her gone when he got back. He reluctantly responded, choosing his words carefully, hoping she wouldn't do something stupid… if she hadn't already.

*Visiting my parents for a week. I'd appreciate it if you could have your stuff out by the time I get back. Thank you, Jessica. I'm sorry it didn't work. No hard feelings, okay? You're a great girl.*

The last part was a lie, but one he had to tell to soften the blow. She was obviously hoping he'd change his mind, but her bipolar messages had only cemented his decision. Meeting Vivian had also offered some assurance that he'd made the right choice by reminding him that other women were out there. Beautiful, intelligent women whose moods wouldn't change at the drop of a hat. Though he'd only spent a few minutes with her, he sensed that Vivian was kind and genuine. However, he knew he shouldn't rush to judgment as Jessica was proof that things weren't always as they seemed. He chastised himself for even thinking of another woman, considering he'd just ended his relationship earlier that day. Getting involved with another woman so soon was the last thing he needed… yet he couldn't stop thinking about Vivian. They shared an energy unlike anything he'd felt before, and it wasn't just lust. If she'd been truthful about running her own business, it showed a relatable drive he greatly respected. Unlike Jessica, or any of his previous girlfriends for that matter, she'd used her intellect to achieve success instead of relying on her looks. Beautiful, self-made women weren't exactly a dime a dozen. Knowing this, he sat in deliberation, conflicted by his two choices. He could let their brief encounter go, or he could act on the undeniable chemistry between them.

A text message alert broke him from his thoughts. A cursory glance showed it was from Jessica, but he didn't bother reading it. He was still feeling good from his few drinks and didn't want her killing what was left of his buzz. He did note the time, however, and tapped his fingers on the arm of the chair as he weighed his options. It was late, but not too late for a visit to be considered rude. He could forget about Vivian and go to bed, or he could take a risk and bravely knock on her door. Calling was out of the question as a loud ringing may wake Samantha, assuming Vivian had managed to get her to sleep.

In a split-second decision, he bolted from his seat and set off toward her room. He'd been completely captivated by her and didn't want to miss out on his only opportunity to get to know her better. In the morning, he would be gone, and so would his chances of seeing her again. It was now or never, and taking risks was the foundation of his success. He generally hit more balls than he missed and hoped he wouldn't strike out this time. He stopped outside her door and listened for any sound coming from inside but was greeted by only silence. A faint light from under the door hinted at somebody being awake, but he lingered, suddenly unsure of his decision. He was surprised to find his usual confidence gone, replaced by a nervous self-doubt he hadn't expected and seldom experienced. It was the whiskey still in his system that gave him the courage to proceed, knocking gently on her door. He heard the shuffling of somebody approaching from the other side, and a moment later, the door cracked open. Vivian's face lit up at the sight of him. She'd changed out of her dress and stood wearing only a t-shirt that hung low enough to keep her decent. Even dressed down, she still looked incredible.

"Hello, stranger," she smiled. "What a pleasant surprise."

"Is it?" he asked. "I know it's getting late. I didn't want to disturb you."

"I'm just relieved it's not management kicking us out."

"How's she doing?"

Vivian sighed and rolled her eyes. "She's passed out... finally."

"I'm glad you got her to bed safely. You're a good friend."

"I try." A look of worry crossed her face, and she looked over her shoulder toward the bathroom. "I'm sorry about the smell. She puked everywhere. I cleaned it up best, but it still stinks."

"I didn't even notice," he assured her. "At least she got it all out of her system."

"True. It's probably for the best that the night ended like it did. Another few minutes and she would have been dancing on the bar... topless. That would have gotten us kicked out for sure."

Beau stifled his chuckle when he realized Vivian wasn't joking. "She gets that wild, huh?"

"Boy, you have no idea."

"Well," he said, looking at his watch, "the night doesn't have to be over. I'm still feeling good and have a stocked bar in my suite. If you'd care to join me, I'd love to have you."

His heart raced as he awaited her response. Studying her face, he could see her trepidation and understood why she was reluctant to accept his invitation. They barely knew each other, and she clearly had reservations about leaving her friend behind. He was sure she'd decline his offer and had steeled himself for the rejection when she surprised him.

"You know what? I'd like that," she smiled. "Can I have a second to get dressed, though? Oh, and I should probably leave a note for Samantha in case she wakes up."

"Take all the time you need," he replied, smiling back. He waited outside the door for a few minutes while she put herself back together. She reappeared wearing jeans and looked like she'd touched up her make-up.

"Sorry, but I wasn't about to put that dress back on," she said as she closed the door and locked it. She slipped the key into the front pocket of her jeans, where he could also see the outline of her cell phone.

"You look lovely," he replied, admiring her. Somehow, she looked just as beautiful dressed casually as she did all done up.

"I'm just glad to have those heels off," she laughed, looking down at her sneakers. "This is more my style."

As they walked back to his suite, Beau used the time to learn more about her. She was intriguing, and the conversation flowed freely with no awkward silences. It was almost like they'd known each other forever with how easily he could open up to her. She felt familiar to him in some way, perhaps because they were so similar. They came from different backgrounds yet shared the exact drive for success, both running their independent businesses that relied solely on their mental prowess. That, and a sprinkling of charm. Like him, she seemed to know how to talk to people, which was crucial for anyone making their own way in life.

With what a pleasure she was to be around, it was no surprise to him why her real estate business had taken off.

"And I thought our room was nice," she gasped when she entered his suite.

"Please, make yourself comfortable," he said, gesturing toward the sitting area.

"Thank you for having me," she replied, sitting in one of the red armchairs. She watched as he poured them both a glass of whiskey before seating himself in the armchair across from her. He handed her a drink, and she accepted it with a polite nod.

"I have to admit, I was a little nervous you'd say no."

"I almost did," she confessed.

"May I ask why you didn't?"

She took a sip of her drink as she chose her words. She didn't seem to mind drinking this glass straight, which he assumed was from the amount of alcohol she already had in her system. He didn't bother with a mixer or a chaser, either. The whiskey went down smoothly enough but packed a punch. Within seconds, he felt pretty buzzed again and could tell she was feeling good, too.

"Well," she began, "I've spent the last three years being bored. Not with my job, but with my ex, Marcus."

"Ah, yes. You mentioned him earlier."

"Let's say I could use a little excitement in my life right now," she chuckled. "It was either go to bed annoyed with Samantha or take a chance with you."

"I hope you don't regret your decision." He raised his glass and smiled warmly. "Cheers."

They spent the next hour talking like old friends. He found himself completely enamored with her mind and body, hanging on every word as she told him about her upbringing in Colorado and how she'd dived into real estate with knowledge passed on from her father. As gorgeous as she was, with her waves of long, dark hair and perfectly symmetrical face that could have quickly catapulted her to fame, her humor and kindness sucked him in. It seemed to be a genuine kindness, too, unforced with no facade.

"So tell me," she smiled. "How did you become a big-shot venture capitalist?"

"You really want to know?" he asked, surprised by her interest. In the entire year he'd been with Jessica, she'd never once asked him how he'd got his start.

"Of course. It's fascinating."

"My parents always stressed the importance of saving," he explained, pausing briefly to sip his drink. "While other kids were spending their money on candy and comic books, I was squirreling away every penny I found. My parents gave me an allowance for helping out around the house. I saved that, too. When I was fourteen, I got a job delivering newspapers and tucked away everything I earned. By the time I was eighteen, I'd saved a decent amount of money. A friend wanted to open a bicycle shop but didn't have enough capital to do it. His plan seemed solid, so I took a chance and invested in his business. It took off, and I started turning a profit within a year. I used that money to help overhaul a local tavern, then kept investing in small businesses until, collectively, I had a decent amount of money coming in and could invest in larger businesses."

"Like this place?" she asked, looking around the room.

"Exactly. This is my largest investment and my most profitable… for now."

"Oh?"

"I have a meeting with a company next week that could pay off quite well."

"Care to share?"

Her sincere interest in the machinations of his business took him aback in a good way. Never had anyone shown such a curiosity in his work, and he found himself thrilled by the opportunity to talk about it.

"There's a research laboratory developing a new technology they're calling, 'Sono-Scan.' It's pretty wild stuff. It's an advanced Ariel sonogram capable of detecting artificial caverns and other underground structures. It's so powerful it could show you the basement of this place just from a quick fly-by."

"You're kidding," Vivian replied, her jaw dropping in disbelief.

"Not one bit. It's close to being finished, but they're out of money. The military already agreed to buy the technology at a very hefty price… if they can see a final product."

"So that's where you come in?"

"Bingo. I front them the rest of the money they need to finish things up and make millions when the military buys it."

"You're a smart man, Mr. Sullivan," Vivian replied.

He was stunned she'd remembered his last name but reminded himself that being good with names had indeed played a large part in her success. She was sharp, even with a fair amount of alcohol in her system.

"I thought so until Jessica," he sighed.

"Even smart people make mistakes."

"Listen," he said, setting his glass down. He looked at her apologetically, and his tone turned serious. "I feel like that was too much information earlier. You know, downstairs in the bar."

"What do you mean?"

Seeing her confusion, he leaned in and spoke softly, "With the whole infertility thing."

"You know, had it come from anyone else, it might have been a bit much. Yet, with you… I don't know. I'm very comfortable around you, so it didn't bother me."

"I'm glad you feel the same," he said with a sigh of relief. "You're so easy to talk to."

There was a brief pause filled not with awkwardness but with lust as they looked into each other's eyes. Vivian broke the silence first by clearing her throat and taking another sip of her drink.

"I should probably get going…"

"So soon? I was hoping you'd join me for one more drink."

"What time is it?" she asked.

He glanced at his watch and replied, "A little after midnight."

"I don't know," she muttered as she mulled over the idea. "I've had a lot to drink, and if we're being honest with each other, you're very attractive."

"As are you," he was quick to return.

"I'm not sure if staying is such a good idea. It might lead to a type of excitement I'm not sure I'm ready for… if you know what I mean."

"Say no more," he nodded. "I understand."

"It would just be too easy for us to—"

"Really, I get it," he stopped her. He knew where she was going and felt the same way. With both of them close to drunk and sharing such a strong attraction to one another, the bed in the other room would prove too great a temptation.

"Thank you for having me," Vivian said, setting her glass down and standing to leave. Beau followed her lead, rising to walk her to the door.

"It's been a pleasure," he replied. He was disappointed she was leaving but didn't blame her. The chemistry between them was overpowering, and one more drink may have removed the inhibitions they were barely holding onto.

"I wish you continued success," she smiled.

It looked like she wanted to say more but thought better of it. The faint smell of her perfume quickened his pulse as she brushed by him out the door. In that moment, he desperately wanted her to stay but refrained from asking. At this point, if she wanted to stay, she would have made up her mind already.

"Same to you," he replied, returning her smile. Closing the door, he sighed and removed his loosened tie, tossing it onto the chair he'd just been seated in. He shrugged his suit jacket off, slung it over the back of the same chair, and unbuttoned his shirt when he was interrupted by a soft knocking. With his mind a bit muddled from the whiskey, it took him a second to realize where it was coming from. He hurried to the door in hopes Vivian had reconsidered and was thrilled to find she had returned.

"Welcome back," he grinned.

Without a word or warning, she threw her arms around his neck and pulled him close, kissing him deeply. He didn't resist.

"That was unexpected," he said when their kiss finally broke. He could still taste the whiskey on her.

"I just... I know I shouldn't be doing this, but there's something about you."

"There's something about *you*," he countered, pulling her close again and kissing her soft, full lips. "Stay the night with me."

"Okay," she breathed, eyeing him lustfully as their lips met once more. She unbuttoned the rest of his shirt as they kissed, then stepped back to admire his body. "You're so fucking sexy."

She bit her lower lip while running her fingers down his chest to his defined abdomen. Always one to take charge, he took her by the hand and led her to the bedroom, where he gently pushed her onto the bed, crawling on top of her as their lips connected again. When he slid a hand up her shirt, she pushed him aside and rolled on top of him, straddling him as she peeled off her shirt and threw it to the floor. Smirking, she unclasped her bra and teased him momentarily by holding it to her chest while he watched in eager anticipation. She didn't disappoint when she finally tossed it over her shoulder, revealing her full, perky breasts accented by dark, hard nipples.

"Jesus," he muttered, looking up at her in awe. "You really are perfect. I can't believe—"

"Hush," she smiled, silencing him by placing a finger on his lips. He didn't protest when she began trailing kisses down his body while unbuckling his belt. He moaned softly, loving how her lips felt on his skin. For once, he wasn't the one in control… and he liked it.

After snaking his belt loose, she made quick work of his dress slacks. He helped by kicking his Italian leather loafers off while she tugged his pants down around his ankles. She threw them over the side of the bed, flopped onto her back, and worked her shoes off to pull her own pants down, adding them to the growing pile of clothes on the floor. It wasn't graceful, but in their drunken state, he didn't expect it to be. He was a little surprised to see she wasn't wearing any panties, and although the bedroom wasn't lit, there was enough light pouring in from the other room to see she kept herself well-trimmed.

"You're beautiful," he said, looking over her nude body. She'd been in the driver's seat long enough. It was time for him to take control of the wheel. Climbing on top of her, their lips met again in a heated kiss. He moved down to her neck, and she purred, letting him know he'd found just the right spot. His lips lingered there momentarily before moving down to her breasts, hungrily mouthing a sensitive nipple while she ran her fingers through his dark hair. He moved lower, working his way down her belly to her legs, teasing her with soft kisses along her inner thighs. She moaned when his tongue flicked her clit, and her body writhed as he slid a finger inside of her.

"Oh my God," she gasped, her back arching as he tasted her.

"You like that?" he asked with a playful smile, glancing up at her to find her kneading her breasts. Before she could respond, he ducked his head and licked her again.

"Oh my God," she repeated. One hand moved to clench his shoulder while the other moved to grip the blanket beside her. She was so wet it ran down his chin as he skillfully licked and sucked her swollen clit while moving his finger in and out of her.

"You taste so good," he breathed, his mouth and hand working in unison to please her.

"Don't stop," she panted.

He had no intention of stopping. He doubled his efforts when her moans grew louder. She grabbed the back of his head and gently pushed him into her, her hips rising off the bed to meet his mouth. Not one to miss a sexual cue, he slid his hands under her to grab her by the ass, then ran his tongue up the length of her warm slit, her fingers combing through his hair.

"Does that feel good, baby?" he asked with a coy smirk, already knowing the answer.

"Fuck yes," she groaned.

He squeezed her ass while he licked her clit in between, sucking it gently. He moaned in a low hum as he worked, the vibrations of it adding to her pleasure. Sensing she was close, he removed a hand from her ass to slide a finger back inside of her, continuing to tongue her clit.

"Oh my God!" she squealed, her back arching from the bed again. "Don't stop! I'm... I'm..."

Her fingers slipped out of his hair, and her hands clenched the blanket as she came in his mouth, her chest heaving and body flailing as the powerful orgasm surged through her body. He waited until it had run its course before wiping his chin and kissing his way back up to her breasts, stopping to lick her hard nipples, then continuing on to her neck.

"That was… wow," she said in a purr. Their lips met yet again, and she didn't seem to mind the taste of herself. She broke the kiss and tugged on his black boxer briefs. "How am I naked, yet you're still wearing these? No fair."

"Right?" he chuckled. He'd been so focused on pleasing her that he hadn't even realized he was still partially clothed.

"Off," she replied. "Now."

He did as instructed, pulling them down and brushing them onto the floor with his leg. He heard an audible gasp as she looked at his hard cock, seemingly taken by its size. He considered himself a humble man but had to admit that he was well-endowed. The tip of his impressive member glistened with precum, which was no surprise. Tasting her had turned him on immensely.

He swelled with pride when she whispered, "You're so big."

It was his turn to moan when she wrapped her fingers around his thick shaft and began to stroke him softly. He couldn't help but notice the contrast of her dark skin against his pale complexion as her hand worked his cock. He was taken by the beauty of her chocolate color against his alabaster tone, but this thought was fleeting, gone the moment she lowered her head and took him in her mouth.

"God, that feels so fucking good," he muttered as she sucked him, her hand trailing behind, gliding up and down his throbbing girth. Again, he was glad enough light was spilling into the room for him to watch as she worked his dick with genuine vigor. She seemed to truly love pleasing him, repaying his oral with her own, and enjoying his cock in her mouth. He had no problem vocalizing how good her lips felt wrapped around his hard shaft. "Don't stop, baby. Suck that dick. That's it. Just like that."

The whiskey in his system had removed his inner monologue, his thoughts tumbling out in uncontrollable bursts as he continued to watch her. She didn't appear to mind and, if anything, liked how verbose he was being. His words fueled her effort, her mouth working in expert conjunction with her hand. She was able to read his body language in a way no woman ever had, bringing him close to an explosion within moments. Not wanting him to finish yet, she released him from her lips and kissed her way up his muscular body.

"I want to feel you inside of me," she whispered in his ear after giving him a moment to calm down. He was eager to oblige, grabbing her by the hips and positioning her over his hard shaft that was still wet with a combination of her saliva and his precum. A brief look of discomfort flashed across her face as he set her down on his cock, and she stretched to accommodate his size. However, that look quickly turned to one of pleasure as she rode him.

"Is that what you wanted, baby?" he breathed, still holding onto her hips while he thrust in and out of her.

"Yes," she replied, her eyes closed and face twisted in carnal concentration.

His hands moved from his hips to her ass. He lifted her up and down with his strong arms, controlling their rhythm as he impaled her with his cock.

"That's it," he groaned, watching as her perky breasts bounced in his face. "That's it, ride that dick. Fuck, yes. Don't stop."

"I'm going to… I'm going to…" she began, but was unable to finish, interrupted by her orgasm. The room was filled with her cries of pleasure as she came, soaking his cock with her warm juices. She collapsed on top of him, breathing heavily as she recovered from the intense climax. He was still inside of her and somewhat surprised by how hard he still was given the amount of whiskey he'd drunk. A part of him had worried he wouldn't be able to perform and would let her down, embarrassing himself in the process. Thankfully, that wasn't posing a problem. He slipped out of her and, in one swift movement, rolled her onto her back. After repositioning himself between her spread legs, he slid his cock deep into her pink slit as she gripped his shoulders tightly.

"Give it to me," she demanded. "I want it."

He didn't hesitate, slowly pumping himself in and out of her like a piston. Their eyes met, and in that moment, something changed. It no longer felt like they were having sex. For the first time in his life, it felt like he was making love. Their lips met passionately, the energy between them almost palpable. The intense connection he felt with her mind and body was a whole new experience for him and made him realize what he'd been missing out on over the years. Sex had just reached a new level, and he wasn't sure if there was any going back.

"Baby…" she breathed, running her hands through his hair as his hips thrust into her. Her eyes remained locked on his, and he knew she was sharing the same overpowering feeling. What that feeling was, he wasn't exactly sure, and he didn't think she knew, either. It almost seemed like she wanted to profess her love for him, but she stopped saying the words. Had she said them, it surely would have seemed silly later, but it would have felt somehow right in that instant.

"You're so beautiful," he told her, lowering his head to hers for another charged kiss. He drove himself into her harder and faster while her fingers dug into his shoulders.

"I… I…" she began, closing her eyes and clenching his shoulders tighter. "I'm cumming. I'm…"

Her entire body shook as yet another orgasm shot through her, followed by another seconds later. He wasn't sure if multiple orgasms were regular for her, but it did wonders for his confidence either way. He slowed down long enough for her to enjoy each climax, and when she was done riding them out, he picked up his pace again, pumping into her with a steady, deliberate rhythm. He could feel himself getting close and closed his eyes to focus on lasting longer. Picking up on his restraint, she pulled him close and whispered in his ear, "Give it to me."

"Yeah?" he asked. He wasn't entirely sure what she wanted but suspected she was permitting him to finish inside of her. Hoping he wasn't wrong, he thrust into her and groaned as he emptied himself, filling her with his warm load. It was the longest, most intense orgasm he'd ever had, draining him completely. Weakened by how powerful it was, his arms gave out, and he lay on top of her, brow damp with sweat as he struggled to catch his breath.

"Feel better?" she teased, softly rubbing his back as he regained his wind.

He moaned, enjoying her touch for a few seconds before finally speaking. "I've never cum so hard. That was... wow."

"You're telling me," she smiled. "I got off four times. That's unheard of for me."

"Really?" He lifted his head to study her face and could tell she was being sincere.

"Really. Hell, I'm usually lucky if I get off once."

"You know how to make a guy feel special," he grinned, carefully rolling off of her. He wrapped an arm around her and pulled her close, marveling at how perfectly she fit by his side. She was like the puzzle piece he hadn't realized he was missing.

"I'm exhausted," she said with heavy eyes.

"Me too. It's been a long day, and that killed the little energy I had left."

"Do you mind if I sleep here tonight? I don't think I could walk if I tried."

"Of course," he replied, smiling as he kissed her forehead. He was hoping she'd stay and was thrilled that she'd asked. There was something special about her, and he wasn't ready to let her go.

"I feel so safe next to you," she told him, running a hand across his muscular chest.

"Good. I want you to."

"Your ex didn't deserve you. You're a really great guy."

It had been far too long since a woman had said such genuinely sweet things to him. Insincere flattery had become a regular part of his life over the years, usually from women with an ulterior motive. Unsure of how to take it, he chuckled and replied, "You're making me blush."

"Sorry," she said, continuing to feel his chest. "I didn't mean to make you uncomfortable. I get a bit emotional when I'm sleepy."

"It's okay. I like it."

"Yeah?"

"Yeah."

"Ugh," she groaned. "I so don't want to get up right now."

"I thought you were staying?" he asked, confused.

"I am, but that was the most I've drank in years. I need to pee." She glanced at her crotch and added, "I also need to clean up. I'm leaking. You came a lot."

"Sorry," he replied, trying to gauge if she was upset.

"Don't be," she smiled, alleviating any concern he had. "It was hot."

He watched as she crawled out of bed and stumbled to the bathroom, returning to his side minutes later. Still naked, she kissed his cheek and snuggled beside him, falling asleep within seconds. He was asleep moments later, drifting off to the sound of her gentle breathing.

# Chapter Five

## *Vivian*

Vivian groggily awoke and glanced at the clock on the nightstand. It was just past 9:00 a.m., and Beau was still sleeping soundly beside her. She wasn't too surprised that he was still so out of it, considering the emotional wringer he'd been through the day before. Breakups were mentally exhausting, and traveling was draining as well. Adding to that, he'd cum so hard it had been pouring out of her as she'd drunkenly scurried to the bathroom. She'd had to hold it in with one hand, but it had still dripped down her leg. Figuring he'd be asleep for a few more hours, she quietly crept out of bed and collected her clothing that was still scattered on the floor, dressing herself in the suite's main room so as not to wake him. She checked her phone and was relieved to find that Samantha hadn't messaged her. In a last-minute decision, she found a pen and jotted a quick note for Beau on the notepad beside it.

*Beau,*

*Thank you again for a beautiful night. Forgive me for not waking you for a proper goodbye. Given the day you had yesterday, I didn't want to disturb your rest. Spending the night with you here in this beautiful castle is an experience I'll never forget and will surely reflect on often. You're an incredible man, Mr. Sullivan, and meeting you was truly an honor. I wish you nothing but continued success in life.*

*Yours,*

*Vivian Clark*

She set the note between the two sinks on the bathroom counter, figuring he had the best chance of finding it there. If he thought as much like her as she suspected, he'd want to take a shower right away. She reeked of whiskey and sex and knew he did, too. As fantastic as their night had been, she was ready to wash off the smell of it.

She stole another glance at him before leaving. He could have been a sculpture with how gorgeous he looked: one strong arm resting above his head, a muscular leg sticking out from under the sheet that was low enough to showcase his toned abdomen. He was truly a sight to behold, but staring at him any longer would have crossed into creepy. She left without a sound, wanting to stay but knowing she had to return to her friend.

Nodding politely to the guests she passed, she made her way back to her room in hopes of finding Samantha still asleep. "The Walk of Shame" is what she would have called the trek under different circumstances. However, she didn't regret the night she'd spent with Beau and felt no shame in having slept with him. With how thoroughly average the sex with Marcus had been—and the other men before him, for that matter—Beau had introduced her to a whole new world. For a moment, it felt like they were making love. She wondered if he felt it, too, or if she was just being fanciful.

Slinking back into her room as stealthily as she could, she found Samantha still asleep... or so she thought. Laying on her side with her back to Vivian, the redhead surprised her by asking flatly, "Did you have fun, you slut?"

"Busted," Vivian laughed, flopping down on her bed.

Samantha rolled over and looked at her with a smile. "How was it?"

"Amazing!" Vivian gushed, kicking the bed excitedly with both feet like a little kid.

"Did he have a big cock?"

"Samantha!"

"Come on, Viv. Details!"

"If you must know… yes. Very big. And he knew how to use it."

"Well, I'm glad one of us had fun," Samantha groaned. "I'm so sorry about last night. I made such an idiot out of myself."

"I'm surprised you can even remember it," Vivian chuckled. "You were wasted."

"Oh, trust me, there are a lot of gaps in my memory."

"That's probably a good thing."

"It was that bad, huh?"

"Uh, yeah."

"I remember doing shots with you and that hot guy and sitting on the arm of a chair."

"And?" Vivian prodded. "Anything else?"

Samantha groaned again and covered her face with her hands. "Please tell me I didn't really puke all over myself."

"Oh, you totally did," Vivian replied. "You made quite a spectacle out of yourself."

"Did anyone see?" her friend asked, her face still covered in embarrassment.

"Just that hot guy."

"Shoot me. Please… just shoot me."

"Remind yourself that you're happily married. That puking in front of a gorgeous, rich guy doesn't matter because you have Brian."

Samantha thought over Vivian's words for a moment. "I'm not sure if that helped or made things worse."

"It was supposed to make things better. How are you feeling?"

"Like I got hit by a bus." She paused for a second. "Humiliated, and like I got hit by a bus."

"My hangover's kicking in, too," Vivian said, realizing she'd likely woken up partially drunk. With the alcohol finally running its course, her head was beginning to throb.

"I really wanted to show you more of the castle today, but it might have to wait for another time. It hurts even to move."

"I'd be just fine with lying in bed all day," Vivian agreed. She silently thanked herself for having the foresight to close the curtains before leaving the night before. The dark room was ideal for curing their hangovers, as were the complimentary bottles of water the hotel had provided.

"Thank you for taking care of me last night. I saw my dress in the tub when I got up to pee earlier. That was sweet of you."

"You did a number on that bathroom, but I cleaned it up."

"I did?" Samantha asked. "I don't even remember that. I'm so sorry."

"You're lucky I love you," Vivian muttered.

"So I'm guessing after I passed out, you went back to the bar to talk to that guy?"

"Actually, he showed up here. I left you a note. I'm guessing you didn't see it."

"Nope. I'm so hungover that I barely know what planet I'm on. How did he get our room number?"

"Turns out he has some pull around here."

"Oh, a big shot. You two went back to his room?"

"Sammy, you should have seen it. Deluxe suite. It made this room look tiny."

"Whoa, fancy. So who made the first move?"

"My memory's a bit hazy, but I'm pretty sure it was me."

"Damn, girl. I'm glad you had fun. Now give me the details. All of them."

Vivian briefly recounted the events of their night. Never one to kiss and tell, there were specific details she kept to herself, the most significant being their failure to use protection. She was still chastising herself for that mistake. Beau had told her about his infertility, so she wasn't worried about getting pregnant, but a playboy like him had probably been around the block a few times. If he hadn't worn a condom with her, the chances were good he hadn't worn one with the plethora of women he'd likely slept with over the years. She made a mental note to get checked out when she returned to the States. Better safe than sorry.

Samantha hung on every word as Vivian relived her encounter with the handsome entrepreneur. The redhead waited until her friend had finished telling her story before peppering her with questions.

"He made you cum?"

"Yes."

"How many times?"

"Four."

"Jesus, I've never cum that many times. Did you suck his dick?"

"Yes."

"Did he go down on you?"

"Yes."

"You lucky bitch. He had a nice body?"

"Amazing."

"Are you going to see him again?"

"No."

"Why not?"

"I just got out of a relationship, Sammy. I'm not looking to jump into another one. Not right now."

"Even with a guy who's hot and rich?"

"Even with a guy who's hot and rich."

"Even with a guy who's hot and rich and can make you cum four times?"

Vivian had to laugh at that. "Look, he's perfect, okay? Gorgeous, smart, funny, great in bed… but I'm finally single again. I want to focus on myself for a while. Besides, I don't do long-distance relationships."

"He lives here?"

That question stumped her. During the course of their time together, she couldn't recall if he'd told her where he lived. If he had, she couldn't remember. She blamed the whiskey for that one.

"He lives in the States… I don't know where."

"Did you at least exchange numbers?"

"No."

"Oh my God, Viv. Why not?"

"Because I'd be tempted to call him, and that's not what I need right now. I need to focus on my career and settle into my new place."

She wouldn't admit it, but she did regret not adding her number to the note she'd left him, even though she knew it was for the best. Their connection had been very real, but jumping into another relationship so soon didn't seem smart. Even with that awareness, she would have been thrilled if he called.

"You could have just kept in touch as friends. Then, make it more when you are ready."

"Maybe," Vivian shrugged dismissively. She knew she wouldn't be able to keep Beau at arm's length; he was simply too hard to resist. She changed the subject with, "Have you talked to Brian?"

"I will in a bit. I don't think I can read or write yet. I feel like death."

"Mark last night on your calendar," Vivian smirked. "I finally outdrank you."

"You totally did," Samantha conceded, burying her face in her pillow.

An hour later, an unexpected knock on the door interrupted the television show they'd absorbed themselves in as a distraction from their hangovers. Vivian's heart raced in excitement, hoping it would be Beau. Her heart sank when she opened the door to find a young man dressed in hotel staff attire. However, her disappointment quickly turned to delight at seeing the food cart by his side and the aroma wafting from it.

"Breakfast," the man smiled.

"I'm sorry, we didn't order room service," Vivian replied. She feigned confusion but knew who'd ordered the food.

"It's from an admirer," the man said, his smile widening.

Her suspicions were confirmed, and she stood aside, allowing him to push the cart into the room. As he removed each lid from its respective plate, he rattled off the dishes found under each. Bacon and eggs, sausage, pancakes, waffles, fresh fruit, and orange juice were just a few of the things Beau had surprised them with. The young man pointed out the note that had been folded in half and positioned between two of the plates.

"For you," he nodded. With a knowing grin, he added, "From your admirer."

Vivian reached for the note and couldn't contain her smile as she read it.

*Vivian,*

*Last night was terrific, and the honor was all mine. Thank you for the memories that will last a lifetime. If your hangover is as bad as I think, I hope this food will help. Wishing you and your friend a speedy recovery. Safe travels back to America.*

*Beau*

She folded the note again and set it aside to keep as a memento. She usually wasn't sentimental, but Beau had left quite an impression, compelling her to save his words.

"What did it say?" Samantha asked, sitting up in her bed.

"Don't worry your freckled head about it," Vivian chuckled. She didn't hold much back from her friend, yet when it came to Beau, she wanted him to herself. She'd already told Samantha too much in recounting their steamy night together. Turning her attention to the young man, she asked, "How much do we owe you?"

"It's been paid for," he assured her, leaving.

"Wait, let me at least give you a tip," she said, moving toward her purse.

"No need," he stopped her with a raised hand. "That's already been covered as well. Your gratuity isn't necessary. Thank you, though. Enjoy your breakfast."

After devouring as much of the breakfast as they could, they spent most of the day lying in bed, commiserating on the hangovers they were desperately trying to recover from. The food had helped, but only so much. The rest was up to time. By the evening, they both felt well enough to see the rest of the castle. Vivian kept an eye out for Beau, hoping their paths would cross one more time. It was a silly, irrational thought since she knew he'd already checked out, but she couldn't stop her mind from going there.

As beautiful as the castle was, the handsome entrepreneur she'd spent the night with had stolen her focus. It was her first one-night stand and likely her last, but it had left an indelible mark.

They shook the rest of their hangovers with a few more hours of sleep and felt much better by the morning. Vivian took one last look at the castle as they drove off, admiring its grandeur while silently reflecting on her time there. It almost felt like a dream. Had it not been for the note he'd left her in time, she may have even convinced herself that it was.

Three hours later, they were back at Samantha's quaint home, which looked and felt tiny compared to the enormous castle they'd spent the weekend in. Over the next few days, they enjoyed each other's company while exploring more of Ireland. When they didn't see the land, they were relaxing with movies and snacks. Samantha proved to be a fantastic host, ensuring Vivian was comfortable, well-fed, and entertained during her stay. She did an excellent job making her feel at home, and Brian was equally hospitable.

The day before she was set to fly back to the States, Vivian got daring and asked Samantha if she could borrow the bicycle she'd seen leaning against the side of the house. She hadn't ridden a bike since she was a young teenager, and regardless of the adage, she was a bit worried she'd forgotten how. It was a beautiful day out, and a ride into town seemed like a fun way to burn off some of the calories she'd packed in while visiting. Between the alcohol and the food, she was feeling sluggish and needed at least some form of exercise. As much as she loved her friend, she also wanted some time alone. Samantha understood and was fine with Vivian taking her bike for a spin, though she watched and laughed as Vivian slowly pedaled off, the bike wobbling as she struggled to relearn something that had once seemed like second nature. Within minutes, she had the hang of it again, smoothly gliding toward Killarney's city center. Along the way, she had to stop to let a small herd of sheep cross the narrow street and laughed at the contrast between life on this British isle and life back in her hometown of Denver.

Arriving downtown, she parked the bicycle outside a small general store. She was reluctant to leave it unattended, but Samantha had assured her it would be fine, reminding her that they were in Killarney, not Denver, where bike theft was rampant. Vivian had protested, insisting she should at least bring a lock, but her friend had dismissed the idea as unnecessary. She wasn't comfortable with it but took Samantha at her word and left the bike on the sidewalk as she headed inside the store. She had no intention of buying anything. She simply wanted to browse. Casting an occasional glance out the window to check on the bike, she walked the aisles, noting the cultural differences in the products.

A pudgy man wearing a blue apron hurried over with a smile to ask in a thick Irish accent if she needed help finding anything. She politely declined, explaining that she was visiting from the States and just wanted a quick look around. Spotting a magazine rack, she picked up a real estate publication and became so engrossed in it that she didn't notice somebody approaching her from behind.

"Fancy meeting you here," a familiar voice sounded, jarring her from the article she'd been reading. She turned to find Beau Sullivan grinning wide and looking every bit as handsome as she'd remembered. This time, he was dressed far more casually, wearing tan slacks and a white polo shirt that hugged his muscular frame nicely. The gallon of milk in his hand looked weightless, given his strength, but it wasn't his powerful arms that weakened her knees. It was the sight of his light blue eyes.

"Beau!" she gasped, trying to wrap her mind around his unexpected appearance. She quickly composed herself and joked, "Stalking me now, are you?"

"Busted," he laughed, throwing his free hand up in mock surrender.

"What are you doing here?" she asked, puzzled by his presence in the little store that looked to be family-owned.

"Mom and Dad were out of milk, so I offered to grab them some," he said, motioning to the gallon he was holding.

"Your mom and dad live here? In Killarney?"

"All their lives," he replied. "I was raised here."

"Small world. This is where my friend lives now. Samantha? You met her the other night."

"Like I could forget," he laughed. "How was she feeling the next day?"

"Very hungover and embarrassed."

"Hopefully you weren't embarrassed, too," he said. She could see him searching her face for any trace of regret.

"Don't be silly," she smiled. Realizing she was still holding the magazine, she stuffed it back in the rack and brought Beau in for a hug. "I had an amazing time."

"Good," he said, sounding relieved. "I was a bit worried you'd—"

"Never," she stopped him. "Never. Easily one of the best nights I've ever had."

That was a lie. It wasn't one of the best nights she'd ever had. It was *the* best night she'd ever had. However, she didn't want to tip her hand by telling him that. She wasn't one for games, but leaving him wondering if she'd had better seemed like the right approach. She wanted there to be some aura of intrigue, after all. A little mystique was never a bad thing.

The nervous jitters from his good looks passed, and within moments, he felt like an old friend again. They walked the store together, slowly making their way up and down each aisle while sharing more details of their lives. He recalled his life growing up in Killarney, and she opened up with more stories of her childhood in Denver. It was like they'd picked up right where they'd left off, with no awkward silences or lulls in their conversation. After their night together, she'd been worried their chemistry had merely resulted from the alcohol they'd drank. Spending time with him sober, however, she was pleased to find it was still there… and quite possibly even stronger.

"I shouldn't keep you," she said, noting the beads of sweat forming on the milk Beau had been carrying.

"I'm in no rush, believe me," he chuckled. "I love my parents, but my mom can be a bit much. I was looking for a reason to get out of the house."

"I wouldn't want the milk to go bad…"

"I'll be fine. Besides, what are the chances of us running into each other like this? I'm not going to ignore a sign from the universe over a gallon of milk."

"Fair enough," she laughed. She wasn't sure if she believed in signs, but Beau resurfacing in this small Killarney store seemed almost kismet.

"You leave soon, right?" he asked as they neared the checkout counter. "To go back to the States?"

"Tomorrow, actually," she sighed. "I've had a great time here, but I have a life to get back to."

"I get it," he nodded. "I leave tonight. I wish I could stay longer, but duty calls."

The chubby man in the blue apron smiled as Beau set his milk on the counter. "Beau Sullivan! I thought that was you. I haven't seen your face around these parts in some time."

"Hello, Benny," Beau greeted, shaking the man's hand. "I don't get back here as often as I should."

"Living in America still, are you?"

"I am," Beau nodded, pulling his wallet from the back pocket of his slacks.

"How are the folks?"

"They're doing well, thank you for asking."

"Such good people they are. Please send them my regards."

"I will. How have you been?"

The two men caught up for a moment while Vivian stepped back and enjoyed their exchange, touched by the friendliness of this peaceful Irish town. All paid up, Beau shook the man's hand again and wished him well before turning his attention back to her.

"You hungry? There's a place right around the corner that has amazing food."

She'd rode the bike into town to burn calories, not take more in, but sitting down for lunch with Beau was too tempting to pass up. "I'd like that. What about your milk, though? It's already been out long enough."

Hearing their conversation, Benny chimed in to help. "Throw it back in the cooler here and get it whenever you're ready, Beau."

"Thanks, Benny. You're a good man."

"Anything for an old friend," the portly clerk replied.

After placing the milk back in the cooler, Beau guided Vivian outside, respectfully holding the door open for her. Stepping onto the sidewalk, her eyes were immediately drawn to the black Range Rover parked on the side of the street.

"Yours?" she asked, nodding her head at it.

"My parents, actually. I bought it for them last year."

"Lucky them."

"They've always been so supportive. The least I could do was replace the piece of junk they were driving."

"That was very kind of you," Vivian smiled, moved by his thoughtful expression. "You're a good son."

"I try," he shrugged. "Call me crazy, but I believe in being good to the people who've been good to me."

He offered his hand, and she was struck by a sudden rush of excitement when she took it. She was so lost in his touch that they'd nearly rounded the corner by the time she remembered Samantha's bicycle.

"Wait!" she said, tugging him back toward the general store. "I'm an idiot. I almost forgot about my friend's bike. I can't just leave it there."

"You rode a bike here?" he asked with amusement.

"Hey, a girl has to keep her figure," she joked.

He looked her up and down, undressing her with his eyes. "And what a beautiful figure you have."

She felt herself blush and was glad her dark skin hid it. "Thank you."

"Well," he began, sizing up the bike. "There's plenty of room in the back of the Rover. It should fit."

"Are you sure?"

"Of course."

She watched as he lifted the bike, admiring his strong arms as he quickly maneuvered it into the back of the SUV.

"Problem solved," he smiled, closing the tailgate and retaking her hand.

"My hero."

Hand in hand, they walked to a tavern no bigger than the general store they'd come from. It wasn't even noon, yet the place was alive with people enjoying a drink, a meal, or a combination of both. They were greeted by a host who thanked them for choosing O'Brien's Tavern and seated them in a booth adjacent to the bar. He was in the middle of handing them menus when another man sidled up to the table.

"Mr. Sullivan!" the man said with a wide smile. He looked to be a few years older than Beau but was slightly shorter and had more of an athletic build than a muscular one. His red hair was thinning, yet he still had an air of confidence that made him attractive. "It's been too long!"

Beau stood to shake his hand. "I know. Life in the States has been keeping me busy. Good to see you, Gabriel."

"And who might this beautiful woman be?" the man asked. His eyes revealed a glimmer of lust as he extended his hand to her.

"Vivian Clark," she nodded, taking his hand. The man was certainly a charmer, but nobody could take her attention from Beau. Sensing he was no longer needed, the host dashed off to greet a group of customers who'd just walked through the door.

The man introduced himself as Gabriel O'Brien, the owner of the establishment. He shook his head as he whistled, adding, "You truly are a wonder."

"I see you haven't changed," Beau laughed, asserting his dominance by patting Gabriel on the shoulder. "But calm down. She's with me."

Vivian swooned. Beau claiming her and being so protective made her heart skip a beat. He was territorial but not in an insecure way.

"You lucky bastard," Gabriel chuckled, acknowledging Beau as the alpha by taking a step back from the table. He looked around the bustling tavern and changed the subject with, "As you can see, business is good."

"I didn't have to see the place to know that," Beau replied. "The monthly financials tell me everything I need to know. You're doing a terrific job, Gabe."

The conversation between the two men jogged a memory she might have forgotten. During the night she'd spent with Beau, he'd mentioned investing in a tavern. It didn't take much deduction to piece together that this was it. It was a nice place, likely due to the renovations Beau had fronted the money for, and she could see why it had become a favorite among locals and tourists.

"Thank you. I owe it all to you," Gabriel told him.

Beau waved his hand. "Nonsense. I made some cosmetic adjustments, but your management skills are what keep people coming back. Behind every successful business is a smart owner."

"You're too kind," Gabriel beamed. "And too modest! You know you saved this place."

"It was a bit run down, but I wouldn't have fixed it up if I didn't have faith in you."

"And I appreciate that. I'm glad I haven't let you down." He turned his attention back to Vivian and flashed her a smile much different from the one he'd greeted her. This time, it was strictly friendly with no hint of flirtation. "I'll leave you two alone now. I just wanted to say a quick hello to the man who turned things around here."

"Keep up the good work, Gabe," Beau said as he slipped back into the booth. The man disappeared, allowing them to enjoy their time together.

"You're a popular guy," Vivian remarked.

"Nah. I grew up with Benny, and Gabriel's just a business partner."

She could tell that he was trying to be modest, a trait she admired. They looked over the menu and ordered lunch, both skipping alcohol in favor of tea. It was nice having a clear mind as she spent time with him, taking in all of his subtle idiosyncrasies. He'd raise his eyebrows when he'd laugh, rub the bridge of his nose while thinking, and run his fingers through his hair when frustrated. He didn't seem frustrated easily, but Jessica was clearly a trigger. She regretted asking if he'd heard any more from her.

"That girl, he groaned, combing his fingers through his dark hair. He'd had a smattering of gel or hairspray in it when they'd met to keep it perfectly in place, but today, it appeared he'd simply let it fall naturally. Even with it unstyled, he still looked ready for a photo shoot in some high fashion magazine. "She's seriously texted me about one hundred times. Called me close to two hundred."

"You're kidding me."

"I wish. Check this out," he replied, digging his phone out of his pants. He called up his text messages and showed her the sea of messages Jessica had sent him, scrolling down the lengthy list as Vivian watched in disbelief. "Crazy, right?"

"Have you replied to her at all?"

"Nope," he said, shoving his phone back in his pocket.

"Why don't you just block her number?"

"Oh, believe me, I have. She's been calling me from different ones now. The girl has a lot of friends, I'll give her that much. She keeps filling up my voicemail, too. It's highly annoying."

"What's she been saying?"

"No idea. I only listen to the first few seconds. Then, I deleted them. She starts off either screaming or crying."

"Beau, that girl's unstable."

He ran his fingers through his hair again and sighed. "I know. I'm changing my number when I get back to the States."

"You never did tell me what part of America you live in."

"No? I thought I did. I'm in—"

He was interrupted by the host, who returned to their table with a smile. "Beau Sullivan? *The* Beau Sullivan?"

"Guilty," Beau answered with a puzzled look.

"I've heard so much about you from Mr. O'Brien!" the man gushed, holding a pile of menus across his chest. "I'm sorry I didn't say something earlier, but I had no idea it was you. He just told me!"

Beau looked a tad annoyed but smiled back politely. "I see."

"I just wanted to meet the guy who fixed this place up. I remember what it looked like before the renovations. It wasn't exactly welcoming."

"Thank you," Beau replied. "The place is in a great location. I knew with a little work, it could make some serious money."

"You weren't wrong. The place is booming now." Realizing he'd intruded on their time, the host nervously cleared his throat. "Anyhow, Mr. O'Brien talks about you a lot, so I just wanted to pop over and say hello. Enjoy the rest of your lunch."

"Thank you," Beau nodded. The man scurried off, but his brief interruption had been just long enough to derail their conversation.

"You need to start a fan club," Vivian laughed.

"Let's get out of here," he replied, pushing his plate aside. They'd finished their lunch and already agreed to steer clear of the bar. He reached into his pocket for his wallet and pulled out a euro, placing it halfway under his plate for the server. She glanced at the bill and converted the currency in her mind. He'd just set down over one hundred dollars. She knew the sandwiches and tea they'd ordered only cost a small fraction of that, meaning he was leaving their server a very generous tip.

"You just made our server's day," she said.

"I'm considered a co-owner, so I don't even have to pay," he shared. "But a lot of the servers here are young and just starting out in life. I'm hoping this will help ours out."

Once again, she found herself touched by his thoughtful nature. He stood and reached for her hand, helping her to her feet. His chivalry was not lost on her, and she appreciated the gesture. He stopped by the bar to say goodbye to Gabriel, promising not to wait so long between visits.

"Thank you for lunch," Vivian smiled, holding Beau's hand as they walked back to his parents' Range Rover. The afternoon sun made his blue eyes look even lighter, and for the umpteenth time, she found herself transfixed by his looks and charm.

"My pleasure. I'd love to drive you back to your friend's place," he offered as they lingered by the SUV.

"I'd like that," she smiled. As much as she would have loved to burn off her lunch by pedaling back to Samantha's, she couldn't resist spending more time with him.

"Wait here," he said, holding his index finger up. "I'll be right back. I just need to grab the milk."

She'd been so caught up in him that she'd forgotten the milk he'd left in the cooler. He darted into the general store, returning moments later with the gallon, and placed it in the trunk next to her bike. Always the gentleman, he helped her into the vehicle before circling around to the driver's side and taking his place behind the wheel. She began directing him toward Samantha's house, but halfway there, he surprised her by veering down a dirt road.

"Slight detour," he told her with a coy smile.

"Oh?"

"I want to show you something. Is that okay?"

"I'm in no rush," she replied, curious about where he was taking her. Had it been anyone else, she might have been concerned as they sped down the unpaved road to an unknown destination, but she was completely at ease with him.

A thick covering of trees began to envelop them as the road narrowed and became rougher. They finally rolled to a stop on the rocky shore of a large body of water surrounded by rugged mountain slopes. Aside from the lone fisherman she spotted in the distance, they were utterly secluded.

"Welcome to Muckross Lake," he announced with a grin.

"It's so beautiful," she replied, absorbing the scenic view. "How did you find this spot?"

"My dad used to take me fishing here when I was a kid," he explained, staring at the gentle waves the light summer breeze created on the water. "I never really saw it as a romantic place… until now."

"It is," she agreed. She couldn't refrain from adding, "I mean, aside from the name."

"Right?" he laughed.

"Muckross. Not exactly sexy."

He took her hand and looked at her longingly. "You're sexy."

"Stop," she blushed, looking away.

"I mean it. You're just…" he trailed off as he looked her over, his eyes dripping with desire. "You're incredible."

She felt her mouth go dry, and her heart began to race. She wanted to pull her hand away from his, yet couldn't. His magnetic effect over her was in full force, preventing her from letting go. Looking down at her jeans and tank top, she made a nervous attempt at levity. "Even dressed like this?"

"Especially dressed like that."

She swallowed hard, knowing where things were heading but too weakened by the temptation to stop it. She feebly began to protest, her voice low and shaky. "Beau, we shouldn't—"

He silenced her with a kiss. As it deepened, she was overcome with arousal and could feel the wetness forming between her legs. She'd never been kissed so passionately. Had never felt so wanted. She pried herself away from him and placed her hand on his cheek, staring intently into his blue eyes.

"How do you do that?" she murmured, flushed from the intensity of their kiss.

"Do what?"

"Turn me on so fast."

"Is that a bad thing?" he smiled.

"No… no, it's not." Grabbing the back of his head, she pulled him close again for another kiss, their tongues meeting in a heated dance. With the center console between them, kissing was as far as they could take things. Beau was also aware of this and broke the kiss, jerking his chin to the back seat.

"Shall we?" he grinned with devilish lust.

"You've got to be joking," she replied, studying his face. Seeing just how serious he was, she whispered conspiratorially, "In the back of your parents' vehicle?"

"I won't tell them if you don't," he smirked.

"You're so bad," she breathed, trembling with excitement. She glanced at the spacious back seat, biting her bottom lip as she considered his suggestion.

"It's your last day here," he reminded her. "Let's make it one to remember."

"I'm all sweaty and gross from the bike ride into town. I wouldn't—"

Before she could finish her sentence, he sprang from the SUV and quickly made his way to the passenger side, opening her door and unbuckling her seatbelt.

"What are you doing?" she asked, yelping in laughter as he scooped her into his strong arms. He pulled her from the vehicle and kicked the door closed. "Beau!"

"Sweaty and gross, you say?" he smiled as he effortlessly carried her toward the lake, leaving the Range Rover idling behind them. He carefully set her down and gestured at the body of water before them. "If only there were some way we could get you clean."

She raised her brow quizzically. "You're kidding, right?"

"Perfect day for a swim," he replied, kicking off his shoes and setting them on a large rock where they wouldn't get wet. When he peeled off his shirt, revealing his sculpted body, she felt her defenses slip away. In that instant, she knew he'd do anything he asked of her. He threw his shirt on top of his shoes and tugged his pants down, tossing them onto the pile of clothes. Standing in his boxer briefs, the sun shining on his magnificent body, he smiled wide at her. "Come on. Your turn."

"You're crazy," she laughed, shaking her head.

"Less talking, more taking your clothes off," he joked.

A modest woman, she hesitantly looked around again to ensure they were alone. Deciding the fisherman was too far away to get much of a view, she stripped down to her bra and panties, handing her clothes to Beau so he could add them to the pile on the nearby rock. Using the hair tie she'd forethought to wear on her wrist, she tied her hair up and took a deep breath.

"I can't believe I'm doing this," she said, holding onto Beau's shoulder as they stepped into the water. She recoiled at how cold it was but pushed forward anyhow, slowly inching her way in so her body could get acclimated to it. "It's freezing!"

"Shush. It's not bad," he replied, wrapping an arm around her waist to steady her as her feet traversed the rocky lakebed.

"I better not get eaten by the Loch Ness Monster."

"That's Scotland, sweetheart," he chuckled.

By the time the water had reached her navel, she'd adjusted to the temperature and had to agree it wasn't that bad. She ventured farther in but stopped when the water reached her shoulders, knowing her hair would become a frizzy mess if she got it wet. On the other hand, Beau didn't have to worry about that problem. She melted when he wet his hair and slicked it back, looking as if he were shooting a commercial for some sort of fragrance.

"What?" he asked when he caught her staring.

"You're a good-looking man, Mr. Sullivan," she replied. She didn't look away. Rather, she continued to admire him in an effort to sear his image into her mind.

"That means a lot coming from you," he said, moving toward her and pulling her close. Their lips met again, and she didn't stop him when he slipped her bra straps down around her shoulders. With her breasts submerged, nobody could see him rubbing her hard nipples, and with how turned on she was, she almost didn't care if they could. She pulled his boxer briefs down and took his cock in her hand, jerking him slowly as their lips remained locked in a heated kiss. She jumped into his arms, wrapping her legs around him, and he helped support her with a firm grip on her ass. He gave it a gentle squeeze, and she playfully swatted his shoulder.

"You're trouble, you know that?"

"You like it," he grinned, his eyes locked onto hers.

She purred when he began kissing her neck and closed her eyes as she enjoyed the sensation of his mouth on her skin. She could feel his hard cock pressing into her and seized the opportunity to feel it inside of her one last time. Sliding her panties aside, she guided him, moaning as he filled her completely.

"Oh my God," she murmured, her hands clutching his back tightly.

"Vivian..." he began softly. She could feel his warm breath on her neck, and it sent chills down her spine. "You're so beautiful."

The buoyancy of the water made her feel as light as a feather. It also made it exceedingly easy for him to move her up and down, his thick shaft pumping in and out of her warm slit. She buried her face in his shoulder, lightly biting his flesh to muffle her cries of pleasure that surely would have carried across the lake, potentially garnering unwanted attention.

They made love in the water, the sun beaming down on them as they experienced each other in the most intimate of ways. When he noticed her shivering, he carried her out of the water and moved them to the back seat of the SUV that he'd left running. Concerned their dripping bodies might damage the leather upholstery, she protested, but he stopped her with a kiss that her entire body felt. The wetness of their bodies worked to their advantage, preventing them from sticking to the leather seats as they picked up where they'd left off in the lake. Tugging his soaked boxer briefs off, she took his cock in her mouth, her hand trailing behind it, sucking him until he was fully erect again. She'd never had a man precum so much but liked it, considering it a testament to how desperately he wanted her. She hungrily lapped up every drop, loving the sounds he was making as she continued to suck him. He was just as vocal as she'd remembered, and it only added to her arousal.

"I want you," she said in a low growl that surprised even her. Her desire for him had reached a boiling point, and she couldn't hold out any longer. She peeled her wet panties off and tossed them aside, then reached behind her to unclasp her bra, letting it fall to the seat beside her. Straddling him, she positioned herself over his cock and guided it into her again, slowly lowering herself until every inch was inside of her. Grinding her hips into him, her hands on his bare chest, her moans grew louder as she rode him harder and faster. The combination of her clit rubbing against him while his throbbing shaft filled her quickly brought her to orgasm. She moved her hands from his chest to the headrest behind him, squeezing it hard as she came.

"That's it, baby," he breathed. Her eyes were shut, but she could tell he was watching her cum. "That's it. Cum for me."

Her arms gave out, limp from the powerful climax, and she fell against his chest, breathing heavily. He rubbed her back, his cock still inside of her, and kissed her neck while she recovered.

"I... I need a second," she panted. "I just came so hard."

"I could tell," he smirked, looking quite proud.

"Damn you for being so good," she groaned, her fingers kneading his muscular chest. "I think you've ruined me for other men."

He laughed, but she could tell from his eyes how hard he still was inside her that he wanted more. Still shaking, she summoned the strength to rear up and ride him again. With his hands on her ass, he lifted her up and down, repeatedly driving his sizable cock into her. As the SUV gently rocked, the front tire of her bicycle slowly spun in the trunk. Had she not been so preoccupied with his cock, she might have found it amusing. She rubbed her swollen clit with one hand while the other clenched his shoulder, closing her eyes to focus on cumming again. It didn't take long. As the orgasm shot through her, he pulled her close and took a breast in his mouth, sucking her dark, sensitive nipple.

"Oh, fuck! Oh, fuck! Oh, fuck!" she repeated, digging her fingers into his shoulder as she rode out the orgasm. He squeezed her ass as she came, intensifying her climax, taking everything out of her. She collapsed onto his chest again, winded and weak, but mustered up the strength to roll onto the seat next to him. She could tell by his breathing that he'd been close, too, and she didn't want to leave him hanging. She worked him with her mouth again, sucking her juices off of his hard cock as he grunted his approval. Remembering how much he was capable of cumming and knowing she wouldn't be able to take it all, she pulled away as he came, finishing him with her hand. He shot streams of warm, white cum into the air as she stroked him, painting his abdomen and chest.

"Don't stop," he pleaded, his voice shaky. "Don't stop."

She didn't disappoint, jerking him as she watched his cum fly, making a mess of his body and her arm. Had she not been so spent from her own orgasm, she might have been turned on by the sight of his. The look on his face as he exploded and his prominent, thick cock shot an impressive amount of cum was something she wouldn't soon forget.

"That was really hot," she said when she'd finally drained him completely.

"Oh my God," he said, his breathing labored. "I usually don't cum so much, I swear. You're just so fucking sexy."

"Yeah?"

"Yeah," he replied, looking down at the load covering his body. "That's a lot for me."

"I'm flattered," she smiled.

He used his wet boxer briefs to clean up the cum, then rolled down the window and tossed them out. Both of them damp from a mixture of lake water and sweat, they cuddled naked in the back seat together as they recharged. Although they'd never met before Ashford Castle, he had a familiar warmth to him that made her feel safe and secure. His arms wrapped around her. They held each other close, affectionately exchanging kisses and sweet nothings. When enough strength had returned, Vivian put her bra and panties back on, which wasn't a pleasant experience given how wet they were from the lake. Beau checked to make sure they were still alone, and confident nobody had joined them, dashed from the vehicle nude to retrieve their clothes from the rock he'd set them on. She couldn't help but chuckle at his pale bottom as he navigated the rocky shore, carefully planning each step so he didn't embarrass himself by falling. He returned seconds later, and after they'd dressed, he scooped up the boxer briefs he'd thrown from the window earlier and brought them to the water to wash them.

"Aren't your parents going to wonder why you're coming home with a pair of wet underwear and warm milk?" Vivian laughed.

He looked at them and shrugged. "At least they're not covered in cum. Then I'd really have some explaining to do."

She giggled and shook her head. "You're something else, Beau Sullivan."

Moments later, they were back on the road and heading toward Samantha's house. Neither of them wanted to part ways, but Beau had a flight to catch, and his parents, worried that he'd been gone so long, had called to inquire about his whereabouts. He'd told them a half-truth, saying he'd stopped by Muckross Lake for a quick swim since it was such a lovely day out.

"I feel like a kid again," he'd joked when the call had ended. "Sneaking out and having to lie to my parents."

Arriving at Samantha's home, Beau helped Vivian out of the SUV before popping the trunk and carefully removing the bicycle. Samantha, who had likely been wondering why a black Range Rover had pulled into her driveway, had stepped outside and smiled when she saw her friend with the handsome entrepreneur she remembered from Ashford Castle.

"Well, if it isn't Beau Sullivan," she greeted, shaking his hand. "We meet again... and this time, I'm not puking on myself."

"I'm surprised you remembered my name," he chuckled, flipping the bike's kickstand down.

"A certain somebody over here may have mentioned it a time or fifty," she smirked, glancing at Vivian.

Vivian felt her face flush and looked away in embarrassment. "She exaggerates."

"Sure I do," Samantha fired back, rolling her eyes. She let her friend off the hook by changing the subject. "Listen, Beau, I'm sorry about the other night. I was out of control."

"It's fine," he replied, holding up his palm. "I think we've all had nights like that."

"Where you puke all over yourself in a fancy bar in front of somebody you've just met?" she joked.

"Okay, maybe not that," he laughed, "but don't think I haven't drunkenly embarrassed myself before. I am Irish, after all."

Anticipating the questions her friend was about to ask, Vivian beat her to the punch by explaining, "Turns out Beau's from Killarney. His parents still live here. We ran into each other in town."

"No kidding?" Samantha asked. "Small world!"

"It is," Beau agreed. There was an awkward silence between the three that Samantha proceeded to make even more awkward.

"Maybe you and Vivian can hook up again next time she visits." Immediately realizing how uncomfortable her poor choice of words had made them, she tried to revise her statement but only made things worse. "I mean, maybe you can get together if you're ever here at the same time again. I didn't mean 'hook up,' as in having sex. I meant it as—you know what? I'm just going to stop talking."

"Please do," Vivian groaned, covering her eyes in embarrassment.

Beau, unfazed by Samantha's comment, laughed and shook his head. "You have a way with words."

She pointed over her shoulder at her front door. "I'm just going to go back inside. Let you two say your goodbyes and whatnot. It was nice seeing you again, Beau."

"Likewise," he nodded with an amused smile.

Vivian waited until her friend had disappeared inside the house before speaking. "Sorry about that."

"Don't be. She's funny."

"Really?"

"Yeah, she cracks me up. I can see why you two are friends."

"Thank you. I was worried you might find her a bit... annoying."

"What? No, not at all."

"She tends to speak before she thinks instead of the other way around."

"It's part of her charm," he shrugged. His face and tone turned serious as he closed the distance between them and offered his hand. "Well, Miss Clark, it was truly a pleasure meeting you."

She smiled while fighting back the sudden sadness that had overtaken her. It pained her to admit it, but she'd allowed herself to develop feelings for him. Had they not bumped into each other again at the general store, she probably would have been able to leave things at Ashford Castle. However, the wonderful afternoon they'd just spent together had secured his place in her heart by proving that her memory of him hadn't been skewed by alcohol. He, indeed, was as gentle and kind as he was handsome.

"The pleasure was all mine," she replied, taking his hand. "Have a safe trip home."

"You too." He stepped toward the SUV but stopped and turned back to her, wrapping his arms around her in a heartfelt embrace. He kissed her forehead and whispered, "You're just so beautiful. I don't want to let you go."

Tears welled in her eyes as she held him tightly. "Maybe we'll meet again someday. When we're both ready."

"I'd like that."

"Yeah?"

"The universe already brought us together twice," he pointed out, still holding her. "If it's meant to be, it'll happen again."

She was surprised by how much stock he placed on fate and destiny. It was a nice change from the other men in her life who'd dismissed such things as nonsense. She wasn't sure how much credibility she put into it either, but it was certainly a romantic notion. She'd been tossing around the idea of giving him her number, but after hearing his thoughts on things, she decided to leave things to chance.

"Maybe it will," she shrugged, breaking the hug to wipe her eyes. "Good luck with everything."

She watched as he climbed into the Range Rover. The sullen look on his face suggested that he wasn't ready to part ways either, but she knew he couldn't put his life on hold any longer. He had his bipolar ex-girlfriend to deal with and, if memory serves, an important business meeting to attend. She could relate to having her real estate firm to get back to and a new home to move into.

He backed out of the driveway, then stopped to roll down the window and wave goodbye. She waved back and swallowed her emotions as he sped out of her life.

# Chapter Six

## *Beau*

Beau groaned as he slipped the key into the lock, dreading what he would find inside his townhouse. Between his ephemeral afternoon tryst with Vivian and his long flight home, he was thoroughly exhausted and in dire need of rest. He'd tried to sleep on the plane, but his mind kept swirling with thoughts of the dark-skinned beauty who had somehow stolen a piece of his heart. He'd never forged such a strong connection with somebody so quickly and suspected she could say the same. Believing she shared the same feelings, however, seemed rather presumptuous as there was no way to be certain. She appeared as genuinely enthralled by him as he was by her, but he could have been reading too much into things. Right now, he had other matters to deal with.

Stepping inside his dark townhouse, he could sense something wrong and steeled himself for the worst. He recognized the crunching sound under his feet as the shattered remains of the two vases she'd thrown at him before he'd left and wasn't too surprised she hadn't swept them up. She'd never been big on cleaning, acting as if it were beneath her.

Flipping the lights on revealed what he had feared, and he froze in place as he looked at the mess. Jessica had trashed his home entirely and held nothing back in doing so. The white leather sofa that he'd imported from Italy for a hefty sum of ten thousand dollars had been repeatedly slashed with a knife, its upholstery ruined with cushioning spilling onto the floor. The glass coffee table positioned in front of it had been smashed, leaving shards of glass planted in the carpet. Its frame had been bent beyond repair. The hammer was used to inflict the damage lying nearby. The words "FUCK YOU" spray painted on the rear wall in big, red letters gave him pause. He didn't recall owning any spray paint, which meant she'd gone out of her way to buy some in a premeditated strike. How she'd planned this vandalism reflected a whole new level of depravity.

The screen on the eighty-inch television mounted on the adjacent wall had been bashed in, presumably with the same hammer used on the coffee table. The glass on the framed artwork hanging throughout the living area and kitchen had also been smashed in with such force it had ruined the paintings they were protecting. Their canvases, now cut and embedded with pieces of glass, would make restoring the artwork nearly impossible. All unframed artwork had been spray-painted red, rendering it worthless. The few vases she hadn't rocketed at him before his trip had been toppled and lay in pieces from the fall of her foot. Statues and sculptures were also strewn about the floor, having been brushed from their places on the shelves that had displayed them. Some appeared to have survived intact, while all the glue and spare time in the world wouldn't help the others.

The sight of the defaced artwork hurt his heart. The provenance behind each piece, the stories told by their history, were now silenced by one woman's cruel act of revenge. Such time and effort had gone into creating each painting, vase, and sculpture, most dating back centuries. Their ineffable beauty had been destroyed for nothing. He'd tried to give them a good home, proudly displaying them for their artistic value and not as a financial boast, but had failed in keeping them safe. Anger would come later. Now, as he looked at each piece, he was overcome with deep sorrow and regret.

He heaved and shifted his focus from the artwork to the rest of her destruction. It was mostly overturned furniture—chairs and end tables and such—with random objects lying about that she'd likely thrown in her fit of rage. Predictably, the few items that were hers hadn't been disturbed. If she'd done this much damage downstairs, he feared what awaited him upstairs, where there was plenty more artwork and furniture. He headed toward the stairs and stopped when he heard a noise. Cocking his head, he listened for it again. Seconds later, he heard the sound of somebody shuffling around above him in the master bedroom. He slowly crept forward and had just reached the foot of the stairs when the figure of a woman appeared at the top, silhouetted by the faint light emanating from behind her. Though half in shadows, he could make out that it was Jessica. He hadn't seen her car when he'd pulled up to the townhouse, but that was normal since she typically parked around the corner. She stood there momentarily, looking at him in an eerie silence before finally speaking.

"Welcome home," she said, stepping down the stairs, a bottle of vodka dangling in her hand by its neck. When she took another step down, he could see the bottle was almost empty. She was wearing a pink satin robe that was untied and hanging open, revealing her nude body underneath.

"Jessica," he began, trying to remain calm. "What have you done?"

"Okay, look. I might have gone a little crazy. Don't be mad."

"Don't be mad?" he scoffed. "Are you kidding me right now?"

"You've been gone for a week, Beau," she fired back defensively, her voice slurred from the alcohol. "You didn't reply to me once. Not a single phone call or text message. Yesterday, I just... I just kind of snapped."

He felt his blood begin to boil and clenched his fists so tightly that his knuckles turned white. With the rage that was building inside of him threatening to spill out, he took a deep breath to calm himself. "*Kind of* snapped? You completely trashed the place. Do you even realize how much damage you've done here?"

"Jesus, I said I'm sorry," she muttered. Bracing herself on the railing of the stairway, she took a long swig from the bottle.

"You think 'sorry' is going to fix this?" He ran his fingers through his hair, looking around at the devastation. "Everything else I can deal with, but the artwork? Why the artwork, Jessica? Do you even understand what you did? Do you have any idea how valuable—"

"Oh, wah, sorry about your dumb little paintings," she blurted sarcastically.

His anger welled again, and he fought hard to restrain it, reminding himself that she wasn't worth the jail time he'd face if he lost control. "Those were original pieces," he said through gritted teeth. "They were irreplaceable."

Her body swayed from her intoxication, but it didn't stop her from downing more vodka. The bottle was almost empty, but he suspected it had been full earlier in the evening. "Yeah, well, maybe you shouldn't have been off fucking whores."

"Excuse me?"

"You heard me."

"I wasn't of 'fucking whores.'"

"Then where were you?"

"You know what? You don't need to know where I was. I don't owe you any explanations. I asked you to move out, and you trashed the place instead." He reached into his pocket and pulled out his cell phone. "I'm calling the cops."

"Don't you dare!" she said in a panic, rushing down the stairs while still holding the bottle. She tried to swat the phone from his hand, but he pulled it out of her reach. "We can talk this through!"

"There's nothing to talk through," he hissed as he backed away from her. "You did at least one hundred thousand dollars' worth of damage here. I can't just let you get away with that."

"Beau, I'm sorry! I promise I'll fix everything," she said. Pulling her robe aside, she began to rub a pink nipple while eyeing him seductively. "Just put the phone down. We'll go upstairs, and I'll suck your—"

*"Enough!"* he yelled loudly enough to make her flinch. "You need to learn that there are consequences for your actions. You can't destroy someone's property whenever you don't get your way."

*"Beau, please!"* she pleaded. "We don't need to get the police involved in this."

She moved toward him, but he held his hand out to keep her at a distance. "You need help, Jessica. You're not right."

Lunging forward, she swatted at the phone in his other hand, but it was out of her reach. "Beau, don't!"

"How did you think this was going to go?" he asked, stepping back as he dialed 911 and placing the phone on speaker so she'd know he wasn't playing around. His thumb hovered over the call button, but he had one more question for her. "Did you really think we'd work things out after what you did here?"

"I... I..." she stuttered, unable to come up with any reasonable answer.

"Exactly. You're sick."

*"Put that fucking phone down!"* she shrieked, swinging the bottle at him. He ducked and narrowly avoided what would have been an excruciating blow to the head. She swung the bottle again, but he saw it coming and blocked the strike by grabbing her wrist. The bottle fell to the floor but didn't break, and there wasn't enough vodka left in it to spill out. He pressed the call button with one hand, the other still held out to keep her at arm's length.

"911, what is your emergency?" the dispatcher's voice sounded.

"Yes, I'd like to report a—"

She lunged at him again, punching his face, and sent the phone flying from his hand. It landed on the carpet behind him, barely missing the hard tile floor of the kitchen that surely would have shattered it. She hurried to step on it, but he was too quick, grabbing her by the waist and holding her back as her feet flailed.

*"Fuck you!"* she screamed. *"I'm going to fucking kill you!"*

*"Jessica, stop!"*

*"You piece of shit!"*

He held her back as she fought to break free of his grip. He threw her aside, and she fell to the carpet, allowing him enough time to grab his phone.

"911, can you hear me?" the dispatcher asked.

"Yes, I need assistance. Please send—"

He was interrupted yet again when Jessica sprang up and successfully landed another punch, this one to the opposite side of his face, followed by yet another.

*"Hang up that fucking phone!"* she screamed, trying to snatch it from his hand.

*"Jessica, stop! Stop!"* he pleaded, backing away from her. One hand attempted to shield his face from her blows while the other held onto the phone tightly, the 911 dispatcher still asking questions he wasn't able to answer given Jessica's continued onslaught. She suddenly stopped, her chest heaving and nostrils flaring, and took a step back. An evil grin spread across her face, and in a move proving just how deranged she'd become, she hit herself in the eye with such force that it made her head spin.

*"Stop hitting me!"* she yelled, punching herself in the eye again. *"Beau, stop! Please!"*

The dispatcher's voice sounded as Beau stood in stunned silence, unable to believe what he was seeing. "Hello? Sir, are you still there? Sir?"

*"Stop, Beau, I don't deserve this!"* Jessica begged, punching herself in the eye for a third time. Using the speakerphone to her advantage, she pretended to sob and cried out in pain as she pounded her own face in. He thought he heard a crack when she hit her nose, causing blood to gush from her nostrils and drip onto the floor.

"Send help," Beau told the dispatcher, his jaw hanging slack in disbelief at Jessica's performance. "My ex-girlfriend vandalized my home, and now she's hurting herself."

*"Stop lying!"* Jessica screeched, her right eye already beginning to swell. *"He's hitting me! Please help me!"*

Beau quickly rattled off his address to the dispatcher and, despite being told to stay on the line, disconnected the call after being assured that officers were en route. He was well aware that 911 recorded every phone call and didn't want Jessica making any more false allegations that could later be used against him. Sure enough, when the call ended, she dropped her act and looked at him with a smirk on her battered face. Being a model who took such pride in her looks, he was shocked she'd marred herself in such an outrageous way.

"The cops are on their way," he said. She'd been abusing herself so violently he wasn't sure if she'd heard his brief conversation with the dispatcher. "We're going to get you help, Jessica."

"I don't need help!" she growled, wiping the blood from under her nose with the back of her hand. Brushing by him, she rushed up the stairs, and he followed behind her, unsurprised to find the second story just as trashed as the first.

"Oh, for fuck's sake," he grumbled, pausing in his tracks as he took in the rest of her carnage. More defaced artwork. More overturned furniture. He shook himself from his anger and caught up with her in the master bedroom, greeted by another broken television and several shattered mirrors. She'd thrown her pink robe on the bed and entered the large walk-in closet. He watched as she hurriedly got dressed, tugging on a pair of jeans and throwing on the first shirt she grabbed. She hadn't bothered with a bra or panties.

"I'm leaving you," she told him matter-of-factly. "I'm breaking up with you. It's over between us."

He wanted to point out that he'd severed their relationship a week earlier but let it go, hoping a false sense of victory would keep her calm.

"That's fine," he replied, standing in the closet entrance. It looked like she was readying herself to leave, and he wasn't quite sure how he felt about that. He wanted her to be hauled off in handcuffs for what she'd done, but with her face looking the way it was, he knew they'd both be in for a long night down at the station. She'd accuse him of abuse, he'd deny it, and the back and forth would be a drawn-out ordeal that might not end well for him.

She pushed by him, refusing to make eye contact as she grabbed her purse from where she'd left it beside the bed.

"You'll beg for me back," she laughed as she rooted through her purse for her keys. "You'll beg for me back like they all do."

That comment, clearly a slip of the tongue, shed some insight into her previous relationships, which she'd always been quiet about.

"What are you doing?" he asked, though he already knew the answer.

"I'm leaving," she replied, slipping on a pair of flats and heading for the stairs.

"You can't leave. You're drunk."

"I can do whatever the fuck I want."

"The cops will be here any second," he reminded her, following her out of the room. "They're going to want to talk to you."

She stopped and turned to him with a smirk. "Then they can talk to me when they find me."

"I'm going to press charges, you know."

"Do it," she snarled, "and just see what happens. I'll tell them you trashed this place when I broke up with you. Then you attacked me."

"Please," he scoffed. "I trashed my stuff and not yours? That's ridiculous. They'd never believe you."

"You sure about that?" she asked, pointing at her face. "Rich playboy gets dumped and can't handle the blow to his ego?"

He shook his head and combed his fingers through his hair in frustration. "What is wrong with you?"

"I hope your whores were with it," she said, clumsily descending the stairs. With how intoxicated she was, he knew he shouldn't let her leave but couldn't bring himself to stop her. He'd done a remarkable job keeping his cool, but every man has a breaking point and was close to reaching his. He wanted her gone.

"Expect a visit from the police," he told her as she headed toward the front door. He knew she was serious about pinning her bruised face on him, but he couldn't let her escape with the immeasurable damage she'd done. The value of the artwork she'd destroyed extended far beyond its price tag.

"And you can expect another one," she replied, storming out the door and slamming it behind her.

He took a seat on the only stool she hadn't overturned at the kitchen's breakfast bar and waited for the police to arrive. As the adrenaline left his system, he could feel the soreness on his face from where she'd managed to sneak in a few solid punches. So much had happened so quickly that he hadn't been able to process it all, and with the cops due to arrive any moment, he wouldn't have time to sort out his feelings until later.

He was grabbing an ice pack from the freezer when the doorbell sounded, followed by a knocking at the front door. As expected, it was the police, and the two officers who'd arrived seemed genuinely empathetic as he walked them through the crime scene. He recounted his break-up with Jessica and how he'd returned home after a week away to find the place in its current condition. One officer took pictures of the destruction—a lengthy process given how many items had been destroyed—while the other took down his statement along with his estimate of how much damage had been done, which he could only guess was around the six-figure mark. He'd have to sit down and do the math later, but for now, they had enough information to report the crime as a felony. The two officers flashed each other a look of skepticism when he detailed Jessica's self-abuse, how she'd bruised and bloodied her face after pummeling his in retaliation for having dialed 911.

"You're sure you didn't hit her?" one of the officers gently prodded, trying to coax a confession out of him. "I mean, if I were you and I came home to this mess, I'd have a hard time keeping my cool."

"A lot of guys in your position would have lost their temper," the other officer agreed, studying Beau's battered face for any signs of guilt. His eyes moved to Beau's hands, subtly looking for indication of trauma.

Beau sighed and held up his hands to give the officers a better look at his knuckles. "I didn't touch her."

He could see their incredulity as he retold the story. While they'd initially seemed sympathetic, they now eyed him with suspicion. He didn't blame them since the thought of a model bashing her own face in seemed so outlandish. He silently scolded himself for having dragged his feet with the indoor surveillance system he'd been meaning to install. He had one camera mounted above his front door that gave him a view of the street and captured people coming and going, but that was completely useless in his current situation. If he hadn't procrastinated with the cameras, which he knew he needed, given his growing art collection, he might have had the evidence he needed against Jessica.

They snapped a few photos of his bruised eyes, jotted down a few more notes, and told him they'd be in touch after speaking with Jessica. When they asked if he knew her whereabouts, it occurred to him that he had no idea where she'd drunkenly run off to. That she hadn't moved any of her things out meant she probably hadn't lined up another place to stay, and since she'd established residency at his townhouse, he'd have to go through the eviction process to get her out. He'd hoped to avoid that, but it was clear she would make things as difficult as possible for him. The officers pointed out that, with how much damage she'd done, he could file for an emergency eviction that would have her thrown out in days, not weeks.

Like most beautiful women, she had many men in her life who would take her in without question, so he hadn't felt too bad giving her only a week to pack her things and leave. She was probably crying on one of their shoulders right now, telling them her fabricated version of how he'd beaten her and thrown her out on the street. With no address to give and with her working as a freelance model for no specific agency, he knew the police would have a difficult time tracking her down.

The officers left after assuring him they'd find and question Jessica. Exhausted and relieved to finally be alone, he trudged upstairs, rubbing his left eye as he entered the bathroom to assess his injuries. The mirror above the sink was shattered but still served its purpose, reflecting the bruise that had formed. His right eye was also bruised, but his left had taken the brunt of the attack as the darkness circled it. He groaned, remembering the meeting he had with Sono-Scan in two days. It was a huge investment opportunity that would likely make him millions. They needed his money to finish the project and surely wouldn't turn him away over two black eyes, but it would be embarrassing nonetheless and reflect poorly on his character.

Moving back to the bedroom, he kicked off his shoes and collapsed on the bed, thankful Jessica hadn't sliced up the bedding or mattress. He thought the day he'd left for Ireland had been long, but it had nothing on his return. Under normal circumstances, the damage Jessica had caused, specifically to his prized artwork, would have upset him too much to sleep. However, he was so utterly drained, and perhaps still in a state of disbelief, that he was able to push it from his mind. He didn't even have the energy to get undressed and crawled under the blanket wearing the same clothes he'd flown home in. His thoughts drifted to Vivian and how he could have avoided this predicament had he waited for a woman like her. He reminded himself how silly that was since he was unaware a woman like her even existed until Jessica had pushed him away with her craziness. He also knew that Vivian was a rarity and that he could have gone his whole life without finding anyone like her. She was unique, and he drifted off to sleep, reflecting on their perfect afternoon together.

He awoke four hours later to his doorbell ringing. He'd been in such a deep sleep that it took him a moment to register what had woken him. He looked at the clock on his nightstand through swollen eyes. 7:04 am. The doorbell rang again, and he groaned as he rolled out of bed, both eyes throbbing as he made his way downstairs. He knew it wasn't Jessica since she still had a key and would have let herself in. There was a knock, then the doorbell again as he hurried to the front door.

"I'm coming, I'm coming," he grumbled.

He was greeted by the same two officers who'd arrived at the scene only hours earlier and was surprised they'd returned so soon.

"Mr. Sullivan," one of the officers nodded.

"You found Jessica already?" he asked, still half asleep and trying to make sense of things.

"Actually… she found us," the officer replied.

The other officer said, "She showed up at the station a couple of hours ago with a story that's quite a bit different than yours."

He sighed and ran his fingers through his hair. "That doesn't surprise me. What's she saying?"

"We're going to need you to come down to the station," the first officer told him in a no-nonsense tone.

Beau swallowed hard, realizing just how bad the situation was. "Right now?"

"Right now."

"Let me just grab my things," he said, motioning behind him.

The officers allowed it, stepping inside and keeping him under close scrutiny as he quickly changed his shirt and slipped his shoes back on. He followed the officers outside to their squad car to ensure he had his wallet, cell phone, and keys. As they helped him into the back seat, they reminded him that he wasn't under arrest and was merely going in for questioning. He had an uneasy feeling about it but knew he didn't have much of a choice. If he didn't go in now, he'd have to go in eventually. Getting it out of the way was the best option, especially with the events so fresh in his mind.

After arriving at the station, they guided him into a small interrogation room and asked him to take a seat. A detective who grilled him for over an hour replaced the two officers, hoping he'd crack and admit to hitting Jessica. He stuck to his story, insisting he hadn't laid a hand on her, but the detective, a lanky, gray-haired man in his late fifties, didn't seem convinced. Given how disheveled Beau looked with his hair mussy and traces of stubble peppering his face, he supposed he didn't blame the detective for being dubious. The slacks he was wearing now wrinkled from sleep, and his two black eyes surely didn't help.

"You expect me to believe a model beat her own face in?" the man asked, sliding the X-ray in front of Beau again. In an attempt to make her story more credible, Jessica had evidently stopped by the hospital before filing her report against him. Tapping his finger on the x-ray, the detective added, "You're telling me a beautiful girl like her broke her own nose?"

"I'm telling you, that's what happened," Beau insisted.

"Okay," the detective sighed. "I guess we're done here, then. If that's the story you're going with, I—"

"It's the truth," he snapped, cutting the detective off. Tired and irritable, he was done with the games and didn't have it in him to keep going around in circles. "Now, either let me go, or I'm calling my lawyer."

"Wait here a minute," the detective said, pushing his chair away from the table and rising to his feet. With a look of frustration, he left Beau alone in the interrogation room and returned minutes later with a pair of handcuffs.

"Oh my God, are you serious?" Beau scoffed. "I want a lawyer."

"Please stand up and place your hands behind your back."

His composure finally wavered. A stream of obscenities escaped him, but he did as told, knowing that resisting would only worsen things. The detective read him his rights and informed him that he was being charged with domestic assault.

"This is ridiculous," Beau hissed. "I want my phone call."

"And you'll get it after we book you," the detective told him as he led him out of the room.

"How is it you're taking her word over mine? Your officers saw the damage to my home. You've seen my face. She's got severe issues."

"She's being charged, too."

This news stunned Beau for a brief moment. "She is?"

"It seems to me like you both threw punches," the detective replied, his hand on Beau's elbow as he walked him through the precinct. "We're charging you both and letting a judge sort it out."

In the booking area, Beau caught a glimpse of Jessica, her hands also cuffed behind her back, and took comfort in knowing she was also being detained. It appeared they'd already begun processing her, and she didn't look too happy about it. When she saw him, her brow furrowed in anger, and she mouthed the words "fuck you."

"What happens from here?" Beau asked as the detective sat him down to await processing. Aside from speeding tickets years earlier, he'd never been in trouble with the law and wasn't entirely sure how things would unfold.

"It's still early," the detective began, nodding toward the clock on the wall, "so they should be able to get you in front of a judge this morning for your arraignment."

"Am I free to leave after that?"

"Depends on if you make bail," the detective shrugged.

After processing, he was allowed to make a phone call and dialed his lawyer, who wasn't a huge help as he specialized in business, not criminal defense. He was referred to another lawyer, presumably one of the city's best, and was assured he was worth the staggering price. Two hours later, he stood in front of the judge with his new lawyer by his side. He pled not guilty and was allowed to leave on bail, which didn't come cheap. His court date, where he'd be allowed to defend himself, was set for the following month. If they needed more preparation time, his lawyer assured him they could push the date back to gather evidence. His lawyer, who seemed sharp and worthy of his reputation, was also kind enough to offer him a lift home. Beau didn't feel guilty accepting the ride for the price he was charging.

Back at his townhouse, he sullenly passed the mess and took an overdue shower. The warm water stung his bruised eyes, and he groaned, reliving the nightmare that had unfolded since arriving home. If only he hadn't run off to Ireland and had stayed in Manhattan to oversee Jessica's move, perhaps things would have gone differently. In disappearing the way he had, he'd unleashed the demon hiding inside of her that had been threatening to break loose for months. The flip side to that coin, however, was Vivian. Had he not left, he would have never met her and had his eyes opened to what he'd been missing out on. Despite the drama he'd come home to, Jessica's vindictive actions hadn't soured the memories he'd made with her.

The shower woke him enough to make the phone call to his insurance company. He may have dropped the ball on the security cameras, but he'd at least had the forethought to ensure his more valuable artwork. He was told they'd send an adjuster over the following day to assess the damage and take photos of the defaced pieces. With his Sono-Scan meeting scheduled for the morning, he asked if they could send the adjuster in the afternoon. The next day would be busy between the investment opportunity and the insurance claim. He needed to sleep, and with the Jessica ordeal on hold until he met with his lawyer again, he could finally do just that. Falling onto his bed, too exhausted to ruminate on his problems, he was out within minutes.

He dreamed of Vivian.

# Chapter Seven

## *Vivian*

"'Come to Ireland,' you said. 'It will be fun,' you said."

"Hey, I didn't tell you to sleep with him."

"Actually, you totally did," Vivian reminded her.

"Oh, shit. Maybe I did," Samantha mumbled, then appended boldly, "But I didn't tell you not to use a condom."

"I know, I know," Vivian sighed. Slouched over in her office chair, she held the phone to her ear with one hand while massaging her forehead with the other. Her thumb and the middle finger moved in small circles over her temples, helping to soothe her panic. "He told me he couldn't have kids. That he took a test and wasn't fertile."

"And you believed him, why?" Samantha questioned.

"He seemed sincere."

"You were drunk, Vivian. I don't think you were in the right frame of mine to judge anybody's sincerity."

"You met him. I'm not talking about when you were wasted, but when he dropped me off at your house. I mean, I know you two didn't talk much, but did he seem like the kind of man who would lie about something like that?"

"No," her friend admitted, "He seemed like a genuinely sweet guy."

"Right? This doesn't make any sense."

"Maybe it was just a fluke. One of his little guys was alive and swimming."

"Maybe. Either way, I'm going to have to tell him."

"Why? Wait… are you going to keep it?"

Vivian groaned, and her fingers moved from her temples to the bridge of her nose. "I don't know, Sammy. I just… I don't know."

"Wow. I thought you would have already made an appointment to… you know."

"I thought about it. I even looked up a clinic. But…"

"I totally understand," Samantha replied empathetically. "I'm sure it's not as easy as it sounds."

Vivian burst into tears, her shoulders hitching as she sobbed. "It's not. It's really not. I thought I'd be strong enough to do it, but... I just... I don't think I can."

"Shh... there, there," Samantha spoke softly, gently as she consoled her distraught friend. "It's okay. It's all going to be okay. If you need me there, I'll be on the first flight out. I don't want you going through this alone."

"Thank you," Vivian sniffled. "I just need some time to figure out what I'm going to do."

"Take all the time you need. I'm here for you no matter what."

Vivian wiped the tears from her face and straightened her posture. Her office was no place to have an emotional breakdown. "I appreciate that. I need to get back to work, but I'll let you know what I decide."

"Love you."

"Love you, too."

Ending the call, Vivian removed her compact from her purse and used its small mirror to fix her makeup.

She believed in presenting herself as a strong leader and didn't want her employees to know she'd been crying. Only two crew members were left in the building, the others out showing property, but she knew how the rumor mill worked. If one person found out, the others would know, and her personal affairs were something she preferred to keep to herself.

Two months had passed since her visit to Ireland, and after her second missed period, she'd known something wasn't right. It usually came like clockwork, so for her to miss it once raised a flag. After missing it again, she'd bought a pregnancy test on her way to work with the intention of taking it when she got home. Curiosity got the better of her, however, and unable to wait, she'd nervously taken it in the bathroom before any of her employees had arrived. As suspected, it read positive and confirmed that she was, in fact, pregnant. She'd locked herself in her office to ride out the emotional storm as she struggled to come to terms with the results. After returning home from Ireland, she'd finished settling into her new home. She had completely engulfed herself in her work, keeping herself as busy as possible to forget about Beau. The impression he'd made on her had proven greater than she'd thought, and she found herself reliving their time together more than she should. She knew dwelling on a man who was little more than a vacation fling wasn't healthy, yet she couldn't erase him from her heart.

Her initial reaction was to terminate the pregnancy. Just thinking the word "terminate" made her cringe since it sounded so cold, but "abort" wasn't much better and sounded every bit as emotionally detached. Weighing her options, she used her work computer to search for reputable clinics in the area and found one that seemed legitimate enough. She stared at the number with a lump in her throat, unable to make the call. She'd always considered herself pro-choice, but now that she had to make that choice, she found it difficult. Her conscience gnawed at her, reminding her that if Beau's child was growing inside of her, he had a right to know. There was no doubt it was his since she and Marcus hadn't been intimate in several months, and she hadn't been with anyone else.

Talking to Samantha had helped, though she'd chosen a phone call over a video call to hide how broken up she was. She was the proud owner of a wonderful new home, and her career was blooming.

Now wasn't exactly the ideal time to have a baby. If she kept it, she'd eventually have to explain to her friends, family, and coworkers why the child's father wasn't in the picture, and that would undoubtedly get old fast. The thought of telling her parents, who had been married for thirty years and didn't believe in having a child out of wedlock, made her stomach turn.

"The father? Oh, he's some guy I had sex with in Ireland a week after I broke up with my boyfriend."

She could sugarcoat it all she wanted, but that's exactly what had happened, and she wasn't a good enough liar to fabricate a believable story. She knew how bad it sounded and dreaded having that conversation with anyone, let alone her parents. They would be disappointed in her, but she was confident they'd support her if she opted to keep the baby, which offered her a small degree of comfort. Her thoughts returned to Beau and how he'd react to the news. Whatever she chose to do, she couldn't move forward with the decision until she talked to him. She couldn't help recalling the last words he'd spoken to her.

"The universe already brought us together twice," he had said. "If it's meant to be, it'll happen again."

Perhaps this was fate's way of reuniting them. With that thought in mind, she closed out of the tab for the clinic, feeling a twinge of guilt for having looked it up in the first place, and began searching for Beau Sullivan. It occurred to her that he'd never told her where he lived, which was going to make things a bit more complicated. She remembered asking over lunch, but they'd been interrupted before he could answer. If she could at least narrow her search down to a state, tracking him down might be a bit easier, but that wasn't an option.

A Google search for the name "Beau Sullivan" returned far more results than she'd expected. In hopes of finding him quicker, she did an image search, and her heart skipped a beat when she saw his picture. Clicking on it led her to an article on *Forbes'* website titled "America's Best Entrepreneurs," but he was mentioned only briefly, and his location wasn't disclosed. Down but not defeated, she continued to scour the internet, finding a few more articles on the affluent businessman who'd made a name for himself as a successful investor. She finally struck gold, learning that his company, *Sullivan Investments*, was based out of Manhattan. From there, it didn't take long to find a phone number. She reached for her phone and dialed the number with trembling hands.

"Sullivan Investments, Gabrielle speaking. How may I help you?"

"Yes, is Beau Sullivan in, please?" Vivian asked nervously.

"I'm sorry, he's out of the office but should be back shortly. I'd be happy to leave a message for him."

"Can you tell him Vivian Clark called, please? It's important."

She left her number with whom she presumed was Beau's secretary. Sighing, she leaned back in her chair, anxiously tapping on the armrests as she kicked around Beau's possible reactions to the news. Her thoughts were interrupted when her phone rang from a number she recognized as a New York area code. She knew it was him and hadn't expected him to return her call so quickly. Taking a deep breath, she mentally prepared herself for the conversation and answered on the third ring.

"Hello, this is Vivian Clark."

"Vivian!" Beau's voice sounded with genuine enthusiasm. "What a surprise!"

"I wasn't sure if you'd even remember me..."

"You're kidding, right?" he laughed. "You're unforgettable. When Gabrielle told me you called, my jaw just about hit the floor."

"Really?"

"Really. It's so good to hear your voice!"

The sound of his baritone voice, with its subtle Irish brogue, made her pulse race... but she wasn't going to tell him that. "It's good to hear yours, too."

"God, how long has it been?" he asked. "Two months now? This is the last call I expected today."

"A little over two months, that's right. How have you been?"

He groaned, and there was a short pause. "Don't get me started. Yourself?"

His response raised questions, but she left them unasked for now, choosing to cut to the point. With a heavy sigh, she told him, "Well, things were going great until this morning."

He'd clearly picked up on the shift in her tone, replying warily, "I figured there was a reason you were calling after all these weeks. Are you okay?"

"You told me you're infertile, right? She asked, coming out with it. "That you can't have kids?"

"Yes, that's right." There was another short pause before he spoke with concern, "What's going on, Vivian?"

"I missed my period last month and again this month. I just took a pregnancy test, and…" she trailed off, unable to speak.

"And?"

She glanced at her office door. Even though it was shut and locked, she lowered her voice and told him in a whisper, "Beau, I'm pregnant."

"That's… wow," he replied, sounding disappointed. "Your ex must be happy. Are you two back together?"

"No, you don't understand," she said, closing her eyes and massaging her temples again. "Marcus isn't the father."

"Oh. Then who is?"

"Beau... I've only been with one other person."

One more pause, this one longer, as he pieced together what she was trying to tell him. "Vivian, that's not possible."

"Are you sure? Because this test says otherwise."

"And the test I took says I can't have kids, so..."

Sliding open the upper right-hand drawer of her solid oak desk, she removed the positive pregnancy test that she'd wrapped in a paper towel. She'd kept it out of disbelief, occasionally stealing glances at it to remind herself that she really was pregnant and not going crazy.

"I can take a picture of it if you'd like."

"That's really not necessary. You haven't been with anyone else?"

"Just you."

"Think the test could be wrong?"

She'd had the same thought but had quickly dismissed it. "It says it's over ninety-nine percent accurate. And it explains my two missed periods. I'm going to take another one when I get home, just to be sure. What about the test you took?"

"It was one of those over-the-counter male fertility tests," he answered. "I failed it rather spectacularly."

"You didn't go to an actual doctor?" she asked, shocked by this revelation. She'd assumed he'd been tested by a medical professional.

"No. But after I failed that one, I took another one a few weeks later. I failed that one, too. Both tests were from different kits."

She groaned and squeezed the bridge of her nose in frustration. "I don't know what to tell you, Beau. All I know is I'm pregnant, and you're the only possible father. I'll take another test when I get home, but I know it will tell me the same thing."

"Okay, okay. We'll figure this out."

"I'm really sorry for calling you out of the blue to dump this on you. I just wouldn't have felt right keeping it from you."

"Don't be sorry. I'm glad you called."

"You're not angry?"

"What?" he laughed. "Of course not! I've thought about you almost every day. I was hoping we'd find each other again somehow."

His admission lifted her spirits. "Really? I mean, I know it's not the ideal way for me to come back into your life..."

"Hey, I'll take it. I'm still thrilled to hear your voice."

"You're sweet. I wasn't sure how you'd react."

"It's a shock, that's for sure. I mean, I didn't even consider it a possibility."

"We should have used protection either way."

"Agreed. Although a part of me is relieved to find out, I'm not totally defective."

"So... what do you want to do about this?"

There was a moment of silence while he deliberated. "Take another test when you get home. If the results are the same, call me back, and we'll go from there."

"Okay," she sighed. "I think I'm going to cut out of work early so I can get it over with."

"Fair enough. I'll be in my office the rest of the day. I'm calling from my cell, so you should have my number now."

"Alright. I'll leave now and should be able to give you a call back in an hour or so."

"Sounds good. I'll be glued to my phone."

"Beau?"

"Yes?"

"Thank you."

"For what?"

"I was a bit scared to call. I thought you might accuse me of lying and freak out or something. Thank you for being so understanding."

"You've met me, right?" he joked. "Granted, we didn't spend a tremendous amount of time together, but you should know I'd never do that."

"I know, I know. I guess I was just all up in my head about it."

"Well, I hope you're not anymore. Whatever happens, I'm here every step of the way."

"You mean that?" she asked, tears welling in her eyes from his support and compassion. She shouldn't have expected any less from him and felt silly for being so afraid of his reaction.

"Absolutely. Now go take that other test and call me. No matter what it says, call me. I've missed you."

"I've missed you, too," she replied, smiling wide.

When the call ended, she took a few minutes to compose herself and slipped the positive pregnancy test into her purse to dispose of at home. She knew it was a paranoid thought, but didn't want any of her employees spotting it in the trash can. The chances of anyone rooting through the garbage bin in her office were slim to none, but she was irrationally overprotective of the test results and didn't want to take the risk. For now, the pregnancy needed to remain as hush-hush as possible. If she didn't keep the baby, the last thing she wanted was rumors of an abortion circulating the workplace.

She braved her employees to tell them she needed to go show a property, and they didn't question it, each so engrossed in their own work they barely made eye contact. Returning to the pharmacy, she grabbed another pregnancy test and an iced tea, which proved to be an awkward transaction. The same cashier who'd rang her up a few hours earlier looked as if he wanted to say something but knew better. Back in her car, she chugged her drink as she made her way home and had to pee by the time she stepped through her front door. She didn't waste any time, heading straight for the bathroom while tearing open the test. Curiously, she found herself just as nervous taking the second test as she was taking the first. Her hand shook as she held it between her legs, and minutes later, she had confirmation that she was unquestionably pregnant. After cleaning up, she carefully set both of the positive tests on the bathroom counter and snapped a picture of them side-by-side. Beau had said he didn't need a picture, but sending him one anyway seemed like the right thing to do. She sent it to the number he'd called her from and received a text message back within seconds.

*Call me!*

She dialed his number, and he answered on the first ring.

"So it's official?" he asked. The excitement in his voice caught her off guard. She'd expected a groan of disappointment followed by an obscenity or two. Yet again, he'd excellently surprised her.

"It's official," she replied, looking down at the tests. "I'm pregnant."

"Wow. I need a second to process this."

"I understand. I'm still processing it, too. It doesn't seem real."

"And you're sure I'm the father?"

"You're the only man I've been with. I wouldn't lie to you about that."

"Of course not. I believe you. I'm just... I'm in shock."

"Me too."

"I'm going to be a dad," he muttered. With the news sinking in, he repeated it louder and more enthusiastically. "I'm going to be a dad!"

"So... you think we should keep it?" she cautiously asked.

"Yeah. I mean, wait, what?" he stammered, clearly taken aback by the question. "You don't want to?"

"I just know how busy we are with our careers and everything. And you live on the other side of the country…"

"Vivian, I need to know what you want to do," he replied, his tone now serious. "I told you I'd support whatever decision you made, and I meant it."

"It's not just my decision, Beau. It's yours, too."

"Well, to be completely honest," he began, "I'd be on board with keeping it. I'm not asking you to since it's your body and ultimately your choice, but I'd move heaven and earth to be there if we did see this thing through."

"Okay. You've given me a lot to think about."

"Look, I know how busy our jobs keep us, but this is a human life we're talking about. It's nothing to be taken lightly."

"I know it's not. But I just bought a house, and I work so much these days. It's pretty much all I do."

"I get that, it's just..." He trailed off, and she could sense that he was searching for a delicate way to phrase his thoughts.

"It's just that what?"

"It's just... what if this is my one shot at having a child? I failed both of the tests I took, so for you to be pregnant is a miracle. If you don't keep the baby... it could never happen to me again. This could be it."

"You're not infertile, Beau," she pointed out. "If you were, we wouldn't be in this situation. You probably just have a low sperm count. It might take the help of a doctor, but I'm sure you could have another child."

"Maybe. But this could be a once-in-a-lifetime thing."

"Or it couldn't. You really need to see an actual doctor."

"I know, I know. I'll make an appointment with a fertility specialist here and find out what's really going on."

"Please do. If not for me, do it for yourself."

"I will. Any chance I can get you to come with me?"

"Beau…"

"Hey, we're going to have to see each other again at some point anyway."

She knew he was right. If they didn't keep the baby, she wouldn't want to go through it alone and would want him there. In her heart, however, she already knew they were keeping it, in which case she'd still want him by her side. She'd been completely smitten from the moment she'd looked at him, and those feelings had only grown stronger with every second they'd spent together. Since returning home, not a day had gone by that, she hadn't thought of him, secretly wishing they'd somehow reconnect. If this was fate's way of giving them a shot at a future together, she wasn't going to mess it up.

"You're right. We have much to discuss, and I'd rather do it face-to-face."

"Agreed. How about I fly you here next week? I can rearrange my schedule easily enough."

"You think you can get an appointment with a specialist that soon?"

"I don't see why not. It's a big city. I'm sure somebody will have something available."

She groaned at the thought of taking more time off from work. "Okay. I have a few showings next week, but I can let my team handle them. I can fly myself there, in any case. I'm a big girl."

They ironed out the details, agreeing that the following Monday would work for both of them. They made small talk as she booked her flight online, and with the arrangements made, they were finally able to catch up and enjoy each other again. She shared the details of her new home and how work consumed most of her time. He could relate, explaining how busy his investments had been keeping him. His meeting with Sono-Scan, which she'd remembered him talking about in his suite at Ashford Castle, had gone well. The final product was nearing completion thanks to the money he'd invested, and he stood to make a tremendous profit from it.

Switching from work to personal affairs, he asked her about her love life, and she explained that Marcus had kept his distance and not attempted to contact her. When she turned the question back on him, he was vague in his response, offering only that Jessica was still as unbalanced as ever before changing the subject. She made a mental note to ask him about it again in person so she could read his face and hopefully squeeze some information out of him. For now, she was elated just to hear his voice and lost in seeing him again, which hadn't seemed possible before today. It didn't feel real, yet the pregnancy tests still staring back at her as she paced her bathroom reminded her that it was.

They talked for nearly an hour until his secretary informed him of an urgent call he needed to take. Now that he had her number, he promised to stay in touch and assured her once more that he'd be there for her every step of the way. She felt much better having spoken with him and debated returning to work, deciding to take the rest of the day off to absorb everything that had happened. It was a lot to take in, and she didn't want her work to suffer from her wandering mind, which she knew it inevitably would. She was pregnant with Beau's baby, and he was back in the picture. The turn her life had just taken would surely be too much of a distraction to focus on clients. With the rest of the day free, she called Samantha back to share the latest developments. Her friend listened to every word, waiting for Vivian to finish before dropping the question she'd clearly been itching to ask.

"So… you're keeping it?"

"It looks that way. I mean, I haven't told Beau that yet, but I can tell he wants me to."

"Yes, but do *you* want to?"

"I do," Vivian confessed. "If anybody else was the father, I'd say no, but…"

"But you're in love?"

"Shut up."

"I knew it!"

Even though it wasn't a video call, Vivian covered her eyes in embarrassment. "It's stupid, right?"

"It's not stupid at all. I've always believed in love at first sight. When I saw Brian, I knew he was the one."

"I guess. I just… I never believed in that sort of thing."

"I have to admit that I'm a little jealous. Brian and I have been trying to have a kid for months, and you're pregnant with a guy you spent two days with."

Samantha chuckled to hide her hurt, and in that moment, Vivian couldn't help but feel guilty. She knew her friend wanted to start a family of her own, yet here she was, having a child with a man she barely knew.

"I'm sorry, Sammy. It'll happen to you soon. I'm sure of it."

"Forgive me. I should be happy for you, not over here having a pity party. Let's just hope Brian knocks me up soon so our kids can be around the same age."

"I wasn't even sure if I ever wanted kids, and now I'm pregnant. It's the last thing I expected."

"Life's unpredictable. For what it's worth, I'm glad you're keeping it."

"Really? You don't think it's a dumb move on my part?"

"Not at all. You're going to be an incredible mother. And you and Beau are super cute together."

"Slow down, slow down," Vivian laughed. "We haven't even discussed that."

"It'll happen," Samantha insisted. "I mean, you two were obviously crazy about each other. Even a blind man could see that."

"That may be true, but I told you, I don't do long-distance relationships."

"Um, hello. He's rich, remember? And you're doing pretty well for yourself, too. I'm sure you could find a way to make it work."

"Sammy, it's not that simple. My business is here, and I don't want to give it up. I worked too hard for it. His business is there, and I'm sure he feels the same about it."

"Blah, blah, blah. You'll figure it out."

"We'll see."

They spoke for over two hours, covering everything from possible baby names to nursery decor for the baby room. For a woman who'd been on the fence about having kids, Vivian was surprised by her change in attitude. Over the course of the morning, she'd gone from terrified to excited. She was still scared but not trembling in fear like she had been earlier. Her thoughts turned to Marcus and how, after three years, she'd broken things off with him when he'd begun pressuring her to start a family. Now, a little over two months later, she would have a baby with a man she'd had a brief fling with overseas. She couldn't help but feel bad and hoped word didn't get back to him. If he caught wind of it, he'd definitely be hurt, and she didn't want that for him. Marcus may have been painfully boring, but he was a good guy.

Over the following few days, she rearranged her workload, breaking down the listings she was scheduled to show and evenly distributing them among her team. With her employees working off of commission, they were more than happy to take on the extra properties since it gave them a chance to make more money. She explained that she was considering expansion and flying to New York to scout it out. It was a believable story, and three days later, she was on a plane heading for The Big Apple, landing at LaGuardia, where Beau was waiting for her with a wide grin and open arms. She broke into tears as he wrapped her in a warm embrace, and when she finally pulled away, she noticed he'd also been overcome with emotion.

"It's so good to see you," she told him with a sniffle, rubbing the tears from her cheeks.

Wiping his damp eyes with the back of his hand, he replied, "It's good to see you, too. You look every bit as beautiful as I remembered."

"I didn't think we'd ever see each other again." She pointed at her belly and added, "And then this happened."

"Fate," he smiled.

"You really believe that?"

"I do," he replied, taking her hand in his.

A part of her had worried the magic between them would be gone without the whimsy of the Emerald Isle and the scandal of a tryst. She was relieved to find it was alive, her heart fluttering as he guided her to the baggage claim area where they waited for her bag, so captivated by each other that they missed it on its first go around the carousel.

Her flight had arrived late, which made the drive to Manhattan shorter since there was less traffic. She'd never been to New York City before and stared in wonder as Beau drove them through Times Square to watch the look on her face.

"It's breathtaking," she gasped, taking in the sights and sounds. "I've always wanted to see it in person. Thank you for this."

"Can't have you come here and not show you Times Square," he smiled.

She appreciated his consideration and how he'd held her hand along the drive. When they pulled up to his townhouse, he rounded his Mercedes to help her out of the vehicle before grabbing her bags from the trunk. His attentiveness never faltered, but she had to laugh when he tried to help her up the stairs. How delicately he treated her at only two months along showed he didn't know much about pregnancy.

"I'm not made of glass," she teased him with a chuckle. "I got this."

"Sorry," he said as he hurried to unlock the door.

"Don't be," she smiled. "It's sweet."

Inside, she was immediately taken by how luxurious his home was. Its interior was far more excellent than its exterior, with a modern feel and new furniture. It smelled new, the familiar scent of leather drifting from the black sofa, suggesting it was a recent purchase.

"Did you just move in?" she asked.

"I've lived here for a few years."

"You could have fooled me," she muttered. Continuing to look around, she noted the bare walls and empty shelves. "You must not be home very often."

He set her bags down and released a long, heavy sigh. "There was… an incident."

"That doesn't sound good," she replied, picking up on his tone. "Let me guess. Jessica?"

"You're good," he nodded. "Jessica."

"I figured something happened since you avoided the question when I asked about her last week."

"That 'something' has been a total nightmare."

"Oh, I've got to hear this."

He invited her to sit on the sofa and sat adjacent to her in the matching black armchair. She hung on his every word, her mouth agape as he recalled arriving home from Ireland to find his place in shambles. How she'd done damage well into six digits, and how he was still battling the insurance company over the artwork she'd so callously destroyed. Her jaw dropped further when he recounted Jessica attacking him before bruising and bloodying her face, going so far as to break her nose.

"Jesus... Beau, that's insane."

"I know. I called the cops, but she's claiming I'm the one who trashed the place and beat her. She marched down to the police department with x-rays and everything."

"They couldn't have possibly believed her... right?"

He groaned and ran his fingers through his hair. "Apparently, she put on a brilliant performance. They weren't sure who to believe, so they charged us both."

"They can do that?"

"I guess it's common in these he-said-she-said cases," he shrugged.

She'd briefly considered pursuing a career as a lawyer before falling in love with real estate, but her legal knowledge had mostly stemmed from the crime dramas she'd watched after school. Over the years, she'd learned that most weren't as accurate as she'd liked to believe. She still found herself fascinated by the law and was captivated by Beau's case.

"So… what happened with everything? Did you get the charges dropped?"

"Oh, it's not over yet," he sighed. "Our court date was scheduled for last month, but my lawyer pushed it back. We're hoping we can find some evidence against her, maybe some history of mental illness or something, but it's not looking good. So far, all we've got is the 'fuck you' she spray painted on the wall, and there's no guarantee that will even help. We couldn't find the can, so we're hoping to prove it was her handwriting. It's a long shot, I know…"

"When's the trial?"

"In two weeks. We couldn't get it postponed again."

She slid closer to him and took his hand. "Do you want me to stay? You need somebody by your side."

"You're a saint for offering, but I'd never ask that of you."

"You're not asking, I'm offering."

"And I appreciate that, but you don't need to miss more work for this drama. I can handle it."

"Okay, but if you change your mind, I have no problem being here for you."

He steered the conversation away from his legal woes to the reason for her visit. She was more than willing to discuss their options, but after her long day of traveling, she wanted to wait until she was a bit more rested before broaching such a heavy subject. He could understand that and led her upstairs to the guest bedroom he'd prepared for her, carefully carrying her bag and gently placing it beside the bed he'd made up. A small piece of her was disappointed he hadn't invited her to stay in his bedroom, but she had to respect what a gentleman he was and didn't expect any less from a man so chivalrous.

"Do you mind if I take a shower?" she asked. "Traveling all day makes me feel so gross."

"Believe me, I understand," he replied. "There's a bathroom right down the hall with clean towels waiting for you."

Her visit was starting off just as her trip to Ireland had, and the similarities didn't go unnoticed. There, she'd caught up with her friend downstairs before being guided upstairs to a bedroom that had been thoughtfully readied for her. The layout even seemed familiar, with a bathroom down the hall that she'd used to freshen up with a shower, just as she was about to do now. The similar feeling closely mirroring the outset of her stay with Samantha helped ease her mind. Beau had suggested a hotel, offering to put her up in a five-star resort if she wasn't comfortable staying with him, but she'd dismissed the idea and was glad she had. As expected, he was proving to be an excellent host, and she quickly felt right at home in his beautiful Manhattan townhouse.

After a warm, relaxing shower, she changed into a loose t-shirt and shorts, thinking she'd be climbing into bed, and felt underdressed when Beau insisted on cooking her a late-night dinner. With her busy day of traveling, she hadn't had time to eat a real meal and didn't protest, watching as he seasoned and grilled two chicken breasts, serving them with a side of brown rice and broccoli. She was impressed at how well it came out, given his admission that he didn't cook often and wasn't very good at it. They sat at his little dining room table and made small talk as they ate, and when they finished, she contributed by washing the dishes. She was in the middle of scrubbing his plate when she felt him behind her. He slipped his hands around her waist and nuzzled her hair out of the way to kiss her neck.

"Thank you for coming," he told her, speaking softly.

She purred and shut the water off, shaking her hands dry. "Thank you for having me."

She turned to face him, and he gently brushed her cheek with the back of his hand. "What do you think, pretty girl? Think we should do this thing?"

He was clearly referring to the baby. She'd already decided to keep it but now didn't seem like the right time to tell him that. She was waiting for the perfect moment, and as sweet as this one was, it wasn't it.

"I need more time, okay? We'll talk about it soon, I promise. I just… I need more time."

"I understand," he said, pulling her close and kissing her forehead. "Whenever you're ready."

That display of affection was something she'd needed. With it, she was certain she was making the right choice and would be able to tell Beau soon. For now, it was after midnight, and she was ready to call it a day. Heading upstairs with him trailing behind, she said goodnight to him and thanked him again for the hospitality. He looked like he wanted to say something but thought better of it, and she couldn't help but wonder if he was holding back an invitation to share his bed. With what a gentleman he was, even if that's what he wanted, she knew he would never come out and ask. Had he extended the offer, she wouldn't have turned it down. She missed his smell, his touch, and his safety in his arms.

Retiring to the guest room, she closed the door behind her and slipped into bed with her phone to check her messages. She'd just finished replying to an e-mail when she received a text message from Beau.

*It's nice having you here. I've thought about you every day since Ireland. Sleep well, beautiful girl. If you need anything, I'm right across the hall.*

She smiled as she replied to his kind words and what seemed to be a subtle invitation.

*I've thought about you, too. A lot. Probably too much. Thank you for having me and for being so kind.*

His reply came seconds later.

*Thank you for coming. Sleep well. Remember… if you need anything, I'm right here.*

She put her phone down and rolled over, foolishly thinking she'd sleep. After less than a minute of trying, she reached for her phone and texted him again.

*Anything?*

*Anything.*

Playing coy wasn't going to happen at this hour. It had been a long day, and she didn't have it in her to play games.

*Can I come cuddle?*

His reply came quickly.

*I thought you'd never ask. My door's unlocked. Come on in.*

She sprang from the bed and quietly made her way across the hall to his room, where she found him in bed, shirtless. The small lamp on his nightstand was on, casting the perfect blend of light and shadow over his muscular body. He smiled at the sight of her and moved over, patting the bed in a gesture for her to join him.

"There's a handsome man," she said playfully, sliding into bed next to him.

"I was hoping you'd sleep in here with me," he replied, wrapping an arm around her. "I almost asked but didn't want to make you uncomfortable."

"I'm more comfortable by your side," she purred, kissing his chest and taking in his scent. "You always smell so good, you know that?"

"Do I?"

"Yes, I love it," she answered, breathing him in again.

"I could say the same about you, you know."

"Yeah?"

"I've missed the way you smell. I've missed everything about you."

He lifted her chin and placed a soft kiss on her lips. Pulling back, he looked into her eyes with such intensity that her pulse began to race.

"What?" she asked, her dry tone caused by the lump that had formed in her throat.

He brushed a lock of stray hair from her face. "You're just so beautiful. I'm sorry, I just… I love looking at you."

"I couldn't stop staring at you when we first met."

"I'm a model, and you're an actress, remember?" he smirked, referencing their introduction at Ashford Castle.

"I can't believe you remember that!" she grinned.

"I remember everything when it comes to you."

He kissed her again, and it quickly deepened, their tongues mingling as their breathing grew heavier. Her heart pounded in her chest when he rolled on top of her and kissed her neck, his eyes dripping with desire. One hand worked its way up her shirt to find she wasn't wearing a bra, and he smiled, pleased with this discovery. She moaned, and her back arched slightly when he cupped her left breast, gently rubbing her hard nipple between his thumb and index finger. She missed his touch and welcomed the feel of his hands on her body. He continued kissing her neck, rendering her defenseless to his advances, while she tightly held onto his broad shoulders. Pushing her shirt up to expose her belly, he trailed kisses down her midsection before hooking his fingers in her shorts and pulling them off. Her panties came with them, and after tossing them onto the floor, he crawled between her legs.

"I've missed the way you smell," he said, repeating his sentiments from earlier. He licked her swollen clit and added, "And the way you taste."

She swallowed hard and asked quietly, "You like that, baby?"

"I love it," he moaned, softly sucking on it while sliding a thick finger inside her.

"Oh my God," she breathed, "T-that feels so f-fucking good."

In the weeks following Ireland, she'd drained countless batteries with her vibrator, but her imagination could never come close to the real thing and always left her unfulfilled. His mouth was just as magical as she remembered, and she couldn't contain her cries of pleasure as he skillfully licked and sucked her pink slit, his finger moving in and out of her in a twisting motion that quickly brought her to orgasm. She held the back of his head as she came into his mouth, riding out the powerful climax while he looked up at her with his light blue eyes.

"A girl could get used to that," she smirked, running her fingers through his hair. She'd never been with a man who was so giving. He seemed to love tasting her genuinely and appeared to take pride in wearing her cum on his face. She could see the wetness glistening on his chin as he flashed her a devilish grin.

"I'd do it all day, every day, if you'd let me."

She laughed, pulling him up to her lips, and could taste herself on him as she gave him a quick kiss. "I need to be able to walk every now and then, you know."

"Okay, okay. Maybe just once a day?" he smiled.

"I can work with that." She reached down and felt the hard bulge in his boxer briefs. "You better give me this once a day, too."

"Just once a day?" he asked with a chuckle.

"I'll take it as many times as you can give it."

"Be careful what you ask for. I can give it a lot."

A mischievous smile spread across her face. "Prove it."

"Really?"

"Really."

"Okay, but this needs to go," he teased, tugging on her shirt that was still bunched up just below her breasts.

"It goes when these go," she teased back, snapping the waistband of his underwear.

"Deal."

Not wasting any time, he pulled his boxer briefs off, and she made good on her word by losing her shirt. She took his shaft in her hand, and a few strokes later, he was impressively hard.

"I want it," she breathed. "Give it to me."

Never one to disappoint, he positioned himself between her spread legs. A wave of electricity shot through her when he pressed the tip of his cock against her opening and slowly worked himself inside of her.

"God… you feel so good," he groaned.

She gripped his shoulders tightly again, watching as he slid in and out of her, his thick member soaked with her juices.

"T-that's s-so hot," she panted. In that moment, she was glad they'd left the bedside light on. She'd never considered herself a visual person, but seeing Beau's hard body pumping away at her was almost enough to make her cum again.

Their eyes connected, and she was transported back to Ashford Castle. Like that first night in his palatial suite, it felt like they were making love. She ran her fingers through his hair again and fought the urge to say the words, fearing they might scare him off if he didn't feel the same.

He supported himself over her with one strong arm, the other wrapped under her leg with his hand gripping her bottom. She could hear the bed faintly squeaking as he thrust into her, his eyes still locked onto hers.

"You're so beautiful," he breathed, holding his gaze while his hips worked in a slow, steady rhythm.

Her hands moved from his hair to her breasts, kneading them with her fingers. He seemed to like that, his pace quickening and the grip on her ass tightening. He watched her for another moment, then closed his eyes in concentration as he gave it to her harder and faster. Her eyes also closed to focus on the climax she felt drawing near.

"That's it, baby," she moaned. "Don't stop. Don't stop. I'm... I'm..."

Another orgasm coursed through her before she could finish her thought. Her hands shot to his back, her nails digging into his skin as she came. He slowed down while she rode it out, allowing her to enjoy every second of it. Needing time to recover, she gently pushed him onto the bed beside her and crawled on top of him, covering his powerful chest with kisses.

"You're so sexy," she whispered, working her way down his body. She looked up at him with a smirk and licked the tip of his cock that was dripping with a mixture of their juices. He groaned, and his hips thrust upward, instinctively wanting more. She didn't tease him by keeping him waiting. Rather, she took him in her mouth and hungrily sucked him with her hand trailing up and down his thick shaft. His size caused slight discomfort in her jaw, but seeing and hearing his pleasure was worth it. He was close, and she knew it, but she didn't want him to finish yet. She needed to feel him inside of her again and took him out of her mouth, licking his shaft from the bottom to the top before slowly kissing her way back up to his chest, purposely taking her time so he'd calm down and last a bit longer.

Straddling him, she lowered herself onto his cock and moaned as she felt him fill her. He reached up to cup her breasts, his thumbs rubbing her hard nipples as she began to ride him. She started off slowly, sensing he was still close and not ready for him to cum. When she finally let him, she'd make it worth his time. She needed a bit more of him for now and hoped he could hold out another few minutes. The entire bed rocked, its headboard slamming against the wall as she rode him faster, grinding her hips into his while their moans sounded throughout the room.

"Oh my God. Oh my God. Oh my God," she repeated, feeling a third orgasm coming. With the combination of his long, thick cock inside of her and her clit rubbing against his pubis, she could tell it was going to be another strong one. She wasn't wrong.

"That's it, baby," he said in a low growl, seeing how close she was. His hands moved to her ass and squeezed it tightly as his cock slid in and out of her. "Cum for me."

As if on cue, she was rocked to her core by the most intense orgasm she'd ever experienced. She'd underestimated just how powerful it would be and cried out loudly as her hands clenched his muscular chest.

"That... that was," she stammered. Losing her ability to speak, she slouched over, still straddling him, her shoulders hitching while aftershocks from the climax shot through her. After a moment, she fell to the bed beside him, reduced to a trembling heap as she fought to regain her breath.

"Are you okay?" he asked with a smirk.

"I… I just… need a minute," she panted, winded from the unexpectedly searing orgasm. She rolled onto her side, her body heaving as she recovered.

"Take all the time you need," he replied, kissing her shoulder softly.

"I… that… I can't…"

He laughed and kissed her shoulder again. "Don't speak. Just lay there. It's okay."

She did just that, laying by his side for nearly five minutes before she'd recharged enough to function. She felt bad keeping him waiting so long, but he'd assured her it was okay and seemed to take pride in knowing he'd rendered her immobile. When she could finally move again, she kissed her way down his body and used her mouth to bring his cock to full attention. Crawling back up to meet his lips, she kissed him while stroking his hard shaft, then positioned herself on all fours beside him.

"I want it," she said. Waving her ass invitingly, she looked over her shoulder at his hard cock and bit her lower lip. "Give it to me."

Never one to miss a beat, he hurried to his knees and moved behind her, working every thick inch of himself into her slit. She groaned at how deep he was, uncertain she could take it, and for a brief moment, found herself concerned about the baby. It was an irrational thought that she quickly dismissed, but that it had even crossed her mind was a testament to his size. Her discomfort turned to pleasure when he began pumping away, his hands on her hips as his tempo slowly increased. She buried her head in a pillow to muffle her cries as he took her from the back, the headboard thumping into the wall again as he gave it harder. She could hear his grunts and groans getting louder and glanced over her shoulder to see his face twisted in sexual focus. He was close again; she was fine with that since she couldn't take much more.

"You feel so good," he moaned, his hands tightening on her hips.

"Don't stop," she lifted her head to say through gritted teeth. "I want you to cum for me."

"Yeah?" he grunted, slamming into her even faster.

"Yes, I want it. Give it to me."

In one fluid movement, he flipped her onto her back and stroked himself until he finished. He winced and released a loud groan, his defined muscles tensing as his orgasm overtook him. She watched as he painted her breasts, holding them together for him to cover with his warm cum. As expected, it was an impressive amount that went beyond its intended target, and she closed her eyes as it made its way up her neck, a few drops landing on her face.

"I-I'm sorry," he panted, bracing himself over her with shaking arms. She felt a sense of accomplishment, having weakened such a muscular man.

"Don't be," she said, wiping the stray globules from her cheek. She knew he hadn't done it intentionally, so that she couldn't be too upset about it. And even if he had, in that moment... she might not have cared. "I take it as a compliment."

He rolled onto the bed beside her, his chest moving up and down from his labored breathing. "That was... wow."

"I think we both needed that," she smiled, still dripping with his cum. He noticed the rivulets beginning to run down her side and sprang from bed, disappearing for a moment and returning with a towel. He used it to clean her, gently wiping his cum from her breasts and neck while looking at her affectionately.

"You're so beautiful. I probably tell you that too much, but I can't help it. It's true."

She blushed and took the compliment. She'd been called beautiful before, but it somehow meant so much more when Beau said it. She admired his body as he moved across the room to toss the towel into the wicker clothes hamper just outside the walk-in closet. He switched off the light on the nightstand on his way back to the bed and settled in next to her, pulling her close. They talked as they cuddled and made love twice before she finally fell asleep in his arms, giving her that same sense of safety she'd felt in Ashford Castle.

She awoke sometime later, having drifted from his arms, and snuggled close to his side again. Her movement stirred him from his sleep, and he wrapped an arm around her protectively.

"Beau?" she said in an almost whisper, running her fingers over his chest.

"Yes?"

"I want to keep it."

"Really?"

"Really."

With the soft glow of the street lights creeping through the bedroom window, she was able to see the smile spread across his face. "Thank you. You've made me a very happy man."

"You'll really be there for me, right?"

"Of course. Have you seen a doctor yet?"

"I called an obstetrician and have an appointment in two weeks since it's still too early for an ultrasound. By my math, I'm only ten weeks along."

"I'll be there."

"Your trial is in two weeks, remember?"

"Damn, you're right. What day is your appointment?"

"The fourteenth."

"The trial is on the tenth, so that works. I'll fly out after it if..."

"If?" she asked, her fingers pausing on his chest.

He sighed and stared up at the ceiling for a moment. "Look, there's no telling what the outcome will be. I'd love to say the odds are in my favor, but they're not. If Jessica puts on a good show, who knows what will happen? I could get locked up."

"Don't say that. Everything will be fine."

"Will it? I'd be lying if I said I wasn't a bit nervous."

She rolled on top of him and kissed his lips softly. "You believe that everything happens for a reason?"

"I do," he nodded, holding onto her hips.

"Then relax. The universe wouldn't put us together again just to tear us apart like that."

He smiled up at her. "You have a point, but still. I have to be prepared for anything."

"Shush," she said, placing her index finger over his lips. "I was never big on the fate and destiny thing, but ever since meeting you… I don't know. I think there might be something to it."

"Yeah?"

"Yeah. I mean, what are the odds we'd meet again in that little market? That I'd be here with you right now, carrying your baby?"

He touched her belly and smiled again. "It seems so surreal."

"We still need to figure out how it happened," she reminded him.

"I'm seeing a fertility specialist Wednesday afternoon. You're still coming with me, right?"

"Of course."

He pulled her down to him and kissed her. "Thank you."

With that conversation out of the way, she sank back to sleep, feeling confident in their decision to keep the child. Over the next two days, their bond grew even stronger as he showed her around the city, pointing out one historic landmark after another while expressing more of his playful side. His quick wit often made her face ache from laughter, and she took pride in making him laugh just as hard. They played off each other well, and although she'd never been one for public displays of affection, she swooned whenever he held her hand or pulled her in for a kiss. She was thoroughly enraptured by him and didn't object when he treated her to the city's finest five-star restaurants. Over dinner at Nobu, a posh eatery known as a celebrity hotspot, he discussed the possibility of them building a life together. She'd been hoping he'd bring it up and was relieved that he'd broached the subject first.

"I'm not glued to New York, you know," he told her.

"You'd seriously consider moving?"

"I love the city but never planned on settling down here. This was just supposed to be temporary. I was going to make my millions, then buy a house in some sleepy little town. A big house. With a lot of land."

"I'm surprised to hear you say that."

"You saw where I'm from. Killarney? That's more my style." He looked out the window at the busy city street and added, "Not this hustle and bustle. I'm a country boy at heart."

"Well... have you made your millions yet?" she asked playfully.

"I've made a lot more than that," he smirked.

She leaned in and whispered, "Billions?"

Too modest to say yes, he shot her a wink that served as his answer.

"Jesus," she muttered, shaking her head in disbelief. "I'm having dinner with a billionaire."

"Let's say that Sono-Scan investment worked out very well for me."

"So... what now?" she asked.

"Well," he began, taking the last bite of his steak and pushing his plate aside. "I could easily retire, but I'm wired like you. I like to work. I need to work. That being said, I don't need to work as much. If you wanted to give this thing between us a shot, I'd close down my office here and buy a house in Colorado. I'd work from home. Part-time, of course, so I could be there for you and the baby."

"Wow. You'd move across the country for me?" She touched her belly and corrected, "For us?"

"In a heartbeat. There's no way I'm going to live thousands of miles away from my child. When I told you I wanted to be there every step of the way, I meant it."

"I just bought a nice house. It's probably not as big or fancy as you'd like, and it doesn't have much land, but maybe you could—"

He put his hand up, stopping her mid-sentence. "Thanks, but I learned my lesson with Jessica. We moved in together way too soon."

"Please tell me you did *not* just compare me to that girl," she said, crossing her arms sternly.

"That's not what I meant," he chuckled. "I just… I want to take things slow. Do things the right way."

"Don't you think it's a little too late for that?" she teased, pointing at her belly.

"I know, I know. I just think we should wait before living together. The whole situation with Jessica might have traumatized me a little bit."

She understood his origin and couldn't fault him for it. Putting herself in his shoes, she wouldn't want to jump into living with somebody again, either. What Jessica had done was scarring, and he had every right to be cautious. Reaching across the table, she took his hand in hers. "I'm sorry. You're right. Let's see how things go between us, then figure it out down the road."

"Thank you," he smiled, gently squeezing her hand.

The following day found them at the fertility clinic, where they could finally get the answers they needed. To their disappointment, Vivian wasn't allowed in the room while he produced his sample, but she understood the clinic's need to keep things professional. As fun, as it would have been to help him, she sat in the waiting room as he made his deposit into a small cup that was later analyzed for count and quality. She suspected he may have slipped them some money ahead of time to expedite the results since they came so quickly, revealing that there was nothing wrong with him. In fact, the analysis proved that his sperm count was quite high and of an excellent grade, with no defects to be found. This news forced Vivian to consider the possibility that he'd been lying about his fertility. As if reading her mind, he pleaded his innocence when they were back in his car.

"I wasn't lying," he said, looking at her sincerely.

"Okay," she sighed. He seemed earnest enough, but she needed to understand what could have happened. "Tell me more about those at-home tests you took."

"I don't really know what to say," he shrugged. "Jessica bought them for me at some pharmacy and—"

"Well, there's our answer," Vivian said, stopping him.

"You think she could have tampered with them?"

"Were they sealed?"

He thought for a moment before answering, "I can't remember. She handed me one, and I took it. Same thing a month later."

"And you trusted her... why?"

"She went to school for nursing, you know. Got a degree and everything. Then, she was offered a modeling job, which led to more modeling jobs. At some point, she realized she could make much more money doing the modeling. Easier work, too. And it gave her a shot at being famous. I think that's what attracted her to it the most."

"I see."

"Anyhow, she had me take those tests before she was acting completely crazy, so I guess I didn't have any reason to question the results."

"I'm sure she messed with them somehow. Soaked them in bleach first or something."

"Why would she do that, though?" he asked, starting the car and looking over his shoulder as he backed out of their parking spot.

"Why do crazy people do anything they do?"

"True."

"Maybe she wanted you to feel insecure so you'd stay with her."

"Now that sounds like her," he groaned, shaking his head as he started toward his townhouse. "I bet that's it, or damn close. She's so manipulative. I've learned that the hard way."

"You must be relieved to know you're okay, though, right?" She rubbed her belly and added, "That this wasn't just a fluke?"

"I am," he nodded. "Granted, it wasn't the most ideal way to find out, but still."

"You're not having second thoughts, are you? About the baby?"

"What?" he laughed. Seeing the concern on her face, he squeezed her leg gently and smiled as he reassured her. "Of course not. I couldn't be happier. I mean it."

"Good," she replied, placing her hand over his.

They stopped to eat on the way back to his place, grabbing a late lunch at an Italian restaurant that left them both stuffed. When they arrived at his townhouse, he changed into his gym clothes, insisting he still needed to burn off some of the meals they'd been eating over the last few days. He was a regimented man with a strict workout schedule he stuck closely to, hitting the gym every day around the same time. Even when showing her around the city, he'd made a point to be home and in his gym gear by 5:00 p.m. She appreciated the effort he put into his body and wasn't going to hold him back. He invited her to work out with him at the gym a few streets over, but her queasy stomach told her that was probably a bad idea. She wasn't sure if the pregnancy, her full stomach, or a combination of both was making her nauseous, but she didn't want to embarrass herself by losing her lunch in the middle of a gym.

"Go get buff," she smiled, kicking her shoes off and laying down on the living room sofa. "Come back all pumped up for me."

He leaned down and kissed her forehead softly. "Will do. Feel better, pretty girl. I'll keep an eye on my phone in case you need anything."

She waited for him to leave before reaching for the television remote on the coffee table beside her. She'd been so focused on her career that she rarely had time to watch television, and when she did, it felt like a luxury. She mindlessly flipped through the channels, recalling the day she'd spent hungover in Ashford Castle with Samantha. That was the last time she'd watched television, but she'd been so hungover she hadn't been able to enjoy it.

She watched Gordon Ramsay scream obscenities on the *Food Network* when a knocking shook her from his antics. Muting the television, she cocked her head and listened for the sound again. When the doorbell rang, she realized the knocking had been coming from the front door and sluggishly made her way to answer it. She had her hand on the doorknob when a niggling doubt prompted her to look through the door's peephole. The neighborhood seemed safe enough, but it was better to check before opening the door to a stranger. Beau was the only person she knew here, and he hadn't mentioned anyone stopping by. On her tiptoes, she peered through the small wide-angle lens to find a tall blonde woman wearing dark aviator sunglasses on the other side of the door. She appeared to be waiting rather impatiently, casting what seemed to be nervous glances up and down the street. A few seconds passed before she knocked again, this time louder, then rang the doorbell three times in a row. The sunglasses hid her expression, but Vivian could sense the woman was frustrated.

She cracked the door and shot the blonde a look of irritation. "Can I help you?"

"I'm sorry to bother you," the woman replied. "My name is Jessica. Jessica Van Buren. Beau Sullivan's ex-girlfriend?"

Vivian felt her face grow heated. With everything she'd heard about this woman, she was the last person she wanted to see. "You're not supposed to be here."

"I know, it's just—"

"You need to leave," Vivian demanded brusquely, her brow lowered in anger.

"Look, I don't blame you for being hostile," Jessica said, taking off her sunglasses and stuffing them into the handbag she had slung over her shoulder. "I'm sure Beau's said nothing but bad things about me."

"You aren't welcome here, so please go."

"Wow, he must have painted quite a picture of me," Jessica chuckled. "I know you have no reason to trust me, but nothing he said about me is true. Nothing."

"Goodbye," Vivian groaned, shutting the door.

Jessica's hand sprang out, stopping the door before it could latch. "Please! I have something you need to see."

"Excuse me? Get your hand off of this door," Vivian growled. "Don't make me call the police."

"Please!" Jessica pleaded again. "I really need to show you this."

"I'm not interested in anything you have to show me."

"Oh, I think you're going to be interested in this."

"Go away!" Vivian hissed, wrestling the door shut.

"There's a video of you and Beau having sex!" she heard Jessica say. The solid oak door muffled her voice, but her words made it through clearly enough.

Vivian cracked the door again and cautiously looked Jessica over. "What did you just say?"

"There's a video of you and Beau having sex," Jessica repeated, pulling a tablet from her handbag. "It's on the internet. Here, see for yourself."

She handed Vivian the tablet, a website with a video embedded into it already called up and waiting to be viewed with the click of a button. Vivian quickly noted that the website's name was "PornHub," a website she'd heard of in passing but had never visited.

"It should be connected to Beau's Wi-Fi," Jessica continued, peaking at the screen to ensure the website was still loaded. "Just press play."

Vivian maintained her cool, confident that Jessica was mistaken since the idea was absurd. She certainly hadn't filmed herself having sex, nor would she allow Beau to record them. She couldn't even imagine him asking such a thing since it didn't fit his character. Still, she had to be sure. With skepticism, she pressed play. It took a moment for the video to load, but when it did, what she saw made bile rise in her throat. The quality wasn't the best, but it was undoubtedly her and Beau and appeared to have been filmed in secrecy from the air vent in his master bedroom. It had been recorded the day before when they'd playfully chased each other upstairs for an afternoon romp, and it left nothing to the imagination. She watched in horror as the video played, the tablet shaking in her trembling hands as the footage continued to roll. Every torrid detail had been captured without her consent and posted online for the entire world to see. The information displayed beneath the video, titled "Hidden Cam 001," showed that it had been uploaded the previous evening by a user with the name "IrishVoyeur" and had already received close to fifty thousand views. She couldn't make it through the entire video. Feeling the queasiness return to her stomach, she shoved the tablet back into Jessica's hands.

"I'm... I'm going to be sick," she said, swallowing the vomit threatening to erupt from her mouth. She turned and rushed to the bathroom, dropping to her knees in front of the toilet.

"You poor thing," Jessica said, having followed behind her. She knelt down to rub Vivian's back as she vomited uncontrollably and consoled her in a soothing voice. "It's okay. Get it all out. It's okay. I know the feeling. I've been there."

"What... what do you mean?" Vivian stammered, wiping away the tears that had been caused by a mixture of the vomiting and the emotions coursing through her.

"He did the same thing to me," Jessica explained. "He recorded us having sex and released it online. He broke up with me when I found it and ran off to Ireland. I think he was scared I'd press charges or something. I should have moved out, but I stayed. I realize it was stupid of me now, but I cared about him and was hoping he could offer me some sort of explanation. That he'd apologize, and we could work through it. Instead, he got home and flew into a rage when he found me here still. He beat the shit out of me and threw me out."

Vivian reached for a handful of toilet paper and dabbed her mouth. "You're lying."

"I'm not," Jessica insisted. "It's his thing. Recording his sexual escapades and putting them on the internet. He gets off on it."

"Beau would never do that," Vivian muttered, using the back of her hand to wipe her eyes again.

"Are you sure about that?" Jessica scoffed. "I mean, how well do you know him? We were together for almost a year. I thought I knew him, but I didn't. He has a side to him that he hides really well. He's twisted."

Vivian considered Jessica's words for a moment. While it was true, she'd only known Beau briefly. She felt she'd established enough connection with him to gauge his morality. She threw the wadded-up toilet paper onto the toilet and flushed it down. "I don't believe you."

"And I don't blame you. He's sick. I'm sure he told you everything was my fault. I know I wasn't perfect, but I didn't deserve what he did to me."

Jessica seemed genuinely sympathetic and concerned for her well-being, but that didn't mean she could be trusted. Vivian shook her head and sniffled again. "No. No, he would never do this. You did it."

"What?" Jessica snorted. "That's ridiculous, and you know it."

The thought of Jessica somehow rigging a camera, getting the footage, and then posting it on an adult website did seem like a reach, Vivian had to admit. However, the thought of Beau being responsible was too incomprehensible, given his kind, gentle nature.

"How did you even know I was here?" Vivian asked. The timing of Jessica's visit seemed a bit too coincidental.

"I check his profile on that website every week to see if he's added any new videos. I happened to check this morning and saw it. It said it was a recent upload, so I stopped by on a whim. I wanted to confront him about it. I didn't expect to find you here."

It seemed plausible, but Vivian couldn't believe it. "No. He wouldn't do something like this."

"Oh, honey," Jessica began with an empathetic voice. "He has you fooled. He's a good actor. He got me good, too. When I saw our video, it was the last thing I expected. A friend of mine sent me the link, and I was floored. I couldn't believe it."

"You're not supposed to be in here," Vivian said, feeling sick to her stomach again. "You need to leave."

"If he's done this to me, and now you… Who knows how many other women he's done it to?"

The sudden realization that her reputation could be affected by the video, her career possibly ruined, caused Vivian to lurch forward, vomiting into the toilet again. When Jessica tried to rub her back, she recoiled from the woman's touch and shot her a nasty look. "Please, just leave."

"Okay. I understand you need some time to sort through this. I'll leave my number so you can call me if you need any—" She was interrupted by another round of vomiting from Vivian and looked at her with worry, still kneeling by her side. "Are you going to be okay?"

"I'm pregnant," Vivian blurted, her face buried in the toilet bowl.

There was a long moment of silence before Jessica spoke. "You're pregnant?"

Vivian began to sob, gripping the toilet seat with both hands as tears poured from her eyes. "Yes."

"With Beau's baby?" Jessica asked. Vivian couldn't see her through her tears, but she sounded upset by the news.

"Yes, with Beau's baby."

Another long pause. "That's not possible. He told me he couldn't have children."

Vivian grabbed another handful of toilet paper, wiped her eyes, and then her mouth. "H-he told you that?"

"Yes, why?"

"He told me you had him take two tests right here at home."

"Wow. He's even more fucked-up than I thought," Jessica chuckled, shaking her head in disgust. "No, sweetie, he always told me he couldn't have kids. I think it's just something he says, so he doesn't have to use a condom. How far along are you?"

Vivian sniffled again as she wiped her nose. "Ten weeks."

Jessica did the math in her head. "You met him here?"

"No, in Ireland," Vivian answered. The words had come tumbling out before she could stop them, and she scolded herself for having given the woman so much information. It wasn't any of her business, and she still couldn't be trusted. "You need to go now."

"Okay," Jessica sighed, rising to her feet. "Look, if I were you, I'd stay far away from him. He's a pervert. A dangerous one. You'd understand how scary he can be if you saw what he did to my face. He may seem like a saint right now, but he's the devil in disguise. Leave here and never come back."

With that, she turned and left, leaving Vivian alone on the bathroom floor with her head spinning. Jessica seemed sincere, but Beau had mentioned what a great actress she was. Even with that, she had to consider the alternative, at least. Had she been so swept up in his looks, charm, and affluence that she'd misjudged his character? It didn't seem likely that she could be so wrong about a man, but she couldn't dismiss the notion entirely. She needed to distance herself from him to weigh the situation objectively. Drying her eyes, she hurried upstairs, packed her things, and waited in the kitchen for her Uber to arrive. She didn't know where she was going. She just knew she needed space. Beau would be home soon, and she feared his spellbinding presence might cloud her ability to think rationally. No, she had to leave and wiped more tears from her eyes when her phone alerted her that her ride had pulled up.

She settled on a hotel in Lower Manhattan. It was pricey, but the seclusion gave her time to think. She'd just checked into her room when Beau called her, but she ignored it. She'd talk to him in time, but at the moment, her top priority was getting their video pulled from the internet. She brought the website up on her phone and easily found the video by searching for its title. She copied the link and used the contact information provided at the bottom of the site to e-mail the owner, insisting they remove the video as it was recorded without her consent. She sent a follow-up e-mail minutes later, expressing the urgency of the video being removed in hopes it would speed the process up. With nothing to do but wait for a reply, she fell onto the bed and stared up at the ceiling.

Her phone rang again. It was another call from Beau, but she still wasn't ready to speak to him and let it go to voicemail. A text message followed the call, and she ignored that as well. She didn't want to mute her phone and risk missing an e-mail alert if the website got back to her since that took precedence over everything else. Knowing it could be a while if they even replied, she debated seeking legal counsel. A lawyer might assist in getting the video pulled faster, and since she hadn't consented to being filmed, she was sure the police might be able to help, too. If anything, they'd go after Beau and slap him with a few new charges. As desperately as she wanted to stop the video from spreading, she opted to wait and see how everything played out. She'd pursue legal action if she hadn't received a reply by the morning.

If Jessica had been telling the truth, which seemed unlikely, how had she gone about getting her video removed? She'd mentioned Beau having secretly recorded them, too. A part of her regretted pushing the girl out the door before she could ask a few questions now swirling through her mind. She didn't know who or what to believe anymore and hated that she'd gotten herself into such a mess. Had she not rushed into bed with Beau, she wouldn't be pregnant with his child and the star of an internet sex video. Her thoughts returned to the footage of them in bed together, and she felt sick to her stomach again. She'd never felt so violated. So exposed. So humiliated. As much as she wanted to call Samantha, she didn't want her to know about the recording. With how nosey the girl was, she'd try to find the video online. As close as they were, she wasn't okay with her best friend watching her have sex.

She laid in bed for another hour, emotionally exhausted but too upset to sleep. The video was getting more views with every minute that went by, yet she was helpless to stop it. Somebody was discovering the footage somewhere in the world and likely defiling themselves to it. The thought of total strangers pleasuring themselves to her made her skin crawl. For the time being, she was at the mercy of whoever ran the website, and all she could do was hope for a reply before having to drop money on a lawyer. She wasn't thrilled with the idea of getting the cops involved since that would be more eyes seeing the video. Whether it be Jessica or Beau, she wanted whoever was responsible for the footage to pay, yet seeking justice wouldn't be easy. The recording may have to be played in a courtroom; she could never handle that embarrassment.

She'd cross that bridge when the time came. Right now, she needed to get the video pulled and figure out who posted it. She hoped Beau hadn't been responsible, but Jessica had been convincing enough to raise doubts. Her mother's favorite maxim had always been, "If something seems too good to be true, it usually is," and that saying replayed in her mind as she weighed Beau's involvement. He had always come across as the perfect man, with seemingly no faults. Had it all been an act? Perhaps she was more naive than she thought and had been duped by his good-guy facade. She'd need to confront him soon, but until then, she had to think long and hard about every interaction they'd had. Maybe she'd missed some small warning sign, something he'd said or done that hinted at a darker side. She pored over their time together, but nothing stood out as unusual.

Another two hours went by. Beau had tried calling again, but she hadn't answered. There was still no response from the website, and the video had already racked up another five thousand views since Jessica had shown it to her. At the rate it was accumulating hits, it would easily reach the sixty-thousand mark by the morning. She was well aware of how the internet worked. Once something was online, it usually existed forever in some form. The chances were good that somebody had already saved a copy of it and could release it elsewhere at any given time. Each view multiplied that possibility and added to the urgency of getting the video removed. She sought comfort in knowing she wasn't famous and that her name hadn't been attached to it, but that thought didn't offer as much consolation as she'd hoped. Groaning, she looked at the time and knew she couldn't wait any longer. If Beau had been responsible, and she could get him to admit it, he might agree to remove the footage. Phone in hand, she dialed Beau, and he answered on the first ring. She didn't waste any time getting to the point.

"We need to talk."

# Chapter Eight

## *Beau*

"Where are you?" he asked, relieved she'd finally called but alarmed by the tone of her voice.

He'd arrived home from the gym hours earlier to find Vivian gone, with no note, text message, or phone call to explain her disappearance. It didn't seem like her to take off without warning, but there had been no sign of foul play. She'd packed her things and left her own volition, offering no reason why and leaving him to wonder where she could have gone. Even more confounding, she wasn't answering her phone or returning any of his text messages, which didn't seem right. He remembered she hadn't been feeling well and called the local hospitals and clinics to see if she'd checked herself in, but they had no record of her. Baffled by her abrupt departure, he searched the townhouse, hoping to find a note that he'd somehow missed, but found none.

Dropping onto the sofa, he ran his fingers through his hair in frustration. Despite his best efforts, he was unable to stop his mind from going to dark places.

Perhaps she'd had a miscarriage and was in the middle of being transported somewhere? He couldn't imagine her packing her belongings if that had happened. If she'd stepped out to go shopping, he couldn't see her bringing her things, either. Had something she'd found in his home upset her? He didn't own anything offensive enough to scare her off. The few movies in his collection were rather benign, and he owned no pornography. The pieces of art that had survived Jessica's rampage were innocuous enough, and he kept no love letters or pictures of ex-girlfriends. Something had chased her away. Whatever it was, he decided, must have been on her end. Maybe she'd had a family emergency and had left so quickly that she hadn't had time to leave a note or call. Picking up his phone, he sent her another text message.

*Really worried about you. Please get back to me when you can. I hope you're okay!*

He headed upstairs again to take a shower, making it quick in case she called back, then ventured to the kitchen to grab a light dinner. He'd worked up an appetite again at the gym but was so wrought with anxiety over Vivian's disappearance that he couldn't finish his meal. For her to up and leave without telling him, especially pregnant with his child, still wasn't sitting right with him. Remembering the lone security camera mounted over the front door, he grabbed his phone to review the footage from the day. The camera was an older model that only captured one small frame per second, sending the frames to his phone via his Wi-Fi connection. He had the application set to store a week's worth of playback before deleting the frames in favor of new ones, preventing it from overloading his phone. It was an outdated system he'd meant to replace, but it worked well enough… in theory. He'd never had a reason to use it and fumbled his way through the application for the first time, growing increasingly agitated as he struggled to view the recordings. The stills, compiled to play in succession as a video, were all black as if nothing had been captured. He assumed he was doing something wrong and cursed under his breath as he browsed a variety of settings, none of them offering any help. All seven videos, each dated and time-stamped, were completely black.

"Modern technology," he grumbled, giving up and gently tossing his phone onto the coffee table as he returned to the sofa. The camera's backend application on his phone had obviously glitched, capturing nothing but darkness. His tech-savvy friend had installed the system for him and assured him that it worked, but it had stopped functioning somewhere along the line. Or had it? A sudden thought sent him shooting from the sofa and bolting across the room. Swinging the front door open, he looked at the camera that had been angled above it to capture anyone entering or exiting his townhouse. Sure enough, its lens had been colored black with either paint or a marker. He stood on the tip of his toes, examining the lens to make sure he wasn't mistaken. He wasn't. Somebody had purposely covered the lens, rendering the camera useless, and it had likely been that way for weeks, if not months, without him noticing. Neighborhood kids could have been responsible, but a gut feeling told him Jessica had done it. The lens could probably be cleaned off, but he wasn't in the mood to deal with it since it wouldn't help him find Vivian. Right now, that was all he cared about. Back inside, he called her again and left her another voicemail.

"Vivian, not trying to blow up your phone or anything. I'm just really concerned. I'm guessing you had some sort of emergency and had to leave? I wish you'd left me a note or something. Kind of going out of my mind over here. Please give me a call back when you get this. I just want to know you're okay."

He flipped on the television in an effort to distract himself but couldn't take his mind off of her. He made another round of calls to the hospitals and clinics in the area, but they still had no record of her. Minutes turned to hours before, at close to midnight, his phone finally rang. He grabbed it so quickly that it almost fell, but he still managed to answer it after only one ring.

"Vivian! I've been worried sick about you. What the hell is going on?"

She told him they needed to talk, and her seriousness filled him with dread. Something was wrong, but she wouldn't tell him over the phone, insisting they speak face-to-face. He was surprised to learn that she'd checked into a hotel not far away that he drove by on a regular basis. Since he already knew where it was, he made a mental note of her room number and hurried out the door with his stomach in a knot, convinced she'd changed her mind about the baby. Twenty minutes later, she greeted him at her door with a sunken face, the faint rivulets of mascara under her eyes implying that she'd been crying.

"Come in," she said, motioning him into the room and closing the door behind him.

"What's going on? Are you okay?" he asked, almost in a panic.

She pointed at the bed. "Take a seat."

Swallowing nervously, he did as told and sat on the edge of the bed. She pulled the room's small armchair closer to him and sat across from him, examining his face. "Vivian, what's going—"

"I'm going to ask you something, and I expect the truth," she said, cutting him off. The no-nonsense look she was giving him and her mannerisms reminded him of his interrogation the morning after Jessica's destructive fit. The detective who questioned him had acted much the same way.

"Okay," he replied nervously. He could sense this wasn't about the pregnancy but something much deeper.

"Beau. Did you film us having sex?"

"What?" he laughed, amused by the question's absurdity. However, his laughter quickly died when he realized she wasn't joking.

"Answer me," she said, her eyes fixed on his. "Did you film us having sex?"

"Of course not. Where is this even coming from?"

She calmly handed him her phone and nodded at the screen. "Look."

He could feel her studying his reaction as he processed what he was seeing. "Is this some sort of a joke?"

"Press play," she told him, leaning back in her chair and crossing her arms. She continued to search his face as he started the video.

"What the fuck?" he muttered as the footage of them in bed together rolled. His eyes broke from the video, and he looked at her with bewilderment. "Vivian, what is this?"

"What does it look like, Beau? It's us yesterday in your bed."

He looked back down at the video, still playing, then at her again. He could feel how flushed his face was as he asked, "Did you do this?"

"Wait, what?" she replied, taken aback by the accusation.

"Did you put this online?"

"Of course not!" she fired back defensively.

"What, you find out what I'm worth and film this video as some sort of... some sort of blackmail?" he hissed, springing to his feet. He threw the phone onto the bed and began pacing the room angrily. "What was your plan, huh? Hope I'd write you a big, fat check so you could retire early?"

"Beau, I didn't do this. I thought—"

"You thought I did?" he scoffed, stopping mid-stride and pointing at himself. "You think I'd really film us in bed and put it on the goddamn internet?"

"No!" she replied, rising from her chair. It looked like she was going to burst into tears again as she told him pleadingly, "Please just calm down!"

"You're right," he said, his chest heaving in anger. Seeing how emotional she has flooded him with guilt for believing she could have done such a thing. The video had been so unexpectedly shocking that it had momentarily stripped him of his senses. He closed his eyes and took a deep breath, regaining his composure before speaking. "I'm sorry. I shouldn't have accused you like that. Forgive me. I guess I've been a bit defensive ever since Jessica."

"She stopped by your townhouse earlier. It's how I found out about the video."

He shook his head in confusion. "What?"

"After you left for the gym. She showed me the video and said you'd recorded yourself with her, too. That you're an abusive pervert who shouldn't be trusted."

"And you believed her?"

"No! Well... I... I don't know what to believe anymore, Beau. I needed time to think, so I came here."

"You really think I'm capable of something like that?"

"No," she replied. "At least... I don't think so."

He recoiled at that, offended by her doubt. "You don't think so?"

"Beau... the video was filmed in your bedroom. How do you explain that?"

He sat on the bed again and pinched the bridge of his nose as he thought for a moment. "Jessica. It had to have been Jessica."

"That's what I thought, too... but..."

"But?"

"It seems like kind of a stretch. You expect me to believe she hid a camera in your bedroom, somehow got the footage, edited it, and put it online?"

Struck by a eureka moment, he snapped his fingers and pointed upward. "That's exactly what she did, and I think I can prove it."

"How?"

"When I asked her to move out, I told her to leave her key on the counter. I just realized... she never did. She's been able to come and go anytime she wants."

"I can't believe you never got the key back."

"With everything that happened, it just slipped my mind. Besides, the court ordered her to stay five hundred feet away from me and my townhouse."

"You really think she's been sneaking in there?"

"Somebody tampered with my street camera. The one above my front door? I noticed it earlier. They colored the lens black. I'm betting Jessica did it so I couldn't see her coming and going." He paused and admitted, "Not that I would have seen it anyway. I never check the damn thing. I only got it in case of a break-in, but nothing's been missing or out of place."

"Okay…" Vivian said flatly. It appeared she was trying to remain neutral and consider his words objectively, without bias. "So, how can you prove it?"

"She'd wanted a laptop, so I bought her one for her birthday last year. I loaded it up with high-end video and photo editing software. She may be crazy, but she's not dumb. She learned them quickly and used them to edit her own promotional material for her social media pages. You know, to help her score modeling gigs. It worked well."

"So?" Vivian asked, trying to piece together what he was saying.

"So she's had access to my townhouse and knows how to edit video," he explained.

"What about the camera?"

"She could have put that in there weeks ago. Months ago, even."

"And she's been going in and out to change the tapes or something?"

"Tapes are a thing of the past," he reminded her. "Everything's stored to memory or a hard drive these days. She could have..." he trailed off as his mind connected the dots. "Jesus, she could have done it using my Wi-Fi."

"That's possible?"

"It's how the camera above my front door works. It sends the feed to my phone using my Wi-Fi connection."

"She definitely still has your password. She showed me the video using a tablet that was connected to your internet account."

"We need to go," Beau said, rocketing from the bed and looking at her urgently. "Right now. We need to go."

"What? Where?"

"To my townhouse," he replied as he hurried toward the door. "If she installed a camera in my bedroom, it could still be there. We need to check. If she hasn't removed it yet, it could have her fingerprints on it."

"You're right," Vivian agreed, quickly grabbing her room key and following behind him.

There was an awkward tension between them for the first time as they raced back to his townhouse. He sensed that she wanted to believe him but was still wary, and he didn't blame her. Had their roles been reversed, he would have been skeptical, too.

She glanced at her phone and groaned. "Still nothing from the website. I contacted them earlier, asking them to remove the video."

"I'm not much for porn, but I'm pretty sure that's a huge site," he replied, fingers anxiously tapping on the steering wheel as they sat at a red light. "They probably get hundreds of emails a day."

"You saw how many views it had, right? Almost sixty thousand already. This needs to come down, Beau. It could ruin me."

"It wouldn't exactly be good for my reputation either, you know," he countered. "I've made quite a name for myself lately. If the media were to catch wind of this…"

"I was going to contact a lawyer in the morning."

The light finally turned green, and Beau stepped on the gas. "Don't bother. I'll have my guy send them a cease and desist first thing. He's good. Really good. They'll pull the video, I promise you."

"They better…" she muttered.

"Look, I want to contain this just as much as you do, believe me." He shook his head and said through gritted teeth, "Jessica is going to pay for this. I will make sure she goes away for a long time."

"I'd be okay with that," Vivian nodded. He thought he heard her mumble, "If she did it."

Pulling up in front of his townhouse, they rushed inside and bounded up the stairs to his bedroom. He pushed his dresser underneath the vent cover and climbed on top of it to peer through the slits, using the flashlight on his phone to illuminate the vent's dark interior.

"Son of a bitch," he mumbled.

"Is it there?"

"Looks like it." He hopped down and disappeared, returning seconds later with a screwdriver. Climbing atop the dresser again, he unscrewed the vent cover and tossed it onto the floor. "Oh, yeah, it's definitely still here."

"Don't touch it," she said, looking up at him.

"I won't," he replied, shining his flashlight beyond the camera. "Damn, she really is a clever girl."

"What do you mean?"

"I was wondering how she would have powered a camera. It looks like she ran an extension cord all the way through the vent. That had to have taken some time and ingenuity."

He jumped off the dresser and helped Vivian onto it so she could see the setup for herself. "Wow, you weren't kidding. Do you think it's still broadcasting?"

"Probably. We need to find where the other end of that cord is so we can unplug it," he said, offering her his hand to help her back down. "I'd unplug it from this end, but I don't want to risk touching the camera. We need it as evidence."

It didn't take them long to find it, and he marveled at her creativity. She'd dropped the cord through the ventilation shaft into the downstairs bathroom below. From there, she'd removed the bathroom's vent cover and punched a hole in the side of the aluminum shaft to run the cord down the inside of the wall and out through a small hole she'd cut in the drywall near the floor. She ran the few inches of remaining cord along the baseboard to a nearby outlet, concealing it with the bathroom's small trash can. Replacing the vent cover, nobody could see her handiwork. She knew the chances of him spotting the cord were slim since he rarely used the downstairs bathroom, typically reserving it for guests.

"I was just in here earlier today," Vivian told him as he unplugged the cord, cutting off power to the camera. "She was standing right next to me. Right next to the crime."

"You let her in?"

"After she showed me the video, I got sick. I ran in here, and she followed me. I'm sorry."

"It's okay," he sighed. "She knew she wasn't allowed inside. She violated the court order. That's something else we can hopefully use against her."

His eyes traced up the wall where the power cord would have been running on the other side. Vivian could see him mentally mapping the cord's route on its journey to the outlet. "Beau... what is it?"

"It's probably nothing, but..." He moved from the bathroom to the living room just around the corner. He pointed up to another vent and looked at it for a moment in contemplation. "That vent right there would give somebody a view of this entire room, and it's directly below the vent in the master bedroom. If she had dropped the cord, it wouldn't have been out of the way for her to hide a camera there, too. The power supply would be running right by it."

"You think there's another one?"

He shrugged and grabbed a stool from the kitchen. "Only one way to find out."

"Careful," she said, holding onto the stool while he climbed up.

Reaching for the screwdriver he'd stuffed in his pocket, he removed the vent cover and snorted in disgust. "Really?"

"What?" Vivian asked, unable to see into the vent from her low vantage point. "Is there another one?"

"There sure is," he replied, shaking his head. "We're going to have to search the entire place."

They did just that, tearing through the entire townhouse but finding no other cameras. It made sense that there would only be the two since wiring power to additional cameras would have started getting complicated. Jessica was smart, but she was undoubtedly no electrician. She'd only been able to rig the two cameras because the ventilation shaft from the master bedroom ran straight down to the living room and onward to the bathroom, allowing her to wire them both with no extra work. The master bedroom and living room were the only rooms she would have any interest in monitoring since the other rooms rarely saw any action.

"So what now?" Vivian questioned, dropping onto the sofa with a sigh. She looked exhausted, and he was right there with her. It was pushing two in the morning, and they both needed sleep.

He took a seat in the black armchair adjacent to her. "I think we should call the cops."

"Yeah… maybe."

He was surprised by her answer. "Maybe?"

"Honestly? I don't know. As much as I want whoever was responsible for this to pay, I really don't want this being played in a courtroom. At this point, I just want the video removed."

"Whoever was responsible?" he asked. "We both know it was Jessica."

She flashed him a look of skepticism. "Do we?"

"Oh, come on! You can't seriously think I did all of this."

"Why would she plant cameras in your home, Beau?"

"Probably to see if I was having an affair. She always accused me of it. It really shouldn't surprise me that she was spying on me. She'd constantly accuse me of cheating."

"Did you?"

"Of course not! I can't believe you'd even ask me that."

Vivian checked her phone for the hundredth time. When she immediately set it back on the coffee table, he knew she hadn't heard back from the website. She groaned and rubbed her eyes. "I don't know what to do anymore."

"I still think we should call the cops. They might be able to get fingerprints off the cameras and put Jessica behind bars where she belongs."

"But then the cops will have to watch it, it'll be shown in a courtroom, and as you pointed out earlier, the media might pick it up. It could become a whole spectacle that does more harm than good. You know, if the news covers it, the video will get reposted somewhere and will get millions of views... which is exactly what I'm trying to prevent."

She was right. He could try to contain the story, but the video might go viral if it leaked. Sixty thousand views could easily turn into millions, affecting their personal lives and careers. As much as it pained him to admit it, getting the authorities involved was a gamble they could very well lose. If he wanted justice, he would have to seek it himself. He couldn't just let this go. Not with the look of doubt Vivian kept casting him. He needed concrete proof that Jessica had planted the cameras if there was ever any hope of her trusting him again.

"You're right," he nodded. "Going to the cops could backfire. I'll flush Jessica out on my own."

"I'm sure you will," Vivian replied halfheartedly. "Look, I need to sleep for a bit. Can you bring me back to the hotel? I can call an Uber again if you're too tired."

"Why don't you just crash in the spare bedroom for a few hours? We'll get up early and call my lawyer."

"I don't feel comfortable here anymore, Beau. I'm sorry."

That hurt to hear, but he couldn't blame her. "Okay, yeah, sure."

He grabbed his keys and endured another awkward car ride with her. Despite his protests of innocence, she was visibly upset and painfully cautious of him, saying very little as they made their way back to the hotel.

"Just drop me off out front," she finally spoke as they drew near.

He sighed and did as instructed, slowing to a stop by the hotel's front entrance. "I'll call you in the morning, okay? After I talk to my lawyer."

"Sure," she said with a forced smile. "Thank you for the ride."

He watched her walk inside, desperately wishing things could return to how they had been. For that to happen, he'd need to find evidence and fast. Vivian didn't seem the type to put up with the drama, and he feared she'd hop a flight back to Denver the moment the video was pulled. He had no doubt his lawyer could get it removed, but unless he could prove Jessica was responsible for it, there was a good chance Vivian could change her mind about the baby when she returned home.

He glanced at the time. It was a hair before two-thirty, but he knew Jessica kept odd hours. As a freelance model, it was normal for her to stay up late and sleep in until ten or even eleven in the morning. They worked around that easily enough when they were dating, with her quietly slinking into bed next to him in the wee hours of the night. Knowing she could still be awake, he hurried back to his townhouse to find her new address. He remembered seeing it on one of the court documents his lawyer had given him but had no idea whether it was truly her address. She could have listed the address of a friend or a fake address altogether, but he could only hope that she'd been truthful for a change. Her phone number was also listed, but this wasn't something a phone call could clear up, nor did he want her to have his new number. He needed to talk to her in person.

With time of the essence and his options limited, he rooted through his legal paperwork and headed to the address listed, pulling alongside an upscale apartment building on the Lower East Side of Manhattan. Double-checking the address, he rounded the corner to a parking garage and paid the exorbitant fee to park his car. He'd lucked out with his townhouse, as it had come with a parking spot right on the side of the street, but most Manhattan residents who dared to own a vehicle weren't so lucky and incurred steep parking fees. He spotted Jessica's steel blue Lexus on his walk from the parking garage, assuring him he had the correct address.

"Ten forty-two," he quietly repeated to himself, memorizing the apartment number. Once inside the building, he rode the elevator up to the top floor, reminding himself that his late visit paled compared to what Jessica had done. Under normal circumstances, he'd never show up at somebody's door in the middle of the night, but given the stunt she'd pulled, it felt warranted.

The elevator stopped at the tenth and final floor, followed by a ding as its metal doors parted. He wasn't surprised that she'd be living in a penthouse. She was used to luxury, and although she made a decent living as a model, it was usually somebody else's money she was living off of. He was confident she'd found a new man to fleece and was caught off guard when a woman wearing only a baggy t-shirt groggily answered his knock.

"Dude. It's three in the morning," the tall redhead said, rubbing her sleepy eyes.

"I'm sorry to have woken you. I'm looking for Jessica Van Buren?"

"At three in the morning?"

"I know it's late, and I apologize. It's important."

Jessica's voice sounded from inside the apartment. "Who is it?"

The redhead looked over her shoulder and answered, "Some hot guy."

The door opened wider, and Jessica appeared, looking like she'd just woken up. She ushered the redhead out of the way and took her place in the doorway. "Beau? What are you doing here?"

"You know what I'm doing here," he replied sternly.

"Let me guess," she said with a smirk, "You're here to beg for me back? I knew it would happen eventually."

He ignored that remark and cut to the point. "Take that video down right now."

"What video?" she blinked, feigning ignorance.

"Stop. You know what video? Take it down now."

"My new promotional video?" she asked, continuing to play dumb.

"Jessica, what you did is a serious offense. You could go to prison for it. I won't get the cops involved if you take it down."

"I have no idea what you're talking about."

He groaned and ran his fingers through his hair in frustration. "You know what you did. I found the cameras. Take the video down right now, or I'm calling the police."

"If anyone should be calling the police, it's me. You're violating a court order by being here," she told him smugly. "We were supposed to stay five hundred feet away from each other, remember?"

"Look, this doesn't have to get messy. Just remove that video, and I'll be on my way. No cops."

"I have no idea what you're talking about!" she snorted, her hands gesticulating wildly. "What video?"

"The one you showed Vivian earlier," he said through gritted teeth.

"Who?"

"Jesus," he muttered, pinching the bridge of his nose. He was trying to remain calm, but she was purposely testing his patience. "Vivian. The woman you spoke to earlier at my townhouse."

"I was never at your townhouse," she insisted, shaking her head. "Beau… are you okay?"

It was a smart move on her part, putting on a performance in case he was recording their conversation. She knew how to cover her tracks. That much was evident. "Cut the act. Go take that video down, or it's going to end very badly for you."

"Are you threatening me?"

The redhead resurfaced behind her, looking concerned. "Jessica… is everything okay?"

"Everything is fine," Beau told her, holding up his hands to show that he meant no harm.

"He just threatened me," Jessica said. "You heard it, right?"

"I did," the redhead replied. "Want me to call the cops?"

There was a long pause as Jessica thought it over. "No. No, that won't be necessary. I'm sure he was just leaving. Isn't that right, Beau?"

"Jessica..." Beau said in a low, pleading voice. "Please. If a modicum of decency is left in you, take that video down."

"I told you, I have no idea what you're talking about. What video?"

Her confusion looked so sincere that his resolve faltered for a moment, but he reminded himself what a fine actress she was. "You know damn well what video."

"I really don't, and I don't have time for this. I have a photo shoot in the morning. I know we've had our problems, to put it lightly, but I don't know anything about a video. Maybe that woman... what did you say her name was?"

"Vivian."

"Maybe Vivian isn't being honest with you."

"She wouldn't lie to me," he scoffed, shaking his head.

"Are you sure about that? Because I wasn't at your townhouse and I don't know anything about a video. Now, if you'll excuse me, I have to get back to bed." She began to close the door but paused, offering him a warm smile. "For what it's worth, it was nice seeing you again. I don't know what's happening, but I hope you get it all figured out."

"I'm sure you do," he fired back sarcastically.

"I'll always care about you, Beau. Don't be a stranger. If you need anything, just call me."

With that, she closed the door, and he heard the distinct sound of its lock clicking. He sighed and rested his head against the back of his hand on the door casing, overcome with a feeling of helplessness. He'd seen their exchange going differently. He was supposed to confront her, demanding she remove the video. She was supposed to admit to everything, tears pouring from her eyes as she pleaded with him not to call the cops. He was supposed to watch as she deleted the footage, ensuring she couldn't upload it again. She was supposed to apologize, sobbing as she begged him to take her back. He was supposed to rush back to Vivian, triumphantly announcing his victory.

Those things were supposed to happen but didn't, leaving him at a total loss. He debated knocking on the door and trying again but knew she'd never admit to what she'd done. She'd called his bluff, knowing he didn't have enough evidence to go to the police. Even if he did, Vivian had already clarified that she didn't want to go that route. Defeated, he returned to the elevator while Jessica's words replayed in his mind.

*Maybe Vivian isn't being honest with you.*

Jessica couldn't be trusted, but could Vivian? He had to remind himself that as much as he cared for her, he didn't truly know her. He felt like he did but knew from experience that feelings could be deceptive. He'd trusted Jessica in the beginning, and it had ended in disaster. Was history repeating itself with Vivian? Perhaps he'd been naive in trusting her so quickly. After all, they'd only spent a few days together in person. It seemed unlikely, but she could have rigged the cameras her second day there when he was at the gym, then lured him upstairs to the bedroom the following day. She'd not attempt extortion, so that scenario seemed illogical. She also didn't strike him as the voyeuristic type who got a thrill from recording her sexual escapades. Jessica had to have been responsible, but he hated that she'd successfully planted a small seed of doubt in his mind. Now he knew how Vivian felt, feeling a deep-seated suspicion that would always linger unless they could prove with absolute certainty that neither of them had recorded the footage, subsequently releasing it online for the world to see. If Jessica tried to turn them against each other, she was doing a good job. He needed hard evidence and fast, but that wouldn't be easy to get. With how clever Jessica had been installing the cameras, there's no way she would have been stupid enough to leave her fingerprints on them. Even getting the IP address she uploaded the video from would be hard, if not impossible. Knowing her, chances were good she'd parked outside his townhouse late at night and uploaded it from his Wi-Fi, making it look like he'd submitted it to the website.

"Fuck," he grumbled, riding the elevator back down to the lobby. He continued to fume over the situation as he walked back to the parking garage, desperate for a way to pin Jessica. He couldn't even prove that she'd spoken to Vivian since the lens on his sole security camera had been blacked out. She'd done a remarkable job covering her ass, he'd give her that, but she had to have made a mistake somewhere, and he wouldn't give up until he found it. He was almost to his car when something else Jessica had said struck him.

*I have a photo shoot in the morning.*

Having lived together for a year, he knew her routine all too well. She hated waking up early. When a modeling gig called for it, she'd pack her bag the night before and leave it in her car so she didn't have to rush when the morning came. She'd go overboard stuffing clothes, makeup, and even her laptop into the duffel bag, for which he'd scolded her numerous times, reminding her that the city was safe but not that safe.

"One of these days, somebody's going to smash your window and take that bag," he'd tell her. She hadn't listened then, and he was pretty sure she hadn't changed her ways since they'd split. On a whim, he changed direction and headed to her car, acting casual to avoid suspicion as he glanced inside. Sure enough, her duffel bag was in the back seat, and he could see the rectangular outline of her laptop pressing against its interior. The car was locked, which he expected, and the idea of smashing her window crossed his mind before a realization stopped him. Jessica may not have given him back her copy of his house key, but he hadn't given her back her copy of her car key, either. She'd given him the spare key after they'd started dating since she was prone to locking herself out of her flashy Lexus, and he still had it on his keychain. He dug into his pocket and pulled out his keys, then glanced over his shoulder to make sure she hadn't followed him. Confident she hadn't, he unlocked the car and quickly unzipped the duffel bag, taking the laptop and stuffing it under his arm before zipping the bag back up. He locked her car and hurried back to his, tossing the laptop onto his passenger seat and speeding off to his townhouse. She wouldn't notice the missing laptop until the morning, and when she did, there wasn't a whole lot she could do about it since he'd paid for it and still had the receipt. If she dared call the police, he could easily claim it was his and that he had the evidence to prove it.

Vivian's hotel was close, but he didn't want to wake her. She needed her sleep, and he did, too. It had been an agonizingly long day, and he could barely keep his eyes open, so tired he was seeing things on the drive back to his townhouse. He made it home and set the laptop on his nightstand to dig through when he could think clearer, then set his alarm, passing out within seconds. The incessant beeping from his phone woke him three hours later. As much as he would have loved another hour of sleep, he had important business to handle. He promised Vivian he'd call his lawyer, but that would have to wait. If there was any evidence to be found, it would be on Jessica's laptop, where she'd likely edited and uploaded the video. He booted it up and was prompted for a password, which he thankfully knew… or so he thought. It had been "ilovebeau," but he should have known she would change that. He tried a few different things and had to chuckle when "fuckbeau" worked. For all the effort she'd put into staging the actual crime, she'd dropped the ball to secure the one place she'd left any evidence as he immediately found a folder on her desktop named "Beau" that was a treasure trove of incrimination.

What he found inside sent shivers down his spine. There were photos of him, hundreds of them, taken at various places around the city without his knowledge. There were just as many videos, all taken from the two cameras she'd hidden in his townhouse, some so disturbing they raised goosebumps on his arms. One particularly alarming video, recorded after they'd broken up according to its date and time, showed her standing by his bed, watching him sleep. At some point in the night, she'd let herself in and crept upstairs, appearing as a dark silhouette by his bedside where she loomed over him for nearly an hour as he slept. She stood stock still, simply looking at him as he lay there, oblivious to her presence.

"Jesus," he muttered, moving on to a video that showed her masturbating in his bed. It was another video filmed after their split, this time in broad daylight when he'd likely been at work. The file names were unsettling, with titles such as "I See You" and "Still Our Bed," and they were mixed in with dozens of videos she'd recorded when they were still together. He was horrified by how far back they dated. Some of them were filmed before she'd even moved in. These older videos, mostly recordings of them having sex in his bedroom or on his old sofa, were given names like "Doggy Style" and "Riding His Dick." He skipped by them in favor of the videos with more incriminating names. A video titled "Fuck You" caught his attention, and he opened it, unsure what to expect. His muscles tensed as he watched a recording of her trashing his living room, laughing as she tore his place apart before spray-painting the vulgarity on his wall. This video was hugely helpful as it proved she'd been the one who'd wrecked his place, but it wasn't the smoking gun he needed. It was the video named "Oscar Performance" that sealed her fate.

"Gotcha," he grinned, watching the footage of their fight the night he'd returned from Ireland. Had they taken a few steps to the right, neither of them would have been visible in the frame, but the camera's lens was wide enough to capture the drama. You could clearly see Jessica land a few blows to his face, then turn her fists on herself. Viewing the video was hard and filled him with a mix of emotions. He was excited to have evidence exonerating himself, relieved that he wouldn't have to suffer through a trial, yet saddened by the sight of somebody so obviously needing help. He was suddenly conflicted, uncertain if he wanted to see her behind bars or institutionalized where she could get psychiatric treatment.

Also in the mix of videos were his recordings with Vivian, their titles so offensive he would never dare repeat them, especially to Vivian. He never knew

Jessica to be capable of such hatred and bigotry. He didn't want to tamper with potential evidence, but he had to rename the files to spare Vivian's feelings. If the authorities needed the entire laptop, they didn't need to know about the small edits he'd made or how he'd obtained the device. He quickly changed the discriminatory titles, then copied the two most incriminating videos onto an old flash drive. The footage of her trashing his place and later bashing her own face in would be enough to clear his name and put her away, either in jail or in a mental hospital. Once the case against him was dismissed, he'd wipe the laptop clean so nobody could ever find the more intimate videos. If some of Jessica's modeling work was lost in the process, he'd chalk it up to collateral damage.

Calling up her internet browser, he wasn't surprised to find her still logged into PornHub. It took him a moment to figure it out, but he could remove the video along with the entire profile. "IrishVoyeur" was no more, and he could only hope the video never resurfaced under another username. With over 70,000 people having viewed it, the chances were good that at least one person had saved it. It could appear again someday, and they'd have to live with that possibility.

For the time being, the footage had been contained, and the source of its dissemination was confirmed as Jessica. He couldn't help but feel guilty for considering, even for one second, that Vivian might have been responsible. He needed to see her, but turning over the evidence he'd found would be his first stop. The drive to his lawyer's office would allow her to sleep a bit longer. Regardless of the drama, she still carried his child and needed rest.

It was 8:00 am when he showered and changed his clothes. He called his lawyer, hoping he wouldn't be in court, and breathed a sigh of relief when he answered. He relayed what he had discovered and was asked for the flash drive post-haste so it could be hand-delivered to the district attorney, hopefully absolving him of any wrongdoing. The videos should be enough to get the charges against him dropped, his lawyer assured him, but he needed them right away. Beau was on the road minutes later, racing toward the man's office in Upper Manhattan. After dropping the flash drive off and exchanging a few words, he darted opposite Vivian's hotel in Lower Manhattan.

He knocked on her door with Jessica's laptop tucked under his arm, eager to show her what he'd found. When there was no answer, he knocked again, fingers anxiously tapping against his leg as he waited. Still nothing. He knocked a third time and listened for any sign of life coming from inside the room. Again, nothing. Thinking she might be in a deep sleep, he knocked even louder and put his ear to the door, hoping to hear her stirring. Silence. Growing concerned, he called her phone, but she didn't pick up, nor could he hear it ringing inside. Returning to the lobby, reception informed him that he'd just missed her as she'd checked out minutes before he'd arrived. Worried and confused, he headed back to his car and had just settled into the driver's seat when his phone rang. It was Vivian returning his call, and he scrambled to answer it.

"Vivian, where are you? I'm at your hotel, but they told me you checked out."

"I did," she replied. "I'm sorry, Beau. I'm just done with this whole mess."

"Wait, you're leaving?"

"I checked the video earlier to see how many views it had, and it wasn't there anymore. I'm assuming they got my emails and deleted it. Now I just want to go home. I want to forget about this nightmare."

"Vivian, don't go. I have the evidence right here. Proof that Jessica was responsible for everything."

"I'm sure you do," she replied dryly. She obviously wasn't convinced, and he needed to change that if there was any chance of salvaging things between them.

"I got Jessica's laptop. The stuff on here is crazy. You need to see it. Where are you?"

"That's convenient," she muttered. "I just got to the airport."

The skepticism in her voice stung his heart. "LaGuardia? I'm on my way. Sit tight."

"Beau... don't bother. I'm about to book a flight. Let's just go our separate ways and forget this whole thing ever happened, okay?"

"You've got to be kidding me. I have the evidence right here!"

"On Jessica's laptop," she said. "Right."

"You don't believe me? I'm looking right at it."

"How do I know it's even hers, Beau?"

"Trust me, when you see this, there will be no doubt in your mind, I promise you."

There was a sigh followed by a brief pause as she considered his words. "I don't know…"

"I'm on my way. Don't leave!" he pleaded desperately. If she left, he had a strong feeling she'd change her mind about the baby. He needed to fix things between them before it was too late and zoomed to Queens, weaving in and out of traffic in a mad dash to get there before it was too late. Other motorists honked and yelled obscenities at him out their windows as he frantically hurried toward the airport, but if there was any chance of catching Vivian, he couldn't slow down.

Arriving at LaGuardia, he grabbed the laptop from its place on the passenger seat and bolted inside, hoping to catch Vivian. She'd hung up before giving him any details of her flight, leaving him clueless about what terminal she'd be flying out of. It was a huge airport, and if she'd already passed through security, he'd have no way of reaching her. He pulled his phone from his pocket and called her again.

"I'm here," he said, thankful she'd answered. "Where are you?"

Learning she was moments away from rearranging her return ticket through Delta, he hurried to their ticket counter and found her waiting in line. She looked exhausted, and he suspected she hadn't slept a wink. He pulled her aside and sat next to her in a row of empty seats, hoping nobody passing by could see the laptop screen.

"So this is Jessica's laptop, huh?" she asked as he booted it up, still dubious.

"It sure is," he replied, typing in the password.

She didn't hide the doubt on her face. "And how did you get it?"

"I snagged it from her car."

She leaned in and hissed, "You did what?"

"I know, I know. It was there, and I was desperate."

"You stole it?" she asked in a hushed tone.

"Well… technically, I'm the one who paid for it, so…" he trailed off, angling the screen so she could get a better view. "Look at this."

He opened the folder titled "Beau" and watched her eyes go wide as he scrolled through the photos Jessica had stealthily taken of him. Her jaw dropped, and she covered her mouth in shock. "Oh my God."

"Right? Just wait until you see the videos. She hid those cameras almost a year ago, Vivian. She's been spying on me the entire time."

He played the video of Jessica trashing his place and felt a rush of relief at Vivian's change in demeanor. Her look of skepticism had been replaced by sympathy for everything he'd been put through. "Oh, Beau. Oh, Beau, I'm so sorry… I… I…"

"It gets better," he stopped her. He called up the video of their fight, and Vivian stared in horror at the sight of Jessica taking swings at him before smashing her own face in.

"She's sick," Vivian muttered, shaking her head in disbelief.

"You want to see sick? Take a look at this." He closed out of that video and opened the footage of Jessica standing by his bed, watching him sleep. "This was taken a month ago."

Vivian covered her mouth again and gasped. "Jesus!"

"How creepy is that?"

"Beau... she needs to be locked up before she hurts you. That's the next step with somebody like her. She's obsessed."

"I know. I already handed the videos of her vandalizing my place and punching herself over to my lawyer. He's confident it's enough to get the charges against me dropped and have her put away."

"Are you going to show him the other videos?"

"Probably the ones she recorded after our fight. They prove she violated a court order by entering my townhouse. They might be enough to get her thrown in a mental hospital. Especially the one of her watching me sleep."

"It's the most disturbing video I've ever seen," Vivian agreed. "If that doesn't get her thrown in a nuthouse, I don't know what will."

"My thoughts exactly. We need to discuss what we're going to do with the 'other' videos, though."

It took her a second to realize what he meant. "You mean… videos of us?"

"Yeah, those."

"There was more than just that one?"

"There were four that I could find. The one of us in bed your first night here is the longest." He blushed and muttered, "And the most graphic."

"How come she didn't upload that one, then?"

"Because she's smart. She wanted me to think you wired the cameras. You couldn't have done that your first night here."

"True. What about the others?"

"The second video is the one she uploaded. The other two are harmless. They're just us on the sofa talking, and you can barely even hear what we're saying. I really don't know why she kept those."

"I don't think I want to know."

"Neither do I. either way, we could use the videos to press charges, or we could delete—"

"Delete them," she blurted. "Delete them right now."

He selected the four videos he'd renamed and deleted them, then emptied the virtual trash can while Vivian looked on. "Done."

"Thank you," Vivian sniffled, her tired eyes filling with tears. She shook her head and looked away in embarrassment. "Beau, I'm so sorry. I can't believe I questioned you. I feel so stupid."

He set the laptop aside and wrapped an arm around her, pulling her close as she sobbed against his chest. "It's okay. I don't blame you one bit."

"No, it's not okay. You must hate me."

He laughed and kissed the top of her head as she wept. A few people stopped to stare, but he paid them no mind. "I could never hate you, pretty girl."

"I didn't want to believe those things. I really didn't. I was just so confused. I didn't know what to think. She seemed so convincing, and we really haven't known each other very long. I just—"

"Stop," he said soothingly, rubbing her back. "You don't need to defend yourself here. I would have been just as suspicious in your shoes."

She sniffled again and held him tight. "Really?"

"Really. I hate to admit it, but for a second there, she even had me questioning you. She wanted to pit us against each other."

"And it almost worked. I can't believe I let her get up in my head like that. I really am sorry, Beau."

"I'm the one who should be apologizing, not you. None of this would have happened if you hadn't gotten mixed up in my crazy life."

"It's not your fault."

"Please don't go," he said, brushing a strand of hair from her face and gently caressing her cheek with his fingers. He knew she'd never feel comfortable in his townhouse again and could relate. He didn't think he'd be comfortable there anymore, either. Jessica had tainted it for both of them. "Let's go rent a room somewhere nice. We can catch up on sleep and try to enjoy the rest of your time here."

"I don't know…"

"Vivian, please. We can fix this."

"You really think things can go back to how they were?"

"Absolutely." He wanted to tell her he loved her but feared it might come across as a cheap device to win back her affection. He settled on, "I still care about you so much. That hasn't changed."

"I care about you, too." She wiped her eyes and added softly, "I just wish things could be like they were before. In Ireland."

"Let's go," he grinned. "Right now. Let's go."

"Yeah, right," she chuckled.

"I mean it. Let's go."

She looked at him in bemusement, unsure if he was joking. "Seriously?"

"Seriously. We're already at the airport. You have all of your stuff. Any chance you have your passport? Mine's still in my car."

"I think I do, actually," she replied, rooting through her purse. She stopped and looked at him again. "You'd really want to go back to Ireland with me?"

"I can't imagine a better place to make things right."

"You're crazy, you know that?" she laughed. "You don't even have anything packed!"

He shrugged and smiled. "Whatever I need, I can buy when we get there."

"What about Jessica? When she finds her laptop missing, she might flip out and trash your place again."

"My lawyer says she'll likely be arrested today once the district attorney sees those videos. She's not going to be a problem anymore."

"Beau, I—"

"Come on," he prodded. He could see her wheels turning and knew he had a good shot at persuading her. "We can surprise Samantha, and I'd be honored if you met my parents. I know you have to get back to work, so we'll just stay for a few days."

"You know what?" she said, slapping her legs and straightening her posture. "Yes. Let's do it."

His face lit up. "Really?"

"Really." She smiled and added, "But only if we can stay in Ashford Castle."

"Done."

"I was kidding!"

"I'm not. It's a great idea."

Two hours later, they were flying across the Atlantic. Exhausted, Vivian slept the entire six-hour flight, and he managed to squeeze in a bit more sleep, too. The much-needed rest they were able to get breathed new life into them both, and they arrived in Dublin with optimism. Beau rented a car and held her hand the entire drive to Ashford Castle, where he needed no reservation as a key investor. They were thrilled to find his favorite suite available and were flooded with memories of their first night together when they stepped through the door.

"This is the spot," Vivian smiled, nodding at the bed as she ran her fingers across its burgundy sheets. He could see her choking back her emotions as she continued, "This is where we made a baby."

He stepped behind her and kissed her neck, placing his hands on her belly. "We sure did. And I wouldn't change it for the world."

She turned to face him, and their lips met. She giggled when he playfully pushed her onto the bed and crawled on top of her, his hips grinding into hers. Looking up at him, she ran her fingers through her hair and smiled. "This was a good idea."

The opulence of Ashford Castle was the bandage their strained relationship needed, the magic between them returning stronger than ever. They spent the next two days exploring the castle and each other, making new memories along the way, before driving to Killarney, where he introduced her to his parents. They immediately fell in love with her, welcoming her with open arms and making her feel like part of the family. When Beau broke the news of her pregnancy, his father couldn't resist asking the question hanging in the air.

"When are you going to marry this beautiful young lass?" he blurted in his heavy Irish brogue.

Beau's face turned red with embarrassment, but he recovered quickly and laughed it off. "Give it time, dad. I'm working on it."

Vivian poked his side and smiled. "You want to make an honest woman of me?"

"That's the plan," he replied with a wink.

After enjoying a lovely dinner together, Beau and Vivian repeated their goodbyes, promising to visit soon. They made the short drive to Samantha's place, surprising her and Brian with their unexpected arrival. Samantha was captivated by the story of the sex video—which Vivian was comfortable telling her about now that it had been pulled—and listened with her mouth agape as she took in every scandalous detail. When Vivian finished recounting the drama, it was Samantha's turn to share her own news. She was expecting as well, with her baby due around the same time as Vivian's. Beau accepted a beer from Brian, and the two got to know each other as the women excitedly talked babies. He watched how alive with happiness Vivian seemed to be, taking in her beauty as she laughed with her friend. In that moment, he knew they were going to be just fine. If they'd weathered Jessica's storm, they were strong enough to overcome any adversity. His heart swelled with love as he stole glances at her, admiring the only woman he could imagine spending the rest of his life with.

# Chapter Nine
## *Vivian*

"You're doing great!" the doctor assured her. "Just one more push!"

Vivian took a deep breath and squeezed Beau's hand tightly. Wincing in pain, she gave one final push, bringing their son into the world.

Seven months had passed since Jessica's stunt, and a lot had happened in that time. Beau couldn't shake the feeling he was being watched, which he knew was irrational since Jessica had been arrested and was serving time for destruction of property and assault. Still, the paranoia persisted, prompting him to sell his townhouse sooner than anticipated. He'd relocated to Highlands Ranch, a small city neighboring Denver, buying the spacious estate he'd always dreamed of that sat on twenty acres of land and came with a breathtaking view of the surrounding mountains. At his insistence, Vivian had helped him choose the property. If things worked out between them, he'd reminded her, she'd be living there too, along with their child. Things had worked out, and she'd moved in two months after he'd professed his love for her. He'd planned a romantic evening, doing his best to cook her dinner, then led her into the backyard, where they watched the sunset from the blanket he'd laid out for them. It had been a little chilly given the time of year but not unbearable, and they'd made love as the sun sank behind the mountains, coloring the sky a magnificent blend of orange and red. After, he'd covered her nude body with kisses before staring intently into her eyes and saying the words she'd been waiting to hear. She'd returned them with equal sincerity, not doubting her love for him. From an early age, she'd understood the significance of those three words and had waited to say them to the right man. That man was Beau, without any question in her mind, and when he began tossing the idea of marriage around a month later, she didn't shy away from it like she had with Marcus. Coming from a traditional background, Beau didn't want their child to be born out of wedlock and proposed to her by his fireplace late one night, dropping to one knee to present her with a ring so stunning it left her without words. He'd nervously waited for her to say something and couldn't contain his tears when she finally regained her voice, agreeing to spend the rest of her life with him.

Her parents loved him. She'd introduced them to him shortly after his move to Highlands Ranch, and they were taken by his success and charm. Their approval meant everything to her and reaffirmed her decision to take him as her husband. She wasn't thrilled about giving up the house she'd bought and furnished months earlier but managed to rent it out at a profit instead of selling it at a loss. Beau helped her move into his sweeping estate, which he assured her was now theirs, not just his, and they quickly began planning their wedding. They wanted to marry before their child was born, and she reminded him she wasn't getting any smaller. If she wanted to fit into a wedding dress comfortably, they had to act fast. He was fine with that, whisking her away to Ireland to marry her in Ashford Castle in a ceremony befitting royalty. He spared no expense, chartering a private jet to fly them there along with her parents, who were floored by the majestic luxury resort. Beau's parents were in attendance as well, and of course, she'd never walk down the aisle without Samantha, who was front and center with Brian by her side.

They chose to spend their honeymoon in Ireland to avoid more flying, and a week later returned to the States as husband and wife. Everything had happened so fast that it almost didn't seem real. Only five months had passed since her split with Marcus, and now she was married to another man, her belly growing larger every day. She didn't let her pregnancy slow her down, returning to work as Vivian Sullivan, adopting Beau's surname with pride and renaming her firm to reflect the change. Beau moved his secretary, Gabrielle, to Highlands Ranch in favor of letting her go, which she appreciated. She was a sweet girl around Vivian's age, and the two quickly formed a strong friendship. Over the last few years, Vivian had been so focused on building her career that she hadn't made many friends. Gabrielle was an excellent addition to her small social circle, even helping her paint and decorate the baby's room. An ultrasound revealed they were having a boy, and when Beau had suggested the name "Ashford," she had fallen in love with it. Her labor had been long and tiring, but after one last push, little Ashford took his first real breath and was quickly placed in Vivian's arms.

"He's perfect," Beau gushed, his eyes filled with tears. When he said he'd be there every step of the way, he'd meant it. He'd accompanied her to every appointment and hadn't sat down her entire labor.

Vivian, exhausted and overwhelmed with emotion, couldn't speak. She lovingly cradled their baby in her arms for a minute before finding her voice.

"Hello, Ash," she welcomed him. Referring to her arduous labor, she whispered, "You were worth it."

She held him gently against her chest, bonding with her baby boy while the doctor snipped his umbilical cord. A nurse took over from there, cleaning the newborn while congratulating Vivian on her beautiful new son. Confident that all was well, the nurse followed the doctor out of the room, leaving Vivian and Beau to spend more time with their little one. Vivian's parents, who had anxiously been waiting outside, were allowed in and burst into tears at the sight of their grandson. They fawned over him for an hour before the doctor returned to check on Vivian, worried about the long labor she'd endured. She assured him she was okay, and after looking her over, he agreed she looked fine.

Nevertheless, he insisted she stay overnight for observation, as was standard procedure. Her parents left so she could mend, promising to return later since they hadn't gotten enough of Ashford. She suspected they never would and braced herself for him to be spoiled by the two.

Beau sat next to her bed, holding their baby as she rested. When Ashford began to cry, a nurse moved him to the hospital's nursery so she could sleep. She didn't want him to go but needed to recover and was out like a light within minutes, healing from the tremendous strain she'd undergone. Waking several hours later, Beau brought her a tray of food along with one for himself, and they ate dinner together before spending more time with their baby. She'd never felt such unconditional love before, a connection so deep and so powerful that no force on earth could shake it. She would do anything for her baby, laying down her life without hesitation if need be.

Gabrielle stopped by to meet Ash, bringing him a cute stuffed elephant that he would appreciate when he got older, and her parents returned for another visit as well. Beau used his phone to video chat with his parents so they could welcome the new addition to their family, and they were delighted, to say the least. They promised a trip to the States to meet their grandson, and Beau assured them he'd cover the cost. They'd been wanting to see his new home anyhow but had been waiting for Ash to arrive.

Her parents left around midnight when Vivian started to fade. Beau, who had been awake the entire time, was looking a little worse for wear, too. He drifted off in the chair next to her bed, and with her baby sleeping soundly on her chest, she used the opportunity to get more sleep. Halfway through the night, Ashford woke crying and needed to be moved to the nursery again. She'd tried calming him back to sleep, but the nurse had recommended moving him one last time so she could get a few more hours of rest before being discharged. She was okay with that, and when morning came, she felt good enough to go home.

Beau was rounding up her things when a commotion in the hallway drew their attention. Just outside the door, a small group of nurses seemed to panic, gesticulating wildly as they conferred with each other. Vivian could hear the alarm in their voices and couldn't help but notice the nervous glances they were casting at her through the door's small window. A moment later, one of the nurses entered the room with a fake smile plastered on her visibly shaken face. Vivian recognized her as the same nurse who had taken Ash in the middle of the night.

"It'll be just a moment," the nurse announced. "We're just having a small issue."

Vivian sat up in her bed. "What's going on?"

"Well," the nurse began, avoiding eye contact as she reviewed Vivian's chart. She fidgeted with her glasses and continued, "There appears to have been a slight mix-up in the nursery. We're working on it now."

"A slight mix-up?" Vivian asked, her pulse beginning to race. It was evident by the woman's behavior that something was wrong.

"Oh, we're sure it's nothing," the nurse replied, waving her hand dismissively. "Just give us a few minutes."

"Please," Beau chimed in. "Just tell us what's going on."

The nurse swallowed nervously and cleared her throat. "There's no reason to get upset, so don't worry. We just can't seem to find your baby."

"*Excuse me?*" Vivian belted. "You can't find my baby, and you're telling me there's no reason to get upset?"

"Calm down," the nurse told her in a soothing tone. However, she wasn't a good enough actress to hide her concern, and Vivian could see her quivering. "We're looking for him now."

"How do you misplace a baby?" Beau asked gruffly.

The woman took a step back and shook her head. "I... I handed him to our new nurse last night. I can't find either of them."

"Your new nurse?" Vivian questioned.

"Yes, that's right. Jessica, our new nurse."

Vivian shot Beau a look of horror as panic coursed through her. "Jessica, who?"

"I don't know her last name," the nurse replied.

Beau placed his hand on Vivian's shoulder in an effort to calm her. "Relax. There's no way it can be her."

"What did she look like?" Vivian asked with a lump of dread in her throat.

"Tall. Blonde. Very pretty. Why?"

"Oh my God!" Vivian gasped, fraught with terror. She looked at Beau and began to hyperventilate. "It's her. Beau. It's her. I know it's her."

"Shh… that's not possible," Beau said, rubbing her back. "It's just a coincidence, I'm sure. They'll find Ash."

Vivian broke down completely, stricken with a panic attack that left her shaking and unable to form a coherent sentence. "It's… she's… Beau, it's her… she's… we need to…"

"Sweetie, you need to relax," she heard Beau say. She tried to reply but was too rattled to speak.

"Everything is going to be fine," the nurse assured her. "You need to calm down. The stress isn't good for you right now."

"She's right," Beau nodded. "You're still recovering. Just cool down a bit, okay?"

"*No!*" Vivian wailed, finding her voice. "*This isn't happening!*"

"We're going to find your baby," the nurse said. "We're looking for him—"

*"Bring me my fucking baby!"* Vivian screeched with such force that it made the nurse jump.

"Babe, calm down," Beau told her, but his words fell on deaf ears. She had a complete meltdown, freaking out to such a degree she had to be restrained and sedated. When she came to, Beau was standing at the foot of the bed talking to two police officers. Still groggy from the sedative, she sat in bed and tried to make sense of their words.

"Beau," she muttered, her mind muddled. When he didn't reply, she spoke louder. "Beau."

He broke from the two officers and rushed to her side, brushing the hair from her face. "Hey, baby."

"What's... what's going on?" she asked weakly.

He looked at the two officers and sighed in frustration. They waited while he explained the situation that had unfolded. "It was Jessica. You were right. I didn't want to believe it, but you were right. It was her. She has our baby."

"What?" Vivian cried. The traces of the sedative in her system kept her from losing her mind again. She shook her head in confusion. "How?"

"She knew you were expecting and applied for a job here last month. She's been waiting for this."

"But... she was in jail."

One of the officers stepped forward to fill in the missing pieces. He removed his hat and held it by his side, greeting her with a polite nod. "Ma'am, I'm Officer Davis. This is my partner, Officer Gregory. It seems Jessica Van Buren was released three months ago after exhibiting exemplary behavior and undergoing a psychiatric evaluation."

Vivian shook her head, hoping to clear her mind of the remaining sedative. She could hear what the officer was saying but was having difficulty making sense of it. Even without the sedative, she would have had difficulty wrapping her mind around this turn of events. "How did she get my baby?"

Beau cut in to explain, "I told you she has a degree in nursing, right?"

"I think so," Vivian replied, searching her memory. "Yeah."

"She used that to get hired here. This is the only hospital in Highlands Ranch, so she knew the chances of you giving birth here were good."

"This... this is impossible," Vivian said, shaking her head again. "This can't be happening."

"Ma'am, we've issued an Amber Alert and have all eyes looking for your boy. We'll find him, we promise you," Officer Davis assured her with conviction.

Officer Gregory nodded and added, "She couldn't have gotten far. We've already established a perimeter."

Vivian looked at Beau again, still trying to process the news. "How did she get a job here? Don't they do background checks?"

"Her charges were reduced," Beau groaned. "They didn't charge her with a felony after all."

"So?"

"She's a smooth talker, and they were desperate for a nurse."

Vivian took Beau's hand and looked up at him pleadingly. "Find my baby. Please, Beau, find my baby."

"*Our* baby," Beau corrected her. "And we're working on it. I've been calling her, but there's no answer. I've left her a few messages already."

As she regained her focus, she could see that he was every bit as broken up over this as she was and barely holding it together. He was trying his hardest to be strong for her, but inside, he was just as distraught.

"Our... our baby has been kidnapped," she mumbled to herself, still trying to digest what had happened. It didn't seem real, nor did it seem possible. She'd long dismissed the idea of Jessica ever interfering in their lives again, assuming she'd serve her two-year sentence and find another man there in New York to fixate on. The last thing she expected was for her to follow Beau to Colorado and resurface to kidnap their newborn baby.

Officer Davis spoke again. "We have security footage of her leaving the hospital with your son. We know what vehicle she's driving. We'll find them. Just sit tight."

"He's only a day old!" Vivian said, bursting into tears. "Beau... I... I can't handle this!"

She began to hyperventilate again, and a doctor rushed in to administer another sedative, this one a bit more mild. It didn't knock her out, but it did calm her. The hospital's Chief of Staff came in to offer his apologies and support, likely hoping to avoid a lawsuit. Though she was drugged, she still had a few choice words for him, and he looked away in shame as he took the verbal lashing that she felt justified in giving.

"Is there any update at all?" she heard Beau say as she sank back into the bed.

"Her apartment has been searched," Officer Gregory replied. He'd been glued to his shoulder radio, listening for any new developments. "No sign of her or the baby. We're still searching the perimeter."

"There has to be something I can do," Beau said, running his fingers through his hair. "Let me try calling her again."

He dialed the number the police had on file for her, and it went straight to her voicemail, suggesting she'd shut her phone off. A smart move since leaving it on would make it much easier to trace her whereabouts. He left another message, trying to remain civil, and ended it by repeating his callback number.

"Still nothing," he sighed. "This is ridiculous. I'm going to drive around and look for her."

"Sir, its best you stay here," Officer Davis told him. "We have our guys on it."

"I can't just stand here doing nothing while she's out there with my son!" Beau snapped.

"I understand. I'd be angry, too, in your position. But we need you here in case she calls you."

"He's right," Vivian said. "She took our baby for a reason. Who knows what that reason is? She's twisted. But she's probably planning on calling you at some point."

Her parents dashed in, having heard the news. The media had picked up the story, but the police kept them at bay, refusing to let them into the room. The last thing she wanted was a microphone shoved in her face, so she appreciated the consideration. She would speak with the press later and plead with Jessica to return their baby if they still hadn't heard anything from her.

Right now, she just needed Beau and the support of her mother and father.

Hours went by with no new developments. Beau held up appearances, but she knew he was a mess inside. Her parents didn't leave her side, holding her hand and trying their best to comfort her. They finally caved and allowed the press in to beg Jessica to return their baby and ask for information from anyone who may have seen her with the newborn. Beau used his wealth to offer a sizeable reward, and calls soon started pouring in. The police department received dozens of leads, all of them dead ends, and Vivian had another breakdown when Jessica's abandoned car was found behind an old warehouse, indicating she'd switched vehicles. This would make finding her even more difficult and could render the perimeter they'd established useless. Chances were good. She'd been on the road for hours, and nobody knew what direction she was headed.

Tossing her blanket aside, Vivian stepped out of bed for the first time since giving birth. Her legs were shaky, and she was still a bit loopy from the sedatives she'd been given, but she quickly regained control of her body.

"Babe, what are you doing?" Beau asked, rushing to her side. He'd been talking to Officer Davis, who had stayed to keep them updated on the search. Officer Gregory had left to join the hunt for Jessica and the baby.

"I can't stay here any longer," Vivian huffed, reaching for her bag of clothes. "I need to go find my baby."

"That's not a good idea," her father said, beating Beau to the words. "You need to rest. There's nothing you can do out there."

"He's right," Beau agreed, taking the bag of clothes from her hand. "We need you here. I need you here."

"I need to find my baby!" Vivian cried. "I can't just leave him out there with her."

Her mother joined Beau at her side to calm her down and tried steering her back to the bed. "Honey, you need to listen to them. You're not in the right frame of mind to go out looking."

Officer Davis tried offering his reassurance again. "Ma'am, we have our best men working—"

*"Your best men haven't turned up anything!"* Vivian spat. "It's been hours now. Hours. She could be in another goddamn state."

"And if she is, you have no chance of finding her," Beau pointed out. "There are hundreds of people looking for her. Hell, more than that with the alerts they put out. Thousands. If they can't find her, you're not going to. Especially not in your current condition."

They were right, and she knew it. Her love for her newborn son and her panic over his kidnapping was clouding her judgment. She let them guide her back to bed, trembling from her shot nerves. She thought Jessica releasing the sex video was bad, but it had nothing on the emotional ringer the disappearance of her baby was putting her through.

Beau turned to Officer Davis. "Okay. You've kept me here long enough. I know you're hoping Jessica will call, but I can't keep waiting. My wife can't go out looking, but I sure can."

"Sir, you just established how pointless that would be," the officer replied.

"For her," Beau fired back, gesturing to Vivian. "Look at her. She's beat. But I'm okay. There's no reason I can't be out there searching. An extra pair of eyes certainly can't hurt."

Officer Davis sighed and nodded his approval. "I have a son, too. I get it. Go. But if she calls you, remember the drill. Get as much information as you can without scaring her off. Keep her on the line as long as you can, and listen for background noises. Anything that could give us a location."

"I got it," Beau assured him, shaking his hand. "Thank you."

"I'm going with you," Vivian's dad chimed in. "And I won't take no for an answer. That's my flesh and blood out there, too."

"I'm fine with that," Beau said, leaning down to kiss Vivian's forehead. "I'll be back, hopefully with Ash. If you need me, call your dad. I want to keep my line free in case Jessica does call."

"Okay," Vivian replied weakly. "Thank you. I love you."

"I love you, too."

She watched the two men leave, praying they'd return with her baby. Her mother sat by her side, running her slender fingers through her hair. "Try to rest, honey. Please."

"If she hurts my baby, I'm going to kill her," Vivian hissed. "I'm going to get a gun, and I'm going to kill her."

Officer Davis heard the comment but let it go. Her mother shushed her and continued to comfort her lovingly. "There, there. We'll get Ashford back. Just calm down. Have faith."

Her words helped. Beau had always insisted that things happened for a reason. That the universe put them together to fall in love, get married, and have a baby. He'd said there would be trials and tribulations along the way, but they would persevere, growing stronger with each new challenge. He'd been right so far. They'd managed to put the sex video behind them, even learning to joke about it as a way to move forward.

Making light of the situation had proven a great way to heal.

"Hold on, let me make sure the camera is recording," he'd often quip before they'd make love.

"Okay, but try to get my good angles," she'd playfully return.

The video hadn't returned to haunt them, and it didn't seem likely it would. Jessica had escaped justice for what she'd done, but perhaps this was the cosmos trying to make things right in a very trying way. If so, Ashford would be returned safely, and Jessica would be locked away again. This time, there would be no early release. She could bat her pretty eyes all she wanted, but no district attorney was going to reduce a kidnapping charge. Abducting a newborn baby was no mere slap on the wrist and would surely get her thrown behind bars for years.

These thoughts offered a small degree of comfort as she waited, her mother by her side. She used the time to prod Officer Davis for more information, but he didn't have much to give. Jessica had moved to Highlands Ranch two months earlier and rented a small apartment across town. She'd traded her steel blue Lexus in for something less flashy to avoid their detection. The hospital had hired her after she'd impressed them with her looks and quick wit, and she'd given them no reason to question her mental stability. That's all they knew so far, and none of it helped.

Four excruciatingly long hours passed before Beau returned with her father, both looking equally crestfallen.

"I'm sorry," Beau said, shaking his head. "We couldn't find them."

Vivian groaned but knew they'd done their best. "It's okay."

"No, it's not. I thought maybe I knew her well enough to figure out where she might go. Nothing. Not a trace."

"Sit down," Vivian replied, motioning to the two empty chairs next to her bed. "You two look exhausted."

"No sleep for me until I find our son," Beau told her. Her father seconded that, and the two took a seat by her side.

It was nearing 8:00 pm. Ashford had been missing for twenty hours, and Officer Davis, in need of sleep himself, had been replaced by Officer Kelsey, an older man who had been with the force for over three decades. Kelsey, a jovial character with a crude sense of humor, was trying to lighten the room's dour mood with stories from his long career when a call came over his radio. It was the moment they'd been waiting for, and Vivian's heart pounded as she listened to the breaking news. A citizen had phoned 911 after spotting a woman wearing what appeared to be a wig and carrying a very young baby through a small market an hour away. She'd been shopping for baby formula and had pulled a handgun from her purse when police arrived on the scene. They were now amid a heated standoff, guns drawn, with Jessica unwilling to surrender.

Vivian flew out of bed, adrenaline surging through her body. "We have to get there."

Beau stopped her with his hands on her shoulders. She could tell his heart was beating just as fast as hers. "You stay here. I'll go."

"You're crazy if you think I'm not going," she told him sternly.

"She has a gun. I'm not taking any chances."

Her parents pleaded with her to listen to Beau, but Vivian wasn't having it. She grabbed her bag of clothes and darted into the bathroom, shrugging off her hospital gown and getting dressed as quickly as she could.

"Let's go," she said, bursting out of the bathroom and breathing heavily from the adrenaline. Officer Kelsey spoke into his shoulder walkie in the corner of the room, but she couldn't make out what he was saying. His words were drowned out by Beau, who still wasn't on board with her going.

"I don't think this is a good idea," Beau protested. "If something—"

He was interrupted by Officer Kelsey, who stepped forward to speak with Vivian. "Ma'am. She's asking to see you."

"What?" she asked, shaking her head in confusion.

"She's asking to see you," Officer Kelsey repeated. "She says she'll only surrender if she can talk to you first."

"Me?" She paused and shook her head again, struggling to understand why Jessica would want to speak to her, of all people. It was an unexpected development that had caught her off guard. "Why me?"

Beau shot Officer Kelsey a puzzled look. "Yeah, why her?"

"No idea," the weathered officer shrugged. "I've been instructed to escort you there right away. We can make it in forty-five minutes if we haul ass."

With no time to spare, they rushed to Officer Kelsey's cruiser and were careening down the highway moments later, his lights flashing as they headed south. Her parents had asked to come, but Officer Kelsey had insisted they stay behind since the scene was already, as he succinctly put it, "a complete clusterfuck." An entire SWAT team surrounded the small market, and a sea of onlookers circled the area to watch what was unfolding. Adding to the circus was the media, who had also swarmed the scene. The standoff had become a national story, attracting major news outlets hoping for a tragic ending to draw ratings.

Vivian sat in the back of the cruiser with Beau seated next to her, holding her hand. He assured her that everything would be fine and that Jessica wanting to talk was a good sign, but she could see the doubt in his eyes. He was scared, and that wasn't an emotion she'd ever seen from him before. When he was facing assault charges months earlier, he had looked nervous, but he'd never looked afraid. He was trying to hide it now but wasn't a good enough actor.

The drive felt agonizingly long. Officer Kelsey had radioed ahead to let them know he was en route with the baby's parents in tow, and when they finally arrived at the scene, she was ushered out of the car and briefed on the situation. Jessica was still inside the market wielding a gun, with Ashford strapped to her body in a baby carrier. While she'd been distracted by a negotiator, a sniper had worked his way inside the building using the back entrance. He had a clear shot but wasn't about to pull the trigger unless absolutely necessary. With the position of Ashford, any shot would run the risk of Jessica falling on top of him when the bullet brought her down. Given the newborn's age, there was no guarantee he'd avoid injury—or possibly even death—and his safety was their main priority. The country was watching. The last thing their department needed was to botch this and embarrass themselves on live television. They wanted to get Ashford out alive, so Vivian seemed like their best bet. Jessica had agreed to surrender, but for unknown reasons, she was demanding to speak with Vivian first.

In the privacy of the SWAT van, she was given very specific instructions after assuring the commanding sergeant that she was up for the task. She was to approach Jessica slowly with her hands up, and under no circumstance was she to provoke her. Remaining calm and feigning understanding were crucial to Jessica turning herself in without incident. It was dangerous, as Jessica had proven to be quite unpredictable, but it was a chance Vivian had to take. They strapped a bullet-proof vest onto her and radioed into the negotiator that she was ready. She took a deep breath and stepped toward the market when Beau stopped her by grabbing her shoulder, spinning her around, and pulling her into his arms.

"I love you," he said, pressing his forehead to hers.

"I love you, too," she replied, cupping his face with shaky hands.

"Go get our baby back."

The crowd looked on as the sergeant walked Vivian to the market's double doors. He held one of the doors open for her and gave her a small nod. "Remember, stay cool. Don't instigate anything. Say what you must say to get her outside so we can take her into custody."

"Okay," Vivian said, taking a deep breath. "I can do this."

The negotiator, who had been inside dealing with Jessica, stepped out of the market and looked Vivian over. "I take it you've been briefed?"

"She has," the sergeant assured him.

"We only get one shot at this," the negotiator explained to Vivian. "She's edgy and scared, so stay calm. Don't spook her any more than she already is."

"I got it," Vivian nodded, anxious to get things underway.

The negotiator flashed the sergeant what appeared to be a look of doubt. Moving aside, he motioned for her to take his place inside the market. "Well, then. Showtime."

Vivian swallowed nervously and cautiously stepped inside with her hands up. She heard the door gently close behind her as she took in the family-owned market. It looked like it hadn't seen any updates in decades but appeared to serve its purpose well enough, suiting the needs of locals who didn't feel like driving to a large chain store in a neighboring city just to save a few cents. The place felt empty, but she knew Jessica and her baby were inside somewhere. According to the commanding sergeant, a sniper had also made his way inside without Jessica's knowledge, but there was no sign of him. She was about to call out when Jessica's voice sounded from one of the aisles.

"Vivian? Is that you?"

"It is," she replied, moving in the direction of Jessica's voice with her hands still up.

"I'm over here. Aisle six."

Vivian made her way closer, her pulse racing, and slowly rounded the corner. Sure enough, Jessica was standing in the middle of the aisle with Ashford strapped to her front. She soothingly bounced the baby up and down with one hand while her other hand hung by her hip, holding a gun. On the floor by her feet lay the black wig she'd been wearing that she no longer had cause to wear. A pair of dark sunglasses also looked to have been tossed onto the floor.

"Y-you wanted to talk to me?" Vivian stuttered, trying not to burst into tears at the sight of her baby.

"Are you wearing a wire?" Jessica asked, eyeing Vivian suspiciously.

It took a second for Vivian to process the question. "What? No."

"Prove it," Jessica insisted. "Lift your shirt up."

"What? I'm not going to—"

"I said lift your shirt up!" Jessica hissed through gritted teeth, tapping the gun against her hip in frustration with her finger on the trigger.

"Okay, okay. Just calm down," Vivian said, her jaw trembling. She lifted up her shirt, thankful she'd put on a bra in her hurry to get dressed.

"Turn around," Jessica demanded.

Vivian did as told, slowly turning in a full circle so Jessica could see that she wasn't wired. Satisfied they weren't being listened in on, Jessica seemed to ease up some and took her finger off the trigger of the gun.

"Good," she said. "I want this conversation to be between us."

"Why do you want to talk to me and not Beau?"

"I'll talk to Beau soon. Right now, my business is with you."

"Why me?"

A deranged smile spread across Jessica's face. She looked down at Ashford and delicately ran her fingers through his thin wisp of hair. "Because I wanted you to see me with my new baby."

Vivian felt a wave of anger wash over her and tried her hardest to contain it. "You mean *my* new baby, Jessica. Ashford is *my* baby, not yours."

"Ashford?" Jessica scoffed. "Is that what you named him?"

Vivian wanted to scream at her. To tell her to give her baby back or she'd tear her from limb to limb. Jessica had the upper hand, though, and she could tell by the crazed look in her eyes that she was dangerous. She swallowed the anger that had boiled inside her and took a deep breath. "Yes, that's his name."

"That's fucking stupid," Jessica laughed. She looked down at Ashford again, who was still sleeping against her body. "No. I'm going to call him Beau Junior. Do you think Beau will like that? I do."

"Jessica, please, it's over. This place is surrounded. Just give me my baby back."

"*My* baby," Jessica corrected her. She gave Ashford a light kiss on the top of the head and looked at him affectionately. "He loves his new momma; yes, he does. We've spent the whole day bonding. I was hoping we could have some more time together, but that's okay. We'll be together again soon."

"You're not making any sense," Vivian groaned, her hands still in the air. She was having a hard time maintaining her composure and could feel it beginning to crack. "Look, you said you'd turn yourself in if you talked to me, so here I am. I made good on my word. Now you make good on yours. Hand me over my baby, and let's go."

Jessica threw her head back and laughed, but not loudly enough to wake Ashford. "I'm walking out of here, Vivian, but not with you. You're not going to be walking anywhere."

"Excuse me?"

"You're so stupid," Jessica spat. "You really thought I was just going to hand my baby over and walk out of here with you?"

*"Stop calling him that!"* Vivian barked, unable to control herself. "He is *not* your baby!"

Her raised voice woke Ashford, and he began to cry. Jessica shushed him and gently bounced him again while whispering, "It's okay, baby. Go back to sleep. Momma's got everything under control."

"Jessica, please. It's not too late to fix this. Just hand me over my baby."

Behind Jessica, Vivian spotted the barrel of a rifle pointing out from a stack of cans at the end of the aisle. A sniper really had slipped inside and had managed to conceal himself behind the aisle's end cap display. Crouching down, he'd remained almost invisible. Had she not seen the barrel of the rifle jutting out from between the cans, she would have never known he was there. Jessica didn't seem to be aware of him, so she quickly averted her eyes so as not to draw attention to him.

Jessica let out a long, maniacal cackle that made Vivian's skin crawl. "Oh, you're never touching Beau Junior again."

"You bitch," Vivian seethed. "You shouldn't even be here. You should still be in jail."

"Please," Jessica returned, rolling her eyes. "I'm a pretty white woman with money. We don't do hard times."

Vivian couldn't hold her tongue. "You're going to this time. You're going away for a long time, you psychopath."

"Not likely. I'll plead insanity, feed the jury a sob story about my troubled past, and do a couple of years in some cushy country club of a mental hospital. It'll give Beau time to forgive me and realize that all of this was for him. That nobody else will ever love him enough to do something this big for him. He'll take me back, and we'll be happy together with Beau Junior."

"That's your plan?" Vivian asked in bewilderment. She knew she was straying from protocol but was emboldened by the sniper. Having his rifle locked onto Jessica offered her enough comfort to speak her mind. "Because, if so, you're even crazier than I thought."

"Please. We both know Beau, and I would still be together if it wasn't for you, you whore. You manipulated him. You turned him against me."

"I turned him against you?" Vivian scoffed. "Last time I checked, you did a pretty damn good job of that yourself."

"Everything I do, I do for him. He would have seen that and taken me back if you hadn't distracted him by spreading your legs." She looked Vivian up and down and added, "He was only using you to get over me anyway. You were just a fucking rebound."

"Right. Such a rebound he married me," Vivian replied sarcastically.

Jessica stomped her foot angrily, and Vivian saw her right eye twitch. "He only married you to make me jealous! So I'd do something like this to prove my love for him. He... he wanted me to do this."

"Holy shit," Vivian muttered. "You're delusional."

Jessica ignored her comment and continued, "We were supposed to get married. We were supposed to have a baby. We would have, you know. If you hadn't come along."

"I don't know how you figure that since you told him he couldn't even have children. Yet another thing you lied about."

A deep sadness painted Jessica's face, and her eyes grew distant, welling with tears. "I know. I shouldn't have done that. I just... I didn't want him to think that I was the defective one. I'm the one who can't have kids, not him. I was afraid he'd leave me if he found out. I figured he might be willing to adopt if he thought he was the problem, not me."

Vivian was stunned by Jessica's moment of honesty. "I'm sorry to hear that… but it doesn't give you the right to steal a baby. My baby. It would help if you faced reality, Jessica. Beau doesn't want you anymore. He hasn't wanted you in a long time. I don't know if he ever really wanted you."

*"Shut up!"* Jessica shouted, waking the baby again. "What we had was real. I know it. I can feel it."

"Just because you feel something doesn't make it real."

*"It was real!"* Jessica stomped her foot in anger again. Her brow furrowed in rage as she protested Vivian's words. *"Stop telling me that it wasn't! You don't know what we had! You weren't there!"*

"Okay," Vivian said softly, reeling herself back in. She'd been pushing the woman too hard and unintentionally provoking her. If she didn't start feigning empathy, she ran the risk of Jessica doing something rash. "You're right. I'm sorry. I wasn't there. I'm sure he did love you."

"He did," Jessica sniffled, wiping a tear from her eye. "And he still does. He might not know it, but he does. He'll realize. After this. He'll realize."

"He probably will," Vivian lied. "I've never done anything this extreme to prove my love for him. He'll probably leave me and take custody of our baby so you two can raise him together."

Jessica lowered her head, and when she raised it, her face was pure evil. With a scowl, she hissed through gritted teeth, "Don't you fucking placate me like I'm a child."

"I'm sorry," Vivian swallowed, stepping back and raising her hands higher. She could feel her heart racing. The look on Jessica's face was unlike anything she'd ever seen and sent chills down her spine. "I'm sorry. Calm down. Please. Just calm down, and let's walk out of here."

"I told you before," Jessica sneered. "You're not going to be walking anywhere."

In that instant, it all came together. Jessica was going to kill her.

"Please," Vivian began to sob, taking another step back. "Please, Jessica..."

"Beau will never take me back as long as you're around to poison his mind. But if you're gone... we can be happy together."

Vivian saw her move her finger back to the trigger of the gun. "Jessica, you don't need to do this. Stop! Think about it. Think about what you're doing."

"He'll be upset. I'll go away for a while. He'll get over it and forgive me. We'll move on and be happy together," Jessica said, speaking more to herself than Vivian. It felt as if she were trying to convince herself of her words.

"Jessica, they'll lock you up for life. Please, don't do this."

"It's cute how they strapped body armor on you. Like that will help when I shoot you in the fucking face."

Vivian's entire body trembled, and she felt a warm wetness spread down her pants. She'd lost control of her bladder, which had been weakened from the birth and the fear coursing through her. Ashford started to cry again, and the sound bore a hole through her heart.

She began to sob and braced herself for the worst as she continued to plead with Jessica.

"Please… please, don't do this…"

"Goodbye, bitch," Jessica smirked. She was in the middle of raising her gun when a shot sounded, dropping her to the floor. She lay on her side, Ashford still strapped to her chest, with a pool of blood forming by her head. It happened so quickly that it took Vivian a moment to process what had happened. The sniper had taken Jessica down with expert precision, the shot so powerful it had spun her onto her side. Vivian screamed and covered her mouth, standing in shock for a few long seconds before rushing to Jessica's side to check on Ashford. He was scared and crying but seemed to be okay; Jessica's arm had cushioned the fall when she landed. She gingerly pulled him from the baby carrier and wept as she cradled him in her arms.

The sniper rushed over and grabbed her by the arm, helping her to her feet and leading her out of the market, where the commanding sergeant was waiting for them. The crowd erupted, with bystanders cheering and reporters shouting questions as she was guided back into the SWAT van. She ignored them, still in shock from the harrowing nightmare she'd just endured. Paramedics hurried inside the market after the sergeant gave them the green light, but Vivian was reasonably certain they wouldn't find Jessica with a pulse. Seeing that Vivian had wet herself, one of the SWAT members respectfully handed her a blanket to cover herself with, and she mouthed the words "thank you." She tugged the bulletproof vest off and wrapped herself in the blanket, her body quivering from head to toe. Beau was allowed into the van and teared up at the sight of her holding their baby. He dropped to his knees in front of her and gently kissed the top of Ashford's head.

"Thank God," he said, taking her hand. "I was worried you might not make it out of there."

"S-she t-tried to s-shoot me," Vivian stuttered, still reeling from the horror.

"I know. I heard."

"What? How?"

"The sniper's walkie was on. We heard everything, and it was all recorded."

She felt a small pang of guilt for not following the sergeant's instructions as closely as she could have, but he assured her that she did just fine. The baby was safe, which had been their primary objective. Nothing she did or said could have stopped Jessica from taking a bullet. She'd kidnapped Ashford intending to kill Vivian, and the moment she'd raised her gun, it was over for her.

A paramedic stepped into the SWAT van to pass along the news. Jessica had been pronounced dead, the gunshot to the head likely having killed her instantly. It was over. They had their baby back, and Jessica was out of their lives for good. Beau took a seat next to Vivian and held her hand as the paramedic looked over Ashford, determining that the baby was fine but hungry. Using the privacy of the blanket she was given, she offered him a breast and fed him while the police held the press at a distance. If she chose to speak to them, they told the media vultures, she would do it when she was ready. Right now, she needed time with her baby and a few days to rest. She'd given birth the day before, and her body, along with her mind, had just suffered tremendous stress. She could still feel herself shaking.

"Beau…" she said, sobbing. "I want to go home. Please. I just want to go home."

"Okay," he nodded. "Just hang in there a few minutes more."

He wrapped her in his arms and held her tightly while the police finished things up. It took a bit longer than expected, but she stayed strong for Beau and their baby. Officer Kelsey transported them back to Highlands Ranch and walked them inside the hospital, holding off the press that had followed them in hopes of getting at least some statement from her or Beau.

"You've got to be kidding me," she groaned when Beau refused to drive her home, insisting that she spend another night in the hospital for observation. Since she hadn't been officially discharged, her bed was still waiting for her, and he helped her back into it before taking a seat next to her.

"I know you hate me right now," he smiled, "but this is for your own good."

He was right, and she knew it. She was still shaking from the standoff with Jessica and couldn't seem to stop. The red cloud of mist exploding from Jessica's head and the sound of her baby crying as they fell to the floor were going to haunt her for years to come… and possibly the rest of her life. The doctor offered her another sedative, which she refused in favor of a clear head. Even though Jessica was dead, her guard was still up, and she wanted to remain as alert as possible. As desperately as she needed sleep, she didn't want to take her eyes off Ashford, who was resting comfortably on her chest with a full belly. Beau, who had been incredible throughout the whole ordeal, hadn't slept either and was visibly worn down. Officer Kelsey generously offered to keep watch so they could sleep and positioned himself in a chair just outside their room. It was a thoughtful gesture they appreciated dearly, allowing them enough comfort to finally rest. Confident that nobody was getting into the room, Beau slumped over in the chair and was out within seconds. Still a bit too shaken to sleep, she held Ashford and whispered sweet things to him that he was too young to understand, but she hoped he would feel.

"Mommy loves you so much. You're safe now. Everything is going to be okay."

She didn't know if she was trying to reassure herself or her baby. Jessica was certainly never going to be a problem again, but that's what she'd told herself seven months earlier. After Jessica's incarceration, she was sure the woman was out of their lives for good. It was absurd to think she could cause any more harm now that she was dead, yet she couldn't escape the thought. Could she somehow stir up trouble from beyond the grave? Unless the sex video resurfaced, she didn't see how. Still, the worry persisted, and she knew it would for quite some time.

Ashford cooed, and she smiled down at him. She found a degree of solace in knowing he'd never remember the day he'd spent with his abductor. The last twenty-four hours had been a living hell for her, yet Ashford had been oblivious to it all. Next to them, Beau slept with his arms crossed, and she could hear him lightly snoring, something he only did when he was completely exhausted. Even though she'd seen a hint of doubt in his eyes when he'd told her everything was going to be okay, he hadn't been wrong. Ashford had been returned safely, just like he'd said he would. He firmly believed that they'd overcome all obstacles, no matter how challenging, and he was proving to be correct. If the sex video had made them stronger, she could only hope that this would somehow make them stronger, too.

She smiled again and felt her worries begin to fade. Being alone with her husband and their baby was the only medicine she needed. Within minutes, she'd stopped shaking and was able to relax. Everything was going to be okay, she told herself as she drifted off to sleep holding Ashford. Jessica could never hurt them again, and she had the rest of her life to look forward to with the man of her dreams and their beautiful baby boy, who would undoubtedly grow into a fine man, just like his father.

# Chapter Ten
## *Epilogue*

In the days following Jessica's death, details of Jessica's past emerged that shed light on her behavior. At only fourteen years old, she'd been diagnosed with ovarian cancer that had left her infertile. Her sickness sparked an interest in health care, and she went to school for nursing, intent on making a career of it. While attending classes, she fixated on a classmate she claimed to have fallen in love with, and when he broke things off with her, she took a sledgehammer to his car in anger. He pressed charges, but because she was a hair under eighteen, the records were sealed and weren't released until after her death. Her parents, devastated by the loss of their daughter, believed her mental health issues stemmed from the cancer that had left her unable to bear children. As a little girl, she had a wide collection of dolls and dreamed of someday being a mother. When she learned she'd never have children of her own, it created a crack in her psyche that worsened over time. Instead of seeking help for her ailing mental health, she hid her issues the best she could. However, bottling them up only worsened them and resulted in a violent temper when she lost control.

At the recommendation of the police department, Vivian saw a therapist who helped her move forward. It took a few months, but the vivid nightmares of Jessica returning to torment them in some new way finally slowed to a stop. Beau took Jessica's death worse than Vivian did, which was understandable given the emotional connection he'd once shared with her. He would never say it, but Vivian knew her death had troubled him. He began donating monthly to *Mental Health America*, a nonprofit organization helping those with mental issues. Vivian supported this decision, and Jessica's parents were deeply moved by it.

Vivian took an extended maternity leave to recover from the incident and bond with Ashford. Beau took some off as well and flew his parents over to meet their grandson. Shortly after they left, Samantha and Brian flew in to visit with a little one of their own. Shannon, a traditional Irish name, had been born three weeks after Ashford arrived, and Vivian and Beau immediately fell in love with her red hair and big green eyes. The women were overjoyed that their children were the same age and looked forward to watching them play together when they got older. With any luck, they'd be lifelong friends. Maybe even more, Beau had joked with a wink.

Two years had passed since Ashford's kidnapping and Jessica's subsequent death. Vivian and Beau had returned to Ireland to visit, leaving Ash with Beau's parents for a few days while they retreated to the spot that held such a special place in their hearts. Beau had called well in advance to reserve the suite that meant so much to them both, and after taking a long shower together to unwind from the day of traveling, he guided her to the familiar bed their son had been conceived on. Their relationship was stronger than ever, the kidnapping having forged the bond between them in fire. They'd become unbreakable steel, one-piece welded together in an inseparable connection.

Her body had taken a hit from having their baby, but he didn't mind, assuring her that she was every bit as beautiful as the day they'd met. He covered her naked body in kisses and looked up at her with his light blue eyes as her heart began to beat faster. Two years later, his touch could still make her pulse race. They made love with the same passion they had the first night they'd met. Their sex was always good, but the magic of Ashford Castle—the place they'd met and made their child—elevated it to a whole new height.

"Mmm... I love you," she purred, cuddling up next to him after they'd both had their fill.

"I love you, too," he returned, kissing her forehead.

He'd finished inside of her, which was something she'd found him doing more often in recent months. She felt herself leaking and laughed. "Not to ruin the moment, but I must clean up."

"I know the drill," he smiled.

She dashed to the bathroom and returned to his side a few minutes later. "Much better."

"Good," he said, still recovering from his orgasm. "You always make me cum so much."

"If I didn't know any better, I'd think you were trying to get me knocked up again," she teased, lightly bopping him on the nose with her finger.

He flashed her a devilish grin. "Maybe I am."

"About that," she said, breaking from his side again and rummaging through her suitcase she'd set by the foot of the bed.

"What are you doing?" he chuckled, watching as she searched for whatever she was looking for.

"You'll see. Close your eyes."

"What?"

"Come on, close your eyes."

"Okay, okay."

After checking to ensure his eyes were closed, she hopped back onto the bed with her hand behind her back. "Okay, open them."

She presented him with a small plastic bag and watched his reaction as he pulled out the positive pregnancy test inside.

"Are you serious?" he beamed, smiling wide.

"I found out two weeks ago," she told him excitedly. "I've been waiting to tell you. I wanted to surprise you here."

"We're having another baby!" he laughed, sharing her excitement.

"We're having another baby!"

"I love you so much," he said, tossing the test aside and pulling her into his arms. He rolled on top of her and covered her body in kisses again while she giggled.

Beau had been right. Their love was strong enough to conquer anything; she'd learned to trust in that. She'd had her doubts with the video and again with the kidnapping, but their love had prevailed and hadn't wavered since. Their thriving businesses were making money hand over fist, allowing them to live a life that most could only dream of. Nothing had been handed to them. They'd both achieved success through their hard work and were able to live in luxury while spreading their wealth through various charitable organizations. They made sure to take care of their friends and loved ones, setting up a college fund for Samantha and Brian's child after paying off the couple's home. Beau spent an extraordinary amount of time and money securing citizenship for his parents so he could move them to Highlands Ranch to be a part of their grandchildren's lives, and Vivian was able to repay her parents for their lifelong support by surprising them with a posh home close by that she'd paid for in full.

She ran her fingers through Beau's dark hair and smiled, knowing everything would be just fine. Jessica's meddling had cemented their relationship instead of destroying it as she'd hoped. Over time, she became little more than a distant memory. Ashford would grow up without recollection of her, and neither would his little sister, who was born without incident, surrounded by love.